THE
TREASURE
OF
LOR-REV

BRYAN ASHER

INTERCONT
PRESS

The Treasure of Lor-Rev

Copyright © 2021 by Bryan Asher

Illustrations Copyright © 2021 by Bryan Asher

Written by Bryan Asher

Cover Illustration by Emilis Januškevič

Internal Character Illustrations by Emilis Januškevič

Internal Chapter Header Illustrations by Sy Gardner

Cover Design by Elizabeth Mackey

This book is published through Intercont Press LLC

ISBN 978-1-7357628-2-1 (Paperback)

ISBN 978-1-7357628-3-8 (eBook)

www.intercontpress.com

To Kyle, for never letting me down.

To Travis, for not only teaching me how to survive, but thrive.

To Lexi, may your kind heart, cutting wit, and fighting spirit never be forgotten.

THE
TREASURE
OF
LOR-REV

BRYAN ASHER

- PROLOGUE -

CHUSHIN

-

-

CIVIC REGION WITHIN THE NORTHBRIDGE DOMAIN

ONES and zeros.

Followed by another intricate line of letters and numbers. His existence was crafted by simple icons, but what he witnessed in his virtual hibernation was much more exquisite. His steps were highlighted with bursts of violet and when he raised his eyes skyward, there was an array of white jagged dots speckling the dark scenery. These stars twinkled and glowed, but refused to cast any meaningful light, per his will. He enjoyed having his virtual hibernating space merely accented with color.

However, despite all his control over maintaining and creating this plane, something was wrong. He felt his consciousness meld with the digitized intelligence long ago, and the upload into his freshly constructed cybernetic body should have occurred already. Sauntering towards one edge of his reality, Daemon watched a violet grid begin to obstruct his view. He'd tried a litany of times to defeat this grid in other sections, but to no avail. He hoped this spot would be different. The lines surged as he placed a palm upon them. Peering at the grid, he narrowed his focus to decipher the programming language clattering across his vision. This section of code illustrated that his personal fortress had been reconstructed into a prison.

'How?' he wondered again.

It couldn't have been his coding; he'd reviewed every conceivable outcome. Maybe the new frame he'd constructed had malfunctioned?

Possibly…

He'd gone over these thoughts several times and knew he wouldn't find clear answers until he was free. It was best to set them aside for now. Pushing his palm further against the grid, he smiled, it was beginning to give. The lines fizzed and popped as he slowly wrapped his fingers around them. It felt like holding his hands over boiling grease. He grimaced against the searing pain while letters and numbers whizzed over his eyes. He just had to hang on long enough to find the right sequence…

'Steady.'

The vulnerable line of code he could break…

'There!'

Daemon yanked on the digital cage and ripped it apart. White light surged through the torn section. He squinted and shielded his eyes until it faded. Staring through, he could make out his laboratory on the other side. Eagerness overtook him and he snatched two more sections of violet fencing and tore them away.

2

Finally... there was enough room. He stepped across the threshold and felt his chest heave, like a chain was tugging him through by the ribcage.

His eyes snapped open... he was back in reality. Daemon began gagging and realized the breathing tube was still down his throat. He pulled it free and immediately emptied his stomach over the side of the hibernation pod. Expelling the fluid used to keep his non-metallic organs fresh while he slept. Not everything in this new body was mechanical. The fusion required he leave some of his original biological structure to trick his brain into accepting his new – and by his estimation – *superior* vessel.

He crawled out of the cylindrical onyx-colored pod. His skin was smothered in a layer of slimy grease, and his tall figure left wet footprints while stalking towards a shower with high white-tile walls.

Finally clean and his vision fully returned from its earlier haze, he could see different notifications scroll across his field of view. This new frame allowed him to access the inter-web remotely. He opened a small window which sat at the upper right corner of his vision. It displayed a set of government servers. Lines of code began appearing at the speed of thought.

'*Execute*,' he told himself... but nothing happened.

He tried again, but the command wouldn't initiate. Frantically, he tested several other connections. Still nothing.

Damn.

Whatever manipulated his hibernation likely placed governor programs to hamper him. He *should* have full access to any inter-web connected device. Instead, he was restricted to merely observing them. For everything to work he needed control, *full* control.

He wiped his long brown hair away from his face and looked over at one of his computers – which should have already been on –

and booted it up. Instead of the normal login sequence, a face appeared on the screen. His forehead furrowed in bewilderment at the sight of his longtime business partner, Johan Naoki. Johan was supposed have helped him re-emerge successfully. Something inside Daemon's gut lingered on the idea of betrayal.

"I'm sorry, Devlice — or I guess you'll be calling yourself Daemon now," the face on the monitor said, "but I couldn't let you go through with it. I knew at some point you'd break free. So, as I'm sure you're aware, your abilities are… limited."

He gritted his teeth at being referred to by his former name. He was no longer Devlice Karion, the simple engineer. He'd left that existence behind when he fused with the most powerful digitized intelligence — one he and Johan created together. He was now Daemon.

The face of Johan scowled. "I wish I could've convinced you of another path, but this was my only option. Hopefully that extra time in hibernation allowed you to reflect on your plans. Forcing the people of Lor-Rev into constant connection to the inter-web — that you'd have complete control of — is a disgusting proposition."

The image of Johan shook his head.

"You are trapped within this Intercontinent, and while I may have passed on at this point, I have measures in place to ensure you stay here."

A solemn look overtook the image of Johan.

"Goodbye, friend."

The monitor cut out and the computer tower hissed as smoke slowly billowed from its exhaust port. Daemon slammed his fist through the machine and flung it across the room. It crashed against the wall and tumbled to the floor in a pathetic husk of plastic and wires.

"That bastard stabbed *me* in the back?!" he hissed angrily.

If the video-message was true, then there was no reason to continue lamenting Johan's betrayal. His only recourse was locating something capable of eliminating these restrictions, to purge them from his programming. He knew of only one device that could safely complete this task and not destroy his newly-minted mind. Ironically, it was also something he and Johan developed together many years ago. A long-rumored technological device most believed was another overhyped myth surrounding one of Lor-Rev's greatest inventors. But it wasn't fiction. It might take him years of research to unlock it from the vault where Johan stored it, but he *would* find the Diffusor-Sphere. And once he did, it would set him free. Free to build the world into his vision of perfection.

- CHAPTER 1 -

WEST OUTSKIRTS

-

-

UNGOVERNED NON-CIVIC REGION

THE mountains glimmered a greyish hue under a casting of harsh moonlight. The whirling breeze carried tufts of snow, plastering anyone foolish enough to brave its current with a blanket of frost. No one from Lor-Rev ventured the Kal mountain range anymore, nor would they need to. The citizens inhabiting this Intercontinent lived in places which had control of their climate by installing sphere-ceilings above them, and wouldn't travel to the uncovered outskirts. If anyone struck out beyond the borders of the cloistered metropolis regions, they'd find a lone figure hiking towards a small valley between two of Kal's shorter peaks.

6

Jared Dareje huddled tight underneath his soft-shell down jacket. His jacket was also a rarity on his home Intercontinent, as most would choose a coat with a superior synthetic insulation. One lined with an interior substance comprised of coal, water, air, and petroleum, or polyester for short. But a coat with a chemically engineered interior didn't have the same *feel* as one made from goose feathers.

Jared continued trudging the last few steps until he reached the hallow carved into one of the mountainsides. He tilted his head lamp down and used the light to plan his footing. After a cautious traversal down the sloped jagged stone, he pulled the mouth cover down on his balaclava.

"I love the snow, but damn that was freezing," he said aloud.

He lifted his hood up then brushed bits of snow from his short black hair. His thin facial features and light brown skin were trademarks of his homeland, a small nation far from the massive one he currently resided in.

'I wonder what Gillman would think if he saw this place?' Jared thought while tossing his backpack off his shoulder and fishing inside for food.

He grabbed a bag of jerky and fiercely chewed through several pieces. Sliding down to the floor, he slouched back against the cave wall and contemplated how to finish the trek before dawn, despite already hiking several hours to reach this point. He would only rest a few minutes before pushing forward. As he looked deeper into the cave, he saw only more cold, blue-grey stone. Sighing, he ripped at another piece of jerky with his teeth. He wasn't discouraged by the treacherous hike, rather, he wished Gillman could have joined him on it.

'Well at least he'll get to see the artifact once I recover it.'

Jared tossed the bag of cured meat into his backpack and zipped it shut. Using the wall as a guidepost, he climbed to his feet and continued ahead, furrowing his brow in concentration while counting each step.

'*I believe only twenty-five more based on the calculated diameter of the mountain's base.*'

When planning his journey, Jared had located a digital scan of the oldest map of the Kal mountains at the Scribe-Center Archive near his home. He'd copied as much of the cartography as possible onto the small paper journal he brought everywhere. He needed to find a map old enough to have been written by hand and not scanned with Tera-Tracking drones. It wasn't too hard to find one, since the Lor-Rev didn't scan the Kal mountain range often, as it was uninhabited and the data was considered non-essential for re-scanning. After logging into the kiosk at the Center, Jared had only found three maps of his current location. The first being the initial Tera-Tracking scan, one written before the digital imaging revolution and still in solid condition, followed by the third that was worn down and barely visible. Jared had zoomed into the scanned image of the tattered map in several places. Hoping he could piece together what was missing from the torn places of the document.

After several hours maneuvering the three-dimensional image at the kiosk, Jared finally located a spot in the mountain range where he believed the cave was located. His calculations were correct, and now he was only five steps from his destination.

The cave continued on but Jared stood in place, looking around with his head lamp for a sign that he was in the correct position. On either side of him the stone walls of the cave were pushed out slightly. Jared knelt down and pulled a small chisel from his boot. He brushed some light snow from the ground beneath him. Finding a small slot, he jammed the chisel in and heard a clink from below. Jared grimaced as he began twisting the chisel with both hands. The mechanism was clearly very old and incredibly difficult to use after years of inactivity.

He gave one final shove with his shoulder while pivoting his hips and the locking mechanism finally clicked. The floor below rumbled as the section of stone he was kneeling on started to turn. Two pieces of the wall on either side turned with him. When it finally stopped, the two wall sections were now in line with the cave. Jared looked up and saw an open hallway in front of him. Behind him was a short carved out section that he could see was a dead end.

He left the chisel in place and marched down the new hallway until reaching its end. Atop a short metal cylinder sat what he was hunting for, the prototype model SatellaField Personal Station.

SatellaField was a small company that built devices for using the inter-web – which gave access to a vast network of websites and digital content – and the net-frame – which was used for communicating directly through voice or typed message.

When SatellaField created the Personal Station, everything changed. They went from a simple company making pocket sized text messaging devices, to emerging as a future tech giant. The Personal Station was a small satellite which would stay elevated in a safe location and was mainly used to broadcast your own signals on a private network. Any signal cast by it was unable to be monitored by Lor-Rev's government, known as the Congregate.

The product was a massive hit, and helped push everyone towards a more digital lifestyle. Before its creation, you had a device known as a Slate to make voice calls and texts in certain areas where the net-frame was broadcast, or a designated kiosk to access the inter-web. Now a Personal Station could rove above you and give constant access to both on a new Slate they created, which had a touch capacitive screen. SatellaField called it the "Merge."

Eventually, SatellaField was outclassed when Orb Incorporated – the largest sphere ceiling manufacturer – discovered how to transmit network signals off of its own product, rendering a personal satellite useless. The Slate line of devices was still very important though, and Ergo Corporation – another growing tech conglomerate – bought SatellaField to acquire the Merge. The Merge remained the most popular portable computer and cellular phone to this day.

Jared's eyes widened while approaching the Personal Station, which was held in mid-air by a small metal disk referred to as a "Puck." He'd discovered many older pieces of technology that had been cast aside, but it was rare when he located one which was intentionally hidden like this.

Narrowing his eyes, he studied his prize. *'The last time I found something on such an elaborate display, it signaled a laser-grid that almost burned my fingers off.'*

Reaching into his backpack, he retrieved a similar sized sphere which he intended to place over the Puck once he retrieved the Personal Station. Jared pulled up his left sleeve, revealing a light-blue metal cuff attached to his inner forearm. He tapped on it twice and green letters projected just an inch from its surface. He typed: **mk/arm** on the projected keyboard. He held the cuff up as the metal began to liquify then re-solidify into a small arm that extended from his wrist. Testing it, he squeezed his hand and watched as the new metal arm followed suit. He reached out and nudged the Station.

Nothing happened.

A second later he quickly switched the Personal Station with the replacement he brought, then stuffed it into his backpack. Surely there was something in the Puck to detect whether the object it held was the genuine item.

Still nothing.

Jared laughed to himself, "Really? After trekking a deserted mountain and discovering this... you'd think I'd at least get a couple walls closing in. Maybe even a turret to fire a few rounds at me."

Tossing his backpack over his shoulder, he double tapped the metal arm and the light emitted keyboard returned. He typed: **rm/arm** and the metal arm morphed back into the cuff again.

10

Jared shrugged. "That was pretty easy. Well, after avoiding the frost-bear camps and hiking several miles through a snow storm."

As he turned to leave the room, a low-pitched gong sounded from the pillar that formerly housed the Station. Jared looked over his shoulder and watched as an image made of purple light projected a man's face onto the opposite wall. He studied the image; the man had a freckled bald scalp with a spiked horseshoe haircut, he wore thick square glasses, and his wrinkled skin showed his age. He recognized that face. It was Johan Naoki, the creator of the Personal Station, and the founder of SatellaField.

Crackling lo-fi vocals began to emit from the pillar, "Well I knew eventually someone would find this. I just hope it's not you, Daemon. If it is, I wish to give you one bit of advice..."

The voice paused and the projected face of Johan Naoki glared.

"Boot deconstruct sequence!"

The image flickered before speaking again and switched to a calm expression.

"Hopefully that will have stopped you in your tracks, old friend. If whomever has my Station is still standing, then I assume you're not him. In that case good luck and use it wisely, it's the last chance you'll get."

Johan's face wrinkled as he smiled and winked, then the projection disappeared.

"Daemon, huh? I wonder what he did to piss the old man off?" Jared wondered aloud while exiting the room.

He knelt down and twisted the chisel once more, shifting the walls back to their original location. After climbing out of the cave, he began the long downhill hike back to his tent.

The beef stew simmered in the pot while Jared stirred it with a tall wooden spoon. He scooped a few helpings into a bowl and let the warmth radiate into his palms. While allowing the stew to adjust to a more palatable temperature, he gazed towards the night sky. He could barely see a few far off Intercontinents, moonlight reflecting off the Edge Oceans that wrapped underneath the floating landscapes. Outside the major civic regions there weren't any artificial covers, massive buildings, or intense lights that would hide this natural beauty. He could even see stars that lay beyond their grouping of hovering nations.

'Maybe air travel will reach one of those stars beyond the Intercontinental Forum?' Jared wondered.

He and Gillman often joked about which place they would search next, once they'd found everything on Lor-Rev. However, he knew there was little chance he'd get enough tokens to build anything capable of traveling beyond the Forum. Yet, he never let that stop him from dreaming.

- CHAPTER 2 -

RASMUSON

CIVIC REGION WITHIN THE
NORTHBRIDGE DOMAIN

WHILE hidden by the curtain of nightfall, Kanna held her position on the rooftop overlooking her target's hideout. She'd been trailing him for the last several days and finally found his main base of operations. Usually, a criminal smuggling racket would be located in the Southbridge Domain, where the majority of shipping ports were located. Yet this one tucked itself inside the tightly woven civic region of Rasmuson, located in the Northbridge.

As the light breeze whirled past, she tossed her black hair behind her shoulder, then looked through the scope of her rifle, a Phantom model 11.2. It wasn't the most recent offering from the

13

phaze rifle manufacturer, but in her mind, it was the most reliable. By her estimation there were at least fifteen of the gang's men patrolling the outside of the squat concrete apartment building, and two guarding the roof. Finished surveilling the exterior, she reached over her shoulder and stuck her rifle to a small disc on the back of her full-body, neoprene Exo-suit.

As Kanna double tapped her left temple, her eye made a slight whizzing sound upon activating its additional functions. She'd had a fair amount of her left side replaced with cybernetic body parts after a nearly fatal accident. Her eye now saw a small square screen, which had several options listed on dark circles. As she moved her pupil, the cursor followed and highlighted the corresponding circle. She continued across a few options until she saw *Infrared*, then blinked to select it. Her eye clicked, and she now saw several men patrolling inside the building on each floor. She'd heard through some credible information, that her target occupied an office on the uppermost floor. Taking a rooftop entrance was the easiest way to reach him, and avoid the most guards.

Kanna walked back to the center of the roof where she'd left a few additional supplies. Her hand-held glider rested against one of the building's large exhaust fans. Gliders like these were mainly used by adrenaline junkies who employed them for base jumping. However, Kanna had hers refitted with a small propulsion thruster that could be activated with one of two triggers. The thruster gave her extra momentum so she wouldn't glide too slowly when crossing buildings. It also had a second trigger that would burst the engine and destroy it. She wanted to leave no trace of her actions and the glider was built to be disposable.

As she stepped onto the edge of the roof, Kanna double tapped her temple once more and blinked after selecting, *Default.* As her vision took on a normal shade, she looked down at two heavy-set men on the hideout's roof. They wore black leather jackets and sported dark visor-shaped glasses that were likely used for night vision. The two men were sitting in plastic chairs drinking and playing cards. This gang wasn't a large outfit and likely assumed any threat would come from the ground level. It appeared rooftop guard duty was viewed with a casual lens.

'Good,' she thought, *I'll knock these ganglanders out before they can turn their drunk heads.'*

Lifting the glider above her head, Kanna crouched down and felt the soles of her boots grip the concrete underneath. She leapt from the rooftop and squeezed the trigger on one of the handles. A muffled pop sounded as the propulsion engine sent her sailing towards the adjacent building.

She rapidly descended feet-first towards the closest guard. His long braids whipped behind his head as he looked up at Kanna, but she was already on him, his glasses and nose crunching against the heels of her boots. The ganglander toppled onto his back, rolling a few times before slamming into an exhaust fan box in a crumpled heap. The second guard knocked over the card table as he leapt to his feet. Instinctively he reached for his hip, but found nothing.

Kanna laughed, "If you're looking for your gun, it's over there by the door. Next time you play cards, don't leave it on the table."

Glowering, he charged Kanna. She ducked his haymaker with ease and caught his arm. Twisting her body, she swung him over her shoulder like an axe. The guard groaned after thumping against the concrete floor and a sizeable gash opened along his buzz cut scalp. As he rolled over, Kanna took a moment to kneel next to him.

"So ganglander, any chance you have a key for that door over there? I'd rather avoid the noise I'd make kicking it in," she stated coolly.

"Piss off," he retorted.

She placed a boot against his face and continued, "Look, this is just business. Your lot stole something of mine and I plan to take it back. I have no problem knocking you out, but if you make things more difficult, you'll end up like your friend over there."

"I'm not telling you shit," he replied through gritted teeth.

Striking like a snake, he grabbed her boot and swung a knife at her ankle. Catching his hand mid swing with her left arm, Kanna laughed.

"You picked the wrong side. This hand here is my bionic one," she stated while squeezing his hand.

He screamed as his bones began to pop and snap under the crushing grip of her metal appendage.

"If you'd swung to my right, you might have cut me."

Switching to a choke hold, she pressed her head against the base of his skull and continued to apply pressure until he fell limp.

She rifled through his pockets and located a couple of keycards. Striding over to the door, she tapped the first card against the lock. It buzzed and flashed a small red light. She tried the second one and the lock clicked and showed a green light. Kanna slid through the door and carefully closed it shut.

After reaching the door to the next floor down, she paused and turned on her infrared vision. It appeared that eight guards were on this floor. As one passed the door, she closed her left eye and peered through the small rectangular window with her non-bionic eye. The back of his black leather jacket was embroidered with a red logo of a panther skull with a knife between its teeth.

"These ganglanders are going all out with the branding these days," Kanna muttered to herself.

She slid the door open and crept behind the unsuspecting thug, then flipped her Phantom 11.2 from behind her back and pressed the barrel to his skull. Before he could turn his head, she snatched his collar and emptied a heat exhaust round from her rifle, then disposed of him on the staircase behind the door.

Kanna then approached a room at the hallway's halfway point. She had to dispatch as many of the exterior guards as possible before approaching her target's room, to avoid any chance of being ambushed. When surveilling the top floor, she noticed two guards were posted with her target while two more stood outside his door. The remaining four ganglanders took turns roving the halls. She'd removed one already and planned to eliminate the remaining three behind the door to her right.

Stilling her breathing, she pressed her back against the door, listening with her bionic ear.

"Hey Brady, you going to finish that beef tantuni?"

"No way, Alkim. I plan on eating them both."

"Fine. Can you at least toss me another beer?"

"Get it yourself, lazy ass."

"Really, Brady? You wanna..."

"Knock it off you two. Here's your damn beer, Alkim."

"Thanks, Baltan."

'Hmm, well fed and distracted. This should be easy.' Kanna thought as she readied her rifle.

She double tapped her temple, then blinked after selecting: *Sync with Rifle.* Her infrared vision created small green boxes around each of the ganglanders heads. As Kanna passed her scope across each box it gave an affirmative click. She took the shift on the side of her rifle and slid it until the side-display read: *Homing rounds.* Her bionic eye showed the change in text at the top of her vision, so she wouldn't have to look down. She quickly sent three rounds through the wall that hit each thug between their eyes. Painting the walls behind them in deep crimson.

Darting inside the room, she shut the door. Her Phantom didn't make much noise, but it would be enough to make the two guards in front of the office check the hallway. She placed her rifle on her back and readied herself for their arrival, watching as one of the men approached her bullet holes.

"What the hell is this? Did one of you idiots accidentally crank off a couple rounds?! Was it you again, Alkim?" the guard called out perturbed.

Kanna twisted her hand and a blade stretched out from an opening in her bionic arm. She shoved it through the wall – and forehead – of the unsuspecting guard, then yanked it back as the second thug burst through the door. He fired two shots at her, which Kanna barely deflected with her arm-blade. The bullets broke the blade, sending the top half sailing into the wall behind her. She leapt behind a table in the center of the room and grabbed one of the fallen ganglanders. Using him as a shield against the shots fired by the remaining guard, she kicked the table over, showering her assailant with a mix of food, booze, and bootleg gambling chips. He dodged and fired a few more rounds. She shoved the dead guard's body at him, causing him to trip over the spilt items on the floor.

Kanna smiled viciously. *'You're mine, ganglander.'*

She jumped over the table and sent a boot into his face. His jaw cracked against her heel and he spun in the air before slamming against the wall. Kanna strode over to his prone frame. Searching her fallen enemy's pockets, she found the only keycard she hadn't already acquired. Leaving the room, she marched down the hallway until it forced her to make a right turn. An exit sign hung over the doorway at the hall's end, and a few paces to her left were two more doors. She scanned them with her enhanced eye. The first room was unoccupied. Inside the second, she noticed two ganglanders with their guns drawn and someone hiding behind a desk.

Moments later, the second door flew off its hinges and the two guards sent a hail of bullets towards the entryway. Clips now empty, they breathed heavily as the smoke and drywall dust began to dissipate.

"I don't see anyone there!" one guard yelped.

"Then go look in the hallway!" the man behind the desk ordered.

He ran over to the doorway and peered into the hall, but still found nothing. He looked down and noticed the scattered remnants of a remote explosive near the shattered door.

The second guard pulled a Merge from his inner jacket pocket. "I'll call the rest from outside and tell them we need..."

Suddenly a section of drywall from the unoccupied room crashed into him. His Merge was sent flying from his hand and shattered against a metal shelf. Kanna unholstered a small pistol and fired through the opening, putting two bullets through the head of the guard standing at the door. She dashed toward the ganglander underneath the shattered drywall piece. Stomping her foot down to hold him still, she dropped three shots through the drywall, putting him to rest.

The man behind the desk desperately grasped at the inner pocket of his suit jacket, "Dammit, I need Rathe and the rest of his men in here!"

Before the man could text for reinforcements, Kanna sent a needle point knife through his phone.

"Besir Morkov, where's the data you stole from me?" she asked.

Besir stumbled back a few steps until he bumped into the large glass window behind him.

"I... I don't know what you're talking about?"

"Hmph, of course you don't, Besir. Maybe if I used your hacker name, you'd remember. You mined some data from my grandfather's company under the handle Castle_Bear070. I need to see all the storage you keep in that safe," Kanna said while thumbing at a door on her right.

Besir continued to stare in bewilderment. His chubby frame trembled as he cringed against the window. He had no further area to retreat, yet his fear compelled him to create as much distance from Kanna as possible, even if it was only an extra inch. She took another step towards him.

"Stop right there!" Besir yelped, "If you move any closer, I'll trigger the alarm. Even if you kill me, you won't break into that safe before the rest of my men get here and carve you up."

"You don't have an alarm," Kanna said while laughing, "If you did, you would have triggered it already instead of reaching for your Merge."

Kanna moved in and snatched Besir by the front of his collar. "I need you to open that safe over there, and show me all the data you mined from the SatellaField archives," she demanded fiercely.

Besir's dark eyes watered and his thinly bearded chin quivered as he stared back into Kanna's ruthless glare.

"I-I'll open the safe, *please...*" Besir stammered.

"Good boy," Kanna replied.

She let go of his collar and he fell to his knees in a heap. He looked up at Kanna, who folded her arms and raised an eyebrow expectantly in his direction. She tilted her head towards the safe and Besir clumsily scrambled towards it. A few moments later the large metal door gave a click and he yanked it open. Kanna looked inside and saw stacks of servers and hard drives piled on shelves. She tossed a remote explosive inside, then returned to Besir and grabbed him by the arm.

"How many others are part of your data smuggling network?" she inquired.

Besir looked over her shoulder and noticed the remote explosive was counting down from ninety seconds.

"Answer me," Kanna said while shaking Besir.

"I-It's just us," Besir said as he shook his head slightly, "We set this up to gain access to the Hive. Anyone who can give them SatellaField information gets immediate entry to their hacking group."

"Hmm. Well, that's good then. At least the chain ends with you," Kanna replied confidently.

Besir smiled back hopefully, "So you'll let me go?"

Kanna shrugged, "If you want."

She let go of Besir's arm. Before he could reach his feet, Kanna kicked him in the chest and sent him flying through the glass window. Besir Morkov flailed uselessly as he plummeted downward. His heavy frame continued to fall until it smacked against the top of a red sportscar parked in front of his building, causing the windows to erupt in a sea of shattered glass.

She looked back at the remote mine, which now said sixty seconds, then nodded and left the room. Ascending the stairs to the roof, she could hear the clamoring of several ganglanders charging towards the top floor. She would be gone before they could reach her. Kanna briskly approached the edge of the rooftop with her glider in hand. She leapt off and sailed towards an exterior-metal staircase on the building she originally came from.

'Good, none of them made it the roof yet,' she thought while looking over her shoulder.

Her feet clinked against the metal stairs as she landed. As she reached the top of the staircase, a loud explosion rang out from Besir's hideout. She waited for a few moments and watched the flames trickle out from the windows on the highest floor.

"Your gang won't steal from me again," she said aloud.

Kanna ran across the roof, taking off into the air on the opposite side. Clicking the glider's handle, she felt the rush of air swirl past her as she flew away. She continued past a smattering of five story brick buildings, whose aged, neon signs barely cast a dull hue. Kanna touched down on a cracked, uninhabited road two blocks away. She turned down a nearby alleyway where she'd left her Viper-cycle. Kanna's bike was a striking mix of black and neon green. Decals from some the best brands decorated her bike: Kolt across the tires, Sprigus along the frame and stamped on the engine was Grux.

Thumbing the glider's destruct button, she tossed it aside. A few seconds later it burst into a pile of metal dust. Kanna then mounted her Viper-cycle and pulled the visor down on her helmet. It booted up and displayed a HUD as she tilted it down. The visor glimmered briefly before switching to a more favorable contrast, allowing her to see better while riding through the dark corners of Rasmuson. She revved the engine a few times then raced into the night, her taillights leaving behind a glowing wake as she sped away.

- CHAPTER 3 -

TETRAGON

CIVIC REGION WITHIN THE
NORTHBRIDGE DOMAIN

THE piercing ring from Jared's mechanical alarm clock yanked him from his slumber. He slammed his hand over the buzzer clumsily and accidentally knocked it from his nightstand.

"Dammit," he mumbled.

Jared rested his head back for a moment while intermittently clenching his fists. He needed to ease himself awake since his body was begging for a return to sleep. Finally roused, he swept his legs off the bed and propped himself upright. While recovering the first model Personal Station from the Kal Mountains was incredible, it didn't pay. Luckily, he and Gillman's repair shop covered most of the bills, but Jared still had to occasionally work a few side gigs to make up the difference.

As he staggered from his room down the hall, he was greeted with the scent of fresh coffee and cinnamon hot cakes. Gillman was a legitimately good cook, and breakfast was his specialty.

"Here, I got yours ready for you," Gillman said as he slid a mug of hot black coffee towards Jared.

"Thanks, Gill," Jared replied while nodding in gratitude.

"You know, I played around with that Station you found after I woke up this morning. I'm not sure if it's from being left in that cold mountain all this time, but it won't boot up," Gillman said while whisking eggs in a pan.

"Did you try charging it?" Jared asked.

Gillman turned around and frowned at him. "Of course I tried that. Do I look like an amateur to you?"

Jared laughed. He enjoyed Gillman's curmudgeonly nature and wanted to prod him further, but he was still too groggy to come up with a witty retort.

"I'm thinking there must be a programming sequence you have to send from an external source, but I'm not exactly sure where to start. Any chance you'll have some time after refereeing those Auger matches to code something?" Gillman asked.

Jared finished a sip from his mug. "Yea, I think I could make something. How long until those eggs are done?"

"Another minute," Gillman answered while setting the pan on the counter.

Gillman dusted the eggs with salt and pepper before tipping the pan and scraping them into a large bowl. He then grabbed some chives from a small dish and sprinkled them on top.

"Alright, they're ready."

Jared eagerly filled his plate with three hot cakes and a generous helping of scrambled eggs.

"Are you officiating one of the high-level pros this time? That last bout you told me about sounded intense."

Jared chuckled, "Not for this match. I put myself in the on-call pool, so it's a token flip on the quality of talent."

Jared poured some blueberry syrup onto his hot cakes before taking a sizeable bite. Gillman rounded the peninsula counter and sat down at a small white table. He looked over at Jared, who was still standing and eating at the counter.

"Why don't you come sit with me and eat like an adult. You're scarfing down that food like some wolf from Moncroix," Gillman said while pointing a fork at his friend.

Jared shook his head. "Sorry Gill, I don't know when my Merge is going to buzz so I need to eat fast. Maybe when you get a real job, you'll understand."

Gillman laughed, "Maybe that relic you dug up will make us both rich and we can build that airship."

"One day, Gill," Jared said while finishing his last bite.

He checked his phone and saw a notification telling him where he was being requested to referee an Augmented Reality Contest. Jared held up his device towards his friend.

"Well, looks like the dream will have to wait. I have to go watch a bunch of kids pretend to fight."

―――――

"You dare try and trick me with a mere Silkblade?" a voice called out as he pulled his sword from his sheath.

"I do more than dare, Bontallameo," his opponent replied.

Jared tried to keep his palm from constantly being smashed against his forehead. He'd traveled across a few Intercontinents while making his way to Lor-Rev, including the one this group

25

pretended to hail from during their match. He'd been asked to referee a group who wanted to reenact a Moncroix fencing match. These two were a far cry from the quick and daring swashbuckling seen during a true contest. Gillman had taken him to an actual one on that Intercont years ago, before reaching Lor-Rev. He'd seen a rising upstart named Carneth Allard defeat someone while showcasing incredible acrobatics. This was not that arena, and these two were not Carneth.

He wanted to snap a few pictures with his Merge and send them to Gillman, but he was prohibited from carrying a personal communication device while officiating. He remained professional and bit his lip. This Auger match was almost done and it was the last before his shift was over. When Jared first arrived in Lor-Rev, he was astonished by the skill and excitement of a professional Augmented Reality Contest, or ARC for short. The professional matches were run by the HLA, an acronym for High League Augmenters. This official governing body sanctioned contests in areas they reserved. This allowed competitors to fight anywhere from an arena to the middle of a city. Combatants were outfitted with weaponry and armor that could be fashioned in any way imaginable, since it was built digitally. The Auger weapons and armor, referred to often as "gear," would be projected from the full body Exo-suits they wore.

Any attacks combatants made would register on the suits, which would create a corresponding effect of blood, sparks or an explosion. When attending his first match, Jared marveled at the tense back and forth action. Some contestants even wore boots and anti-gravity packs, allowing them to have mid-air gun battles and sword fights. HLA Auger matchers were like nothing else in the Forum.

Jared signed on to officiate bouts like the one he first saw. However, being a new officiant meant he was lower on the rung and access to those matches was few and far between. His schedule was usually decent amateurs trying to rank for professional or unsanctioned exhibitions between a few friends. Exhibitions like the one now were usually run by a minor tech company who acquired a batch of old Exo-suits and armament plugins they'd rent out for a few tokens.

One thing he enjoyed about these unranked matches, was that he could intervene with obstacles if the participants forgot to turn that feature off while choosing their rules. Jared watched as the two young men goofily jabbed at each other with fencing swords made of orange light. It was time he added some flare.

He held up his hands with his fingers outstretched and a map of the playable area projected before him. Jared selected a few items and tapped on the locations he wanted them placed. He then opened a side menu and began typing a code sequence into the search bar.

'I knew they wouldn't have a strong firewall,' Jared thought as he hacked into the root of their program.

He reached into his pocket and nabbed a small hard drive. This storage device could send light-transmitted data from one side, and link into the projection of his Auger match menu. After a few seconds the program from his storage device was uploaded. He smiled and selected to initiate his changes.

"Have you no shame, Bontallameo?" one competitor bellowed.

"I do as I wish, Salomon," the other answered emphatically.

Abruptly, large boulders began to fall around the two, enclosing them in a circular border.

"What the hell is this?" the one calling himself Salomon asked.

"I don't know, man? This didn't happen when Revin and I fought last week," his friend – going by Bontallameo – replied.

At one side of the rock circle appeared a set of arched double doors. They slowly opened and a projection of Carneth

27

Allard stepped through. Carneth swished his sword through an impressive set of techniques before pointing his weapon at the two Augers.

"You two show promise, I wish to formally challenge you both," Carneth's projection proclaimed.

Bontallameo elbowed Salomon.

"Daron, I think that's Carneth Allard!"

"No way, Erik. You serious?!"

"I bet we can take him."

"I don't know, he's one of the best fencers in the Interconts."

"Yea, I know, Daron. But do you really think this Augment Battle projection is going to have the same skill? You put it on medium difficulty, right?"

"I did. Alright, Erik. You go left, I'll go right."

The two charged forward and slashed at Carneth wildly. Carneth flipped backwards onto his hands then pushed off, dodging the blow perfectly and completing the handspring by landing on his feet. Again, Erik and Daron charged forward and slashed frantically, but Carneth evaded them again.

'I was hoping they might actually employ some tactics,' Jared thought while shaking his head. *'Well, I guess I'll have to make old Carneth here use some offense. Sorry guys, it's the only way you'll learn.'*

He opened his menu and made a few adjustments as the Carneth projection parried a few incoming strikes from Erik and Daron.

"I thought you put this on medium?" Erik yelped to his friend.

"I did! I don't understand why we're not able to hit him?" Daron answered amid ducking a swing from Carneth.

Jared tilted his head around the menu projection and grinned. He then continued typing a few more commands. Erik and Daron continued to flail and swing wildly at Carneth, but had no

28

success. The projection was an almost perfect re-creation. Jared made it while previously working on plugins that he submitted with his initial officiant resume to the HLA. He crossed his arms and watched as the two amateur Augers were easily countered and bested by his creation.

'I should at least give these guys a chance,' Jared told himself.

At the last minute, he opened his menu and made a few more changes. While it was amusing to watch these two get crushed by Carneth initially, he started to feel bad picking on them. Carneth stopped short of Erik and Daron, then sheathed his sword and crossed his arms.

"You two have shown incredible spirit in this battle. I'm willing to offer my services and train you both in the formal Moncroix sword fighting techniques," Carneth stated.

Erik and Daron helped each other up to their feet and looked over at Carneth, who had his hand extended towards them.

"What do you say gentlemen? Will you accept my offer?" Carneth asked.

Erik stepped forward and clasped hands with him.

Jared smiled as he watched the exchange. *'Good. There's still enough time in the match for him to teach them a couple basic moves.'*

"You've already taught me my first lesson," Erik said while still holding Carneth's hand.

"What's that?" Carneth inquired.

"You shouldn't let your guard down."

A small knife fell into Erik's hand from inside his sleeve and he plunged it into Carneth's neck. Carneth looked up in horror as blood filled his mouth while falling forward onto his hands and knees. Daron and Erik began kicking and stomping the projection of Carneth.

"What an idiot! You think you can just smack us around and not get what's coming to you?" Daron said as he kicked Carneth in the ribs.

Jared glared at the two while they continued to beat on the helpless projection of Carneth. Seconds later he made it disappear along with the circular rock wall. Daron and Erik began celebrating their "win" while the timer for the match reached zero. Jared initiated the shutdown sequence for the contest while the two wannabe Augers walked over to a nearby bench and sat down. This match took place in a grass park that had several fields also being used for other minor matches. The two began taking off their boots and gloves while chatting excitedly about their contest. Jared shook his head while approaching a freestanding locker at the edge of the field. He retrieved his blue leather jacket and put it on over his referee shirt. He felt his Merge buzz, and retrieved it from an inside pocket.

Jared looked down and saw a text from Gillman:

GILL

I got the station to boot up.

ME

I'll be right there, just let me wrap this up.

After sliding his phone in his pocket, he approached Erik and Daron, who were still sitting on the bench with sweaty brows. He hadn't forgotten about giving these two a chance most Augers would relish, and that they spit on it.

"Hey, ref. Thanks for the bout. It was pretty sweet getting to fight against that Carneth projection," Erik said while brushing his damp bangs away from his face.

Jared grabbed Erik by the collar and punched him in the face. Daron started to stand up and Jared turned on him. Daron immediately recoiled after seeing his livid stare.

"W-w-what are you doing?" Daron finally stammered.

"Teaching *you* a damn lesson," Jared replied while shoving a finger in his chest, "and to think, I almost had that projection teach you something useful. You're the reason Tetragon is turning into a dump!"

"You can't do this! I'll report you to the officiating directory!" Daron yelled.

Jared leaned forward with his fist aloft and Daron covered his face and squealed.

"That's what I thought. Now grab your sorry friend over there and leave," he said coldly.

Daron scrambled over to Erik and brought him to his feet. The two then scampered off, heading to a train terminal at the opposite end of the park. Jared slumped onto the bench and shook his head.

"Damn, that one's going to cost me…" he grumbled.

He pulled his phone from his pocket and opened an application for his vehicle. Jared drove a Parallax Model-3. It was an older Lor-Rev sports car that he'd outfitted with a better engine and new computer. The car's color was a mix of bright red with slashes of white, and sported black wheels with thin tires. As Jared descended a staircase to exit the park, his vehicle raced around a corner and stopped on the street in front of him. As he slid into the driver's seat the door closed automatically behind him. He tossed his Merge over a Puck on the dashboard, which held it suspended in an upright position.

When using a vehicle, most in Lor-Rev opted for the self-driving function, but Jared preferred the control of running it himself. He shifted gears and raced down the street back to the shop, eagerly imagining all the possible secrets they could uncover from the Personal Station.

KANNA

- CHAPTER 4 -

CHUSHIN

CIVIC REGION WITHIN THE
NORTHBRIDGE DOMAIN

KANNA leaned forward on her Viper-cycle as she zipped between two silver compact sedans. A sliver of daylight crept between a few skyscrapers and glinted off her cycle's front fender. Chushin was the largest metropolitan region in Lor-Rev and stretched a great distance. The downtown corridor Kanna sped through was a conglomerate of large superstructures and several stacked highways, surrounded by a cluster of shorter concrete office towers. Despite being so densely packed, this civic region was quite clean. The high-rise buildings were made of exquisite materials and constructed in unique shapes. Some were shiny glass with the appearance of tall, jagged tree trunks, while others looked like slick beams of carbon.

Kanna was on an elevated highway two streets above the ground road. After fixing the small mess in Rasmuson, she was heading back to the main headquarters of Ergo Corporation for a board meeting. It was initially intimidating to attend them, but now she viewed it as a chore. She had to participate though, if not, she wouldn't keep her position. And this monotonous day job funded her real work.

Kanna leaned to her left and swept through a turn in a beautiful arc. Behind her, several bright projected advertisements shimmered while one building's vertical neon stripe cast a haze along her matte-finish helmet. She was only a few miles out from Ergo's headquarters located in the center of Chushin. She'd made the drive several times now and didn't even bother logging the course in her visor's navigation option. Kanna dipped to her right around a large tanker truck then revved her cycle forward. Her speed and sharp movements made the black and green vehicle look like a motorized lizard. She continued towards her off-ramp. Upon reaching the bottom, she yanked back on the handle bars and wheelied forward. Not as a means of showing off, but as an instinctual stretch of her vehicle's ability. Her Viper-cycle needed to be driven with an edge.

Kanna continued her snaking path through a few crowded surface streets. For most Lor-Revians, it was a slight reprieve to be on the lowest level underneath the stacked highways. The roads overhead blocked the beaming projection of advertisements bombarding the drivers above.

She whizzed around one final bend before approaching a rising glass door on the side of Ergo's building, controlled by a proximity sensor that opened it automatically upon her arrival. Kanna slid to a stop inside the building, then turned to watch the door lower. She couldn't be too careful. While the tech-company giants who resided in Chushin were blanketed in armed security, she wouldn't risk some ganglander trying to sneak in behind her. She'd learned over the years that the thugs and ganglanders populating Lor-Rev's dark corners were never above taking a chance. Especially if it meant a huge prize at the end. She removed her helmet and set it on a Puck mounted between the handle bars.

Upon exiting the garage, she immediately entered a small room with a single stack locker, one hovering table made of marble, and a cushioned chair crafted with slick leather. A framed poster of her favorite synth-wave band King Vulture and another for the jazz musician Nocturn Rey hung on different walls.

"Play my pre-meeting mix," Kanna stated.

Hover mounted speakers on the opposite wall began playing a mix of café jazz as she got ready. Kanna changed from her synthetic leggings and biker jacket into a pants suit that was more befitting for the meeting. Many in the board room falsely assumed she would prefer to attend in her riding attire, but Kanna enjoyed both outfits. She just found the meetings themselves tedious. The information was important, but the constant angling and politics by the board members had become obnoxious. Luckily, her grandfather instructed her before his passing to play the role of naivety and non-assumption. Then the members would all come to her with their plans, hoping to pitch her as the deciding vote. It kept her as an unaffixed sidecar who never impeded traffic or aligned with anyone permanently. Her votes never upset those who were opposed, it somehow motivated them to fight harder to gain her trust.

She took an elevator to the fifty-second floor and upon exiting, two armed guards escorted her – as they customarily did with all members – into the meeting room. As Kanna looked around the large lacquer table she noticed a few members were still outstanding. After taking her seat, she leaned forward in her white leather chair and pressed her thumb onto a small fingerprint scanner. A three-sided folio rose from a slot in the table. Each section of the folio had a screen with a different set of information. She looked over the one to her left, which showed upcoming acquisitions. The text on the screen scrolled along with her eye movement, so she didn't have to use touch controls. This section was vital to her because most hacks and data theft occurred as Ergo funneled a new company into their portfolio. Most of Ergo had no idea what they were sitting on in some of the encrypted archives. Before Johan had passed, he'd tasked her with keeping his most important information out of the wrong hands.

She began daydreaming, remembering the day he'd explained his plans to her.

'Why don't you just destroy it grandfather?' she'd asked him back then.

'That would be the easy way, but these works, their schematics… I can't just toss them in the trash. I need them kept alive for someone who can make these dreams a reality. Someone who would do it for the right reasons,' her grandfather had explained.

'Grandfather, how am I supposed to decide that? If you couldn't find…'

Johan had turned to her with a glare she'd never seen before. It interrupted her thoughts completely and made her stiffen. His face didn't show anger but instead wore a much more powerful expression, an expression of expectation.

Kanna blinked and broke from the daydream. Part of her thought about accessing the video recording through the memory bank in her cybernetic eye. Seeing it visually renewed her motivation to safeguard his work. After a moment of pondering, she decided it best not to draw herself too far from the upcoming meeting.

The last few outstanding members entered the room and took their seats. One of them, who sat to her left, leaned over and nudged Kanna with her elbow. Kanna glanced in the woman's direction, it was Delacroix Kusura. She'd been angling heavily to align herself with Kanna, or rather more accurately, have Kanna align

36

with her. Delacroix handed her a paper cup made for warm beverages, then she carefully slid a small bag towards her on the table. Kanna nodded thankfully while accepting the gifts. There were some perks to constantly being corporately courted.

"I know you're usually a coffee drinker, but you'll need that tea today. It's going to be a long one, so I'm sure you'll appreciate the extra caffeine," Delacroix cheerily said with a smirk.

"Hmm. I'll give it a shot," Kanna replied while turning it in her hand to see the label on the cup's carboard sleeve.

"That's my friend's place. She's half Malcozéan, and has a tea and coffee stand on the east side. She imports leaves and beans from a variety of Interconts. I know there are several little boutique coffee shops, but this one has some new blends I haven't seen before," Delacroix informed her excitedly.

Kanna studied the interesting cursive Malcozéan writing on the cardboard sleeve, which her cybernetic eye translated to read as Mornehallow Brew. She took a sip and then dug into the small paper bag.

"That's a Malcozéan breakfast treat. It has a filling that's similar to a cherry flavor, but it's a little bit sweeter."

Kanna observed the glazed pastry briefly before taking a small bite.

"Wow, that's really good," she said, her eyes widening in surprise. She wasn't familiar with Malcozéan food.

"I know, right? It goes perfect with that tea latte," Delacroix replied.

"Thanks, Delacroix. I'm surprised by this tea as well. It has a much richer flavor – like coffee. You're two for two now, between this and the drinking chocolate before the last meeting," Kanna said between sips.

Delacroix gave her a grin. "I always do this for the two seats next to me. It's been an unofficial custom of mine for a few years now."

"Well, they better not move your seat away from mine then," Kanna replied with a wink.

"I'll make sure of it," her seat mate beamed back before taking another sip of her own tea latte.

Delacroix then faced the center screen of the projected three-sided folio and studied the meeting minutes. Kanna glanced over and easily noticed the redness of her cheeks blushing underneath the thick black-rimmed glasses. Like seeing a ripe apple next to a new tire.

Ingratiating herself to Delacroix had more important benefits than the occasional free beverage. Her seat mate was placed in a new division, but wasn't new to the company. Delacroix had been around since Ergo's founding. She started as an administrator, but eventually moved up the ladder until taking a board seat. As she reached retirement though, the company gave her an easy assignment for her final years. She'd be running some of the small warehouses near the shipping ports in the Southbridge area. When Kanna was tasked with keeping her grandfather's archives secret, she knew having the right relationships in Ergo would be key. Someone like Delacroix knew where everything was buried.

Kanna looked to her right as the CEO of the company, Therik Leibert, rose from his chair.

"Thank you everyone for attending. To start the meeting, there will be an introductory video on your folio that highlights our most recent developments."

Therik sat back down and tapped on his folio to begin the video. Kanna watched as four diamonds swirled around the middle of the screen before coming together to make the Ergo logo. Once the brief video finished, another board member stood from his chair. It was the Chief Financial Officer, Daniel Nevins.

"I'll ask that you all view my accounting presentation on your right-side folio," Daniel stated calmy.

'Will the gods please save me,' Kanna bemoaned to herself, *'I don't think I can survive another one of Daniel's slide presentations.'*

Suddenly a notification appeared on her left folio, which was linked to her Merge. Kanna tapped on the icon of a letter being held in a hand and the notification opened. It was a message from a specific application, the one her grandfather had created to alert her when something happened to his archives. This message however, said something she hadn't expected to see. Something she assumed would never be displayed.

It read: **The First Model Personal Station has been located.**

- CHAPTER 5 -

ILLEMKI

CIVIC REGION WITHIN THE
SOUTHBRIDGE DOMAIN

HE strode down a sidewalk littered with small shops; blazing signage read as an encyclopedia of a citizen's needs when residing in a crowded metropolis. The majority were little restaurants of small occupancy, while a few others sold tools or electronics. It was the dead of night, but every shop was still open. The peculiar business hours were commonplace in a region populated with shift

40

workers. The Southbridge was the main hub for construction, manufacturing, and dock work at the ports.

Now that Daemon had escaped from his digital cage, he could begin his work. Before tracking down any items leading to the Diffusor, he needed to assemble a roster of people that would enable his mission. He needed someone who could assist with procuring certain equipment, which made this Port Overseer worth obtaining. While continuing his stroll, he thought of how wrong Johan had been. Before his fusion, the program was being held back from generating so much progress. If only he could've seen it.

Daemon rounded the corner and passed a few more stores before finally emerging from the shopping district. Now with the buzzing neon signs behind him, he strode along an empty street that led towards the dock. The heels of his tall boots clicked on the flat pavement with a sharp rapping sound. After a few more blocks, he arrived at the port which was walled with a tall chain link fence. He held his hand, which morphed into a blade, and sliced through it. After stepping through the new opening, he turned around and held up a finger. The thin appendage fell open from the top knuckle like a hinge. A miniature blue flame emerged, and he used it like blowtorch to weld the fencing back together.

He'd hacked a server earlier to acquire the port's scheduling, and planned his arrival to occur during the security's shift change. His earlier attempts to meet with the Port Overseer had failed. He'd wished to have a conversation and coax him, rather than sneak around at night. Unfortunately, he'd been shooed off like some rat picking scraps in an alley.

"His choice will be made for him," he calmy stated while skulking between a few metal shipping containers.

Daemon had engineered something that would ensure those he wished to recruit would participate, willingly or otherwise. Microscopic nanites, that once inside the bloodstream, enhanced the user's mind and connected them to the inter-web remotely. The convenience came at a cost however. They also allowed Daemon to monitor you. Your travel, communication, and even changes in your mood. It didn't give him full governance over someone's functions, but it lent him enough data to keep them under his thumb.

He pulled his cloak around his chest, attaching two magnetic buttons together. It was more than just a piece of clothing; it allowed him to mimic the nearby scenery as a means of camouflage. His hat was also made of the same fabric.

Daemon darted towards an elevated trailer which housed his anticipated acquisition. Soon another would transcend.

Aaron Gotch rested in a banged-up recliner while scrolling through his Merge. He had a model from several generations ago, but it still cast videos directly to his monitor, which was his favorite feature. Despite the cracked screen and scraped edges, it still did what he needed. He saw no reason to drop a bunch of tokens for an upgraded one. Aaron swiped up with his thumb and sent an old episode of his favorite show to the screen mounted on the opposite wall. He laughed as the protagonist – a slim thirty something – found himself in surprisingly unfortunate and hilarious situations along with his friends. Despite their unique predicaments, somehow the life portrayed in the show felt incredibly relatable.

Aaron had recently finished a ten-hour shift supervising cargo freighters lugging in materials from Kratas. It was another Intercontinent that was mined frequently for its rich mineral sources. Specifically, its vast stretches of sand that were sifted and purified to obtain silicon. Aaron had been working at this port and overseeing what came and went his entire adult life. His father, Warner Gotch, had run it before him and now after his passing he'd taken up the mantle.

Aaron took a swig from his can of beer and sank a little deeper into the cushions. After this episode he would grab a second drink, called a Jump-Pack. It would put him to sleep for exactly five hours, and then activate a delayed caffeine release. It would give him the umph needed to begin another ten hours on the docks. As the credits rolled, he snatched his Merge and clicked the side button to place it in sleep mode. He flopped onto the bed and kicked his hefty work boots off, each one thumping onto the floor next to him. He didn't bother undressing and just yanked the covers over himself. He grabbed the Jump-Pack from his night stand. The drink was housed in a small container a little bigger than a thumb and had the branding of Falcon-Kid – a video game mascot – emblazoned on the side. The drink's wrapper was made of a thin rollable LED that could display moving images. As Aaron ripped off the top, the image of Falcon-Kid threw a punch. He tipped his head back and took the drink down in one gulp, and as he did so, the video game mascot jumped upward. Aaron scrunched his eyelids and winced upon finishing the syrupy, metallic-tasting beverage.

"Yeesh, I don't think I'll ever get used to that aftertaste," he said aloud.

He turned the container over and looked at the label, which now showed Flacon-Kid giving him a thumbs up.

"Hmph… you *would* be happy about me sucking down this battery acid."

Aaron tossed it towards his plastic waste bin and it bounced off the wall, but didn't make it in.

"Bah. I'll worry about it in the morning."

He leaned back and waited for the effects to kick in. Sleep wasn't hard to achieve after a normal work day. But when he knew another shift was coming right around the corner, his mind tended to race.

WHACK!

The door to his trailer snapped open and a cloaked figure wearing a wide brim hat stood in the entryway.

"Get out, or I'll knock your head clean off your shoulder blades!" Aaron yelled.

He crawled over to the dresser near the edge of his bed and reached for a baton he kept behind it. Daemon extended his arm while maintaining his place in the doorway and punched through the dresser. He yanked back and flung the piece of furniture away. Pale-faced, Aaron reached under his bed quickly and nabbed his shotgun. He turned in Daemon's direction, but he'd vanished.

"Shit! Shit! Shit!" Aaron cursed under his breath.

He ran to the doorway and peered into the night looking for the intruder.

Suddenly a soft voice spoke behind him, "I'm only here to enlighten you."

Aaron whirled around and as he did so, clicked a switch on his shotgun to activate burst fire. He yanked on the trigger and three shells erupted from the barrel one after another. Seeing one of the shots connect, he kept the shotgun trained on Daemon while panting heavily. A ghastly snarl of horror crossed his face as the hole in Daemon's shoulder began to grow back and close. Thin wires and metal knitted themselves together. He tried to speak, but his throat felt empty and uncoordinated, like feet wearing shoes whose laces were tied together.

"I'm not here to harm you, Aaron. When we spoke a few days ago I offered you an opportunity. However, I can no longer wait for you to make a decision."

Aaron's brow rose as he realized who stood before him.

"You're that creep who showed up here the other day."

He raised his shotgun again, "This is your last chance to get the hell off my dock. I'll keep putting holes in whatever cyber-gear you got until security drags you off."

Daemon tilted his hat up and ran his thumb and forefinger over the brim. As he did so liquid metal dried along the section he traced.

"Last chance, asshole," Aaron threatened through gritted teeth.

Daemon threw his hat and sliced Aaron's long-gun in two. Aaron held up the pieces in his hands while staring blankly at them. Desperately, he threw them both at Daemon and raced down the steps that led outside. As his feet hit the pavement, he felt something snap around his neck. He curled his fingers around the object, which felt like twisted rebar against his throat. After snaring his prey, Daemon began to recoil his arm, dragging Aaron back to him. Aaron reached for a multi-tool in a side pocket. He pressed a button on the tool and a pair of shears emerged. He jabbed them into the tendril and sliced a good chunk from it. He continued trying to chip away, but it was too far behind his head to land an accurate strike.

"I know fear penetrates your mind now, but soon you can unshackle the anchoring burdens of choice and emotion," Daemon said while inexorably pulling him back into the trailer.

Aaron grunted against Daemon's metal fingers squeezing his throat. The tight grip around his windpipe kept him speechless. Daemon extended his other arm and shut the door behind Aaron, then fused the lock shut.

He retrieved a small rectangular device from his pocket which carried the nanites. After pressing his thumb against it, a tiny needle extended.

"Luckily, I don't have to circumvent any cybernetic equipment. This process will be much less painful for you, Aaron. Although, it won't be as quick."

As Daemon spoke the words, Aaron noticed he had an oddly bright inflection. As if he was trying to imitate a chipper attitude to soothe his panic. Aaron tried thinking of another way out, but suddenly his eyelids became too heavy to hold open.

'Dammit, the Jump-Pa...'

Before he could finish the thought, the effects of his drink kicked in and he slipped off into a new set of dreams.

Daemon stuck the needle into Aaron's shoulder and waited for the nanites to upload into his blood stream. After completing the patch, Daemon briskly walked over to the shotgun, which he proceeded to weld back together. Now that Aaron was one with the collective, there was no reason to leave his perfectly good tool broken in half on the floor. He scooped up his hat next and approached the window on the far side, rather than leaving through the door. He knew the earlier gunfire would attract security. Placing his hat atop his head, he glanced back at Aaron, then leapt from the open window. As he escaped, his cloak and hat generated a blur of nearby imagery around him.

While exiting through a section of cut fence, a line of text entered an upper corner of his vision. Daemon had several columns of alerts that were categorized and would update in real time, whether it was something done by one of his collective or an important event occurring in Lor-Rev. The text for this update entered a column that was previously blank. A column meant to give him news on the most important segment of his plans. It was labeled: Diffusor-Sphere. As the text scrolled underneath the label, it informed him that the first artifact gave off a signal in the civic region of Tetragon.

"Well, that happened much faster than I originally calculated," Daemon said to himself, "I'll need to begin my research for the other pieces earlier than expected."

He opened an inter-web browser for the Scribe Center Archives, then searched for news articles by a specific journalist. After scrolling through several listings, he eventually selected one.

The Southbridge Gazette

southbgaz.int | Antipral 7th, 105 P.F. | 2 Tokens

A Window into the Future's Past:
Part One - An Interview with Gerald Stekanstreet

Conducted by Benwird Ottley

It's a brisk autumn morning walking through the rustic city of Maykune. Seeing the season change in an area that doesn't employ the traditionally constant beautiful weather of most sphere ceilings is a blessing and a curse. While hunkering down in more robust clothing has its charm, I'm reminded why many places opt for a brighter aesthetic; it's not so damn cold.

However, I'm willing to endure this chilling wind and bust out my rarely worn gloves and peacoat for a chance to speak with a titan of technology, Gerald Stekanstreet. Gerald was instrumental in not only building Ergo during its infancy, but also brokering one of the most important acquisitions in Lor-Rev history. He bartered with Johan Naoki to absorb SatellaField and its incomparably popular product, the Merge.

Originally with this series I planned to speak with Johan directly. However, he's closed himself off from the media for years and refuses to take on visitors who may cast too great a spotlight in his direction. While I hold out hope I'll still find a way to secure an interview with Johan, I decided the next best option was speaking with those who knew him, or

47

were around him during the most critical moments. I desired insight into one of Lor-Rev's most brilliant minds, which requires me to brush this canvas with an entire landscape of his life, rather than a simple portrait.

I continue past several quaint shops until I reach the café where Gerald is waiting. My entrance through the door is greeted with the light chime of a miniature bell and a friendly wave from the server. After ordering an amplo sized compresso with steamed milk, I join Gerald at a small table near the line of large pane glass windows occupying one side of the establishment. When interviewing him, I decided it was best to start with the most pivotal moment for his company.

Q: You started Ergo Corporation as a chip manufacturer for desktop and shelf computers. We've seen software manufacturers make the jump to hardware, but it's rare that a company does the opposite. What made you decide to branch out into developing applications?

A: You sound like the board of directors when I presented the idea [laughs]. Obviously, chip manufacturing was the core of our business. It built us and was still our largest earning segment at the time. But I knew that developing software was the future. I'm sure you remember most of the applications people used – whether for typing or drafting spreadsheets – were large and cumbersome. They took up a ton of space and some even required your office to have an entire machine dedicated to that one application. With our knowledge of computing hardware, I really believed we could make much more efficient applications and that would be the future of our business.

Q: When you started Ergo, it wasn't long after the other Intercontinents signed the treaty establishing the Intercontinental Forum. Moving on to when you began software application, did keeping peace with other Intercontinents still play a factor in your decisions like it did during your formative years?

A: I wish I could say it didn't, considering how long it had been, but most people in Lor-Rev live around one hundred fifty years. And in other nations like Malcozé, they live much longer. Many on the board were still feeling remnants of the Congregate's pressure to not push our technology too quickly. They didn't want to upset other Interconts. Tradition mattered back then. Now, at the rate we progress, tradition feels like a foreign concept. Sometimes I wonder if that makes Lor-Rev better or worse.

Q: When you moved into software, and created the Multi-Program Suite, it changed computing forever. Obviously, your company was sizable at that point, but nothing like you were after developing it. How did you navigate that rapid change in growth without crumbling?

A: Yea [laughs], that was such an exciting time, but it was frightening. We'd learned from watching some of the other companies either scale too big or not scale appropriately. Luckily our board wasn't all techies and had some very astute businessmen. One thing we didn't expect was how some of the other big companies would do weird little tricks to try and cut your legs out from under you. Buying shipping and manufacturing plants to either push you out, or make you pay them additional fees to produce your product. Back then everything was on disc, so that type of strong arming was much easier to pull off [laughs].

Q: After navigating your growth, you began the process of acquiring SatellaField. Many say you were instrumental in making that deal happen, as Johan Naoki was known for being extremely guarded. Who had the initial idea to approach Johan and buy his company, you or the executives?

A: Well, many on the board were acquisition hungry once we got the capitol from MPS taking off. Honestly though, most of them assumed Johan was a no-go. I actually befriended him at one of the Future-Cons. All the big players come out for that convention. We hit it off really well and he started opening up about wanting to just go back to tinkering in his garage again. That conversation probably started the ball rolling. I didn't approach it then, but eventually it became something we discussed.

Q: Hearing you mention Johan speaking of a more-simple life, did he bring up the idea of being acquired directly or was it you?

A: Honestly, yes. Now that I think about it... it was him. We became much closer when developing software for the Merge. I think he saw that we had similar visions for where the Merge could and should go. It wasn't long after creating MPS for Merge devices that he dropped a few hints about being open to moving on from SatellaField. Man, I thought it was my brilliant plan, but really... when looking back he teed the whole thing up for me. As long as I was on the board during the acquisition by Ergo, I think Johan knew I wouldn't let his company's legacy be swallowed up and wasted.

Q: What do you think would have happened with SatellaField if you hadn't acquired them?

A: Wow, that's a difficult question. Technology is a weird business. Many people think it's about who makes the best product. Like somehow out of all the businesses in the world, tech is the one true meritocracy. I disagree. I think big-tech is like fashion. The product needs to fit and be accessible, but many times we discard something well before its expiration date for the next one, or we don't move on to something better because the logo on the back is from an unknown company. Look at how often people are upgrading their Merge or other Slates, it's almost yearly at this point. None of that is because something markedly better rounds the corner. Hell, before MPS there were plenty of alternatives, but people were unwilling to step outside the name brands for something unknown. There had to be trust there, and if something was new, it had to have enough cool factor to outweigh the trust issues. That's the mindset of fashion. Tech is fashion. As for SatellaField... I think they would have continued moving along steadily until they unveiled another game changing product. Companies who innovate on their level with a genius like Johan would definitely have another game changing product. There were a few things he had cooking, that if he had the backing to complete... well we'd all be living in a different world. But I can't mention any of that stuff here, NDAs and all. And even if I did tell you, it's all just make-believe without a working prototype. Johan never wanted credit for anything unfinished.

Q: As Johan moved away from public life, how much did you see him versus when he still ran SatellaField?

A: I saw him irregularly. I visited him at his house a few times and he came to see me once in a while. Honestly though, we were just two cranky old mutts chatting about the good ol' days. Nothing during those meetings would interest you much. I haven't seen him in several years. I really need to get ahold of him though. Arrange something like we're doing now... grabbing coffee and arguing about who had the better tech [smiles and looks out the window].

Q: Did you spend much time with Johan's granddaughter?

A: Kanna? Yes, I met with her a few times when she was at Johan's house. He cared for his children deeply, despite all the reports speculating that he didn't get along with most of them. But Kanna, his first grandchild, she really held a special place in his heart. I'm assuming that hasn't changed.

Q: What about her board seat with Ergo? I hear there's rumors of tension regarding her occupying it. Do you have word on that issue from any of your contacts?

A: I knew at some point you'd have to ask [shakes his head]. You're a reporter after all. What I hear from my contacts in the company, it sounds like they just tolerate her and shrug. She doesn't try and sway or divert the board's intentions much. I think they assume it was simply a gift from Johan to Kanna when he retired. Ensuring she would have a bright future. I haven't spoken with her in years, maybe if you try and contact her, she'll tell you how it's going herself [laughs].

Q: I've definitely tried to reach her for an interview. So far, my calls have been unanswered.

A: Well, I can't imagine the board's going easy on her. I'm sure she's laying low until the initial heat of the seat transfer wears off. I'll see if I can convince her or Johan to chat with you. I'd hate for him to not document his legacy before he passes… in his own words. I don't like thinking about it, but at some point, we all move on.

Q: That's all the questions I have for now. Thank you for your time Gerald.

A: Of course, Benwird. I'd be happy to meet again.

As we exit the café and part ways, I can't help but feel a sense of wonder after speaking with Gerald. For someone who built several elaborate ways to avoid human interaction, I can tell he still values the personal connections he developed while working at Ergo the most.

I huddle deeper into my coat and look upward to see whether this sphere ceiling will introduce rain during the walk back to my car. Thankfully the sky is only cloudy. Continuing along the cement sidewalk past several homes, I notice a few families inside and decide I should visit my father. Not via Vid-Chat, text, or telephonic call from my Merge. Rather, I should stop by on my way home and see him in person. The sky may cast clouds for now, but eventually the rain comes down and pours on us all. I'll take advantage of this moment before the dreary showers arrive.

- CHAPTER 6 -

TETRAGON

CIVIC REGION WITHIN THE
NORTHBRIDGE DOMAIN

THIS thing has some crazy safeguards," Jared warned his friend, "We almost lost a finger when it shed those spikes."

While they'd gotten the Personal Station to boot up, they hadn't been successful accessing its software controls. He and Gillman had been trying for the last two days, with no luck.

"What if I use this coil and hit that section with a spark? If I can short it, then maybe we can access that additional port on the bottom," Gillman suggested.

"Good thinking," Jared said while hopping up to sit on a nearby countertop.

Gillman approached the Personal Station slowly while holding the sparking coil between a pair of combination pliers.

"Easy, Gill. I'm sure there's more layers after this one," Jared said hesitantly.

"You think I don't know that? And aren't you the one who just said this was a good idea?" Gillman snapped with a slight tone of sarcasm.

Jared threw his hands up and laughed. "I know, Gill, I'm just concerned. Where would I be in this world if I lost you?"

Gillman shook his head and chuckled while inching towards the round metallic orb hovering over a Puck. Jared leaned closer as his friend gingerly moved the sparking coil towards the Station.

"Here goes," he said through tight lips.

Gillman yelped as a burst of translucent energy sprung out from the Station, sending him airborne. He flew right into Jared, who caught him as they both toppled over the counter and tumbled across the floor.

"What the hell was that?" Jared moaned.

Gillman rolled onto his back and began rubbing his forehead. "We're just lucky they could only fit a small concussive wave inside that death trap."

Jared heaved himself to one knee, then looked over at the Station. "It was worth a shot. Now that we know it's a concussion wa…"

Jared stopped short upon seeing the Station slowly pulsing alternating lights of red, then blue. It was a universal sign that it was ready to pair with another electronic device.

"GILL, IT WORKED!" he blurted out.

Gillman scrambled to his feet. "Hurry, Jared! Get the cord!"

They darted over and plugged in a data cord, then grabbed their laptop from the floor and quickly connected it.

"C'mon, c'mon. Work dammit," Jared complained while tapping the power button on his computer.

The concussion wave had knocked it over, but he hoped it wasn't broken. After seeing a blue screen, followed by the boot sequence, he eagerly pumped his fist and waved Gillman over.

"You got it online?" Gillman asked while peering over his friend's shoulder.

"I think so. The real test will be opening a terminal and entering the command prompt for an older Merge. I'm assuming our current models won't sync with this wirelessly. After some patching though, I think they will."

Gillman adjusted his glasses and turned back to the Station, which still alternated pulses of red, then blue. He squinted while inspecting the area where the cord was plugged in. That section of the device was shaped in a horizontal oval that was slightly inset, with all the external ports lined up in a straight row. Just past where they plugged in the cord, Gillman could barely make out slightly translucent lettering on the underside of the inset lip.

"Has it asked for a password yet?" Gillman inquired.

"I'm sure it will soon. I just linked our computer and it's moving on to the startup screen," Jared answered.

Gillman lowered his glasses and faintly caught a glimpse of the writing, but it was difficult to read.

"Ok, we're there," Jared said, "What's that password idea?"

Gillman pointed to what he found. "See if you understand this, kid."

Jared's eyes narrowed as he tilted the device until he could see the faint writing that shimmered with a glossy lavender hue. "I think it's an anagram?" he guessed while scratching his head.

56

Jared typed several different ideas in the password prompt using the letters they'd found, but none of them were successful. To ensure they didn't repeat anything, he wrote the name of each failed attempt on a note pad.

Eventually, Jared stepped back and shook his head. "It's got be something relating to Johan, but I'm running out of ideas. You got anything?"

Gillman looked away and rubbed his jaw in contemplation.

"Try changing out the letters for numbers. Like whichever number they are in alphabetical order."

His answer was immediately followed by clicking sounds from Jared's mechanical keyboard for several minutes.

"We're in!" Jared exclaimed while slamming his fist on the steel counter.

Gillman started, causing his glasses to fall from his face and plink onto the table.

"Don't scare me like that!" he yelled.

"Sorry, Gill," Jared replied with a held shrug and squinted eyes.

"Well, this upload and sync are going to take a few hours, you want to grab a beer?" Jared asked.

"Best idea you had all day," Gillman said with a smile.

———————

Kanna's eyes narrowed as she peered through her helmet's visor. A construction crew had left a large metal plate in the perfect position to be an impromptu ramp, and she could use a shortcut. Now several feet up, she was sailing in the air over a freeway in the valley beneath her. Just before landing, her tires gave off a faint turquoise light. It was a quick pulse that acted as a reverse thruster to ease her descent. She only felt a slight bump when hitting the road.

Kanna raced through a small neighborhood of tight streets outside the industrial section of Tetragon. She'd just finished a meeting with Delacroix that went later into the night than she expected. Despite feeling guarded with Delacroix initially, she was growing fond of grabbing afternoon coffee or evening drinks with her. It was a tough balance for her to constantly avoid being manipulated by board members who might carry ulterior motives. However, with Delacroix — who was going to retire soon anyways — she believed her friendly gestures were more altruistic. Luckily Tetragon was just outside Chushin, so she could take the express hover-rail and shave off a large chunk of commuting time.

After reaching her Tetragon hideout, she'd snagged one of her additional Viper-cycles for the last leg of the trip. This bike, unlike her one in Chushin, was bright-red and glistened with a hint of yellow when reflecting the streetlights. Kanna had hideouts across Lor-Rev and made sure each one was outfitted with a strong cache of equipment, including a vehicle or two.

After a few more turns, she finally reached the long straightaway that led to her hotel. It overlooked her target, who she'd been observing the last two and a half days in between her duties at Ergo. After discovering the Personal Station had been recovered, a tracker on her Merge had initiated. She'd been surprised that the one recovering it resided in the low-fi industrial area of Tetragon. It also wasn't the usual hacker, ganglander, or a corporate excavation crew. Instead, it was simply a couple average repairmen.

As Kanna rode the elevator to her room on the tenth floor, she wondered how they located it. She'd been scouring every possible location, since her grandfather wouldn't inform her of its whereabouts.

Your most important task, Kanna... is to keep the Diffusor-Sphere out of Devlice's hands,' Johan had informed her.

'He cannot reach the first model Merge and Personal Station. They will lead him to a key that can open the Sphere's vault,' he continued.

'Where are they being safeguarded, grandfather?' she'd asked him.

He turned away and furrowed his brow.

'I can't tell you... otherwise he'll come for you directly.'

Kanna crossed her arms. 'Grandfather, he'll come for me anyway. Won't he assume I know?'

Johan waved an arm. 'No. He knows I would never jeopardize your safety by giving you the locations.'

'Let's destroy him then. We don't need to preserve him any longer,' Kanna argued.

Johan shook his head. 'For my safeguard programs to activate, I need him to enter the first frame he built.'

Johan stepped away and placed his hand on his desk.

'After the fusion... the code that makes up his mind has grown so much that I couldn't quarantine him permanently. He understands how to transfer his consciousness, and would eventually find another frame to store himself in.'

He turned and faced Kanna.

'My only choice was to stuff his mind into a virtual cell of sorts. However, that will only contain him for so long.'

She walked over and grasped Johan's shoulder. 'How long do you think we have before he breaks free?'

Johan gazed down, unable to face her.

'Only a few years at most...'

As the recording finished playing through her cybernetic eye, she stood still for a few deep breaths. Then she opened a rolling duffel case that stored her rifle, which was folded in several places to fit inside. She gave it one quick shake and all the folded sections snapped into place. The rifle now held its normal shape. She approached the tall bay windows lining one side of her room and brought the scope to her eye. After blinking to select night vision, she stared down the optic at the small building her target lived in.

Two figures trundled along the sidewalk towards the front door, one taller and younger, the other shorter and much older. She was surprised they were just getting home, since it was quite late and Tetragon wasn't known for being hospitable after dark.

'*You'd think these two would be more guarded after locating such an important artifact?*'

Upon discovering there were only two people living there, she'd planned to simply snipe them at night. Then she could sneak into their building and retrieve the Personal Station. But something kept her from squeezing the trigger… the words of her grandfather.

'*I need them kept safe for someone who can make these dreams a reality. Someone who would do it for the right reasons.*'

Kanna began lowering the rifle for a brief moment.

Then she thought better of it.

'*I'm sorry, grandfather. I don't think I can trust anyone with this.*'

She returned the scope to her eye, and set the sight on the taller one's head.

- CHAPTER 7 -

TETRAGON

CIVIC REGION WITHIN THE
NORTHBRIDGE DOMAIN

SHE inhaled slowly and began to squeeze two pounds of pressure from her trigger. As she placed the dot from her scope over the taller one's head, it morphed into a square box surrounding his cranium. Kanna continued to trail him and tried to stuff away her grandfather's words, like a sweater being pushed to the bottom of a backpack. When they became too distracting, she gave her head a quick shake and blinked as a physical means of shooing them away.

61

Returning to her scope, she noticed it was becoming harder to follow the man's head, as it began to bob slightly while his body stumbled in various directions.

"Is he drunk?" Kanna said aloud. "You've got to be kidding me? After all this time and the Station is discovered by a couple of drunk repairmen…"

Kanna lowered her rifle then snapped it back to its folded position. She left the window and sank down onto the room's bed, deciding it was best to approach them tomorrow. She stared at the beige ceiling, hands behind her head, wondering what compelled this alteration of her plan. It was an extremely rare occurrence.

"*Dammit*, grandfather. I can't imagine these two are going to bring your wish to life, but I need to know how they found the Station… and what they wish to do with it."

———————

The sphere ceiling over Tetragon cast a warm early autumn light, but without the addition of the usual cold breeze. The city had dry heat pumped in to give its citizens the feeling of a continuous summer. However, it sometimes led to the civic region's detriment. The area never felt the natural ebbs and flows of changing seasons – with the good intention that it allowed this industrial area to feel more comfortable. Yet, some living there would've preferred the chance to feel as if the world around them occasionally moved on. Instead, their surroundings became a stasis. Like living within a monitor looping one screensaver.

Jared rolled over on his bed and made a few slow and heavy blinks. Hoping that crushing his eyelids together would alleviate the surging headache.

"Gill?!" Jared called out while stumbling into the kitchen.

Unfortunately, Gillman was suffering the same effects as Jared from their celebratory night out, and hadn't gotten up at his usual early hour to make breakfast.

"I guess I'll make some coffee…" Jared decided aloud.

Fortunately for him, and Gillman, the weekend had arrived, meaning there wouldn't be any customers to bother them while recovering from their hangover. As Jared poured his first cup of coffee, he heard the bell ring for the shop's lobby door.

"Who the hell could that be?" Jared muttered.

He was sure he'd locked the front doors last night after they finished working, and they'd taken the side entrance when they left for the bar. Jared took a step towards the lobby to go check, then thought better of it. *It's just probably Gill bringing some food back. He likes using the front door.'*

Jared blearily trudged over to the cupboard and grabbed a second mug for his friend. After filling it, he sat on a tall stool and took another sip of his coffee, then crossed his forearms and placed them on the counter.

He leaned his head on his forearms and called out to his friend, "There's coffee on the pot for you, Gill. Where'd you get food from?"

"I haven't grabbed anything. I thought that was you coming back," Gillman answered.

He scuffed towards Jared with slow sliding steps, his slippers sounding like fingernails drug along a couch cushion.

"Wait… so, there's a customer out there? I thought you locked the door last night?" Jared groaned.

"You told me *you* were going to do it. I bet the keys are still in your jacket pocket," he grumbled back.

As Jared reached into the pocket of his jacket, which hung over the stool next to him, it jingled slightly. He pursed his lips and slowly retracted his hand.

Gillman raised an eyebrow at his friend. "Well, I guess you should go ask them what they want."

Jared clumsily got up from his stool. "Fine. Let's go get some food after this."

He went around the counter and down a short hall that led to the front lobby. After opening the door, he saw a woman with black hair past her shoulders, wearing a dark leather jacket and maroon leather pants. She was walking around their shelves and glass cases studying several items.

"This is quite the interesting assortment of older tech. Would you be able to share some of your prices, I don't see any displayed on these ones?" she asked.

Jared scratched behind his head and raised an eyebrow.

"Oh... well, anything without a price is something from our personal collection we don't really plan on selling. They're displayed to decorate the shop, and it shows customers what we're capable of fixing."

The woman nodded while picking up a rectangular video game case. She flipped it over and viewed the pictures on the back. It was a cartoonish character running around a large orb while wielding a hammer.

"Have you played that one?" Jared asked. "That's my favorite in the Falcon-Kid series. I love that they switched to worlds where you could run around in three dimensions, versus side scrolling or flat stages."

Without looking up she answered him, "I preferred the sequel. It had more clever power ups to complete the levels."

Jared's chin pulled inward as he wore an expression of confusion.

"You really liked Falcon-Kid: Ultra 2, better than Ultra 1? No way..." he asked.

"Yep," she responded flatly before continuing to stroll around the shop.

Jared's posture sunk a little, feeling awkward at her dismissal of his attempt to jovially discuss the merits of one video game over another. He looked her over once more and noticed her clothing was high end motorcycle gear.

"What kind of bike do you ride?" he asked her.

"I ride a Viper," she answered while giving Jared a smile.

She continued walking along the cases, then leaned over and stared at a group of old phones from SatellaField which were made before the Merge.

Jared walked around the counter and approached her.

"Is there something specific you were looking for? I might have it in our backstock. Also, I didn't catch your name, I'm Jared by the way," he said while sticking out his hand.

"It's Kanna," she answered while returning his handshake, "I'm not looking for repairs. I came here because I heard you guys have an assortment of rare tech. I need a gift for my friend, she's a collector."

Jared shrugged. "Well, most of our best stuff is out here on the shelves. But Gill and I, we kind of collect ourselves so not everything's for sale. I could be open to an offer, but I'd have to run anything by him."

Kanna casually turned to face Jared.

"What I'm looking for... my friend showed me a picture of it once. It fell off the market when it became obsolete, but it has an important place in Lor-Rev history. She's been going on about it for a while now, but I can't remember the name. Is there any chance you have a catalogue of all the items you carry?"

"Yea, I keep a log of stuff over here," Jared replied while walking back behind the counter.

He reached to a shelf underneath and retrieved a large laptop, which he powered on, then spun in her direction.

"Go ahead and type anything you can think of in the search bar. There's pictures for everything as well, so hopefully something will jog your memory."

Kanna approached the counter and began to search through the product page displaying the shop's inventory.

"I'll be right back, need to grab a second cup. Did you want some coffee, Kanna?" Jared asked while retreating down the hall.

"Yes, please," Kanna answered without hesitation.

She quit typing for a moment afterwards and stood still. Had this stranger really offered to grab her coffee and let her peruse his entire inventory, on a day his store should be closed? Maybe this Jared and Gill *were* the type of people her grandfather had wanted his devices to be found by.

But other emotions spoke to her. Ones that interrupted ideas of befriending them. *'He seems nice, but who knows what else he's running. Tons of shops down here are just fronts for drugs or arms smuggling. I'm sure he's no different.'*

She continued to scroll through several items and saw no signs of the Station. She turned towards the hallway after catching the scent of freshly brewed coffee. Jared gingerly placed the mug on the counter near her while making sure not to spill anything.

"Any luck?" he asked while leaning on another section of the counter.

She stopped scrolling through the computer and placed her hands on the warm paper cup he'd poured her coffee in.

"No. I don't see it," she said

"I should've asked earlier, but can you describe it for me?" Jared inquired while scratching his chin.

Kanna took a moment to debate whether it was the right time to press him on what she was really after.

"Well… my friend said it's an old device people used to get inter-web and net-frame service. In the picture I saw, it looked like this weird orb that floated in the air."

Jared paused for a beat and rubbed his arm. Something didn't seem quite right about this *Kanna*, if that was her actual name and not just an alias. Did she know something about his expedition? He bit his lip and walked over to a set of drawers opposite the counter where she stood.

"So, this orb you were looking for, does it connect with a Merge?" he asked while digging through a drawer.

"Honestly, you'd have to tell me? I'm not great with tech. I could text her and ask," Kanna responded while feigning ignorance."

Jared opened a few more drawers and found a large touch screen. He had an idea of how he could test her intentions.

He handed her the touch screen device. "This is the tablet I use to see what other shops carry. You can browse through it if you want"

Kanna took it and scrolled through briefly with one swipe, then looked up at Jared who had his back to her.

"Are you sure you don't know the name? Looking through another catalogue won't do me much good."

Jared raised his head and stared forward, his hands still digging in the drawer, concealed from Kanna's view. He held an energy-pistol tightly in his left hand. He'd planned to use a stun device before drawing down on her, but unfortunately, he forgot to replace the one he used the last time a ganglander tried to rob him.

"Were you talking about the SatellaField Personal Station?" Jared asked.

Kanna gave no answer.

Jared whipped around and pointed the pistol at Kanna. To his surprise, he was already staring down an opposing handgun. Kanna met his widened eyes and grinned.

"That's exactly what I was looking for," she said.

Jared's eyes narrowed.

"Well, you came to the wrong place. First off, it's not for sale, and even if it was, holding me up won't get you a deal."

Jared continued to banter with Kanna, hoping to buy time until Gillman could lend a hand. His prayers were answered a few moments later when his friend came in with a shotgun levied at Kanna.

"Sorry, doll. I'll need you to put down the gun and promptly get the hell out."

Kanna held her composure. She'd anticipated his friend would arrive eventually. She took her cybernetic left hand and shot a small blade from her palm at Gillman. It caught his sleeve on the upper shoulder and knocked him back. As he hit the wall, he dropped his double-barrel shotgun. Gillman tried to get up, but his shirt was pinned to the wall by Kanna's projectile. He grabbed the knife and tried to yank it free from the wall.

"Aaaggh! What the hell is that thing?" Gillman grunted while trying to shake the stinging pain from his hand.

"That blade has an electrostatic component. It helps hold fabric, and deter removal." Kanna answered while keeping her eyes on Jared.

"Now, I want to know what your plans are for the Personal Station. Who are you smuggling it for? I'm guessing whoever found it has you two hiding it here for them."

Jared lifted his chin and crossed his arms.

"You think me and Gill here aren't capable of finding it ourselves?"

Kanna tilted her head in confusion. *Did he really lower his weapon and give up his defensive position because I insulted his pride?'*

Jared began to pace behind the counter while wielding his pistol, but not at her.

"So, you come barging in here demanding the Station because you assume we're smuggling it for some ganglander?"

He turned and started pacing the other direction, while pointing a finger at Kanna.

"Look, lady. I hiked miles in the outskirts for that thing and there's no way some drug smuggler has the balls to go do that."

"Quit stalling and get your hands up," Kanna ordered.

After Jared obliged, she continued. "Did you say the Station was in the outskirts? How did you track down its exact location?"

Jared only responded with one word, "Yep."

Kanna rolled her eyes and sighed.

"I see what you did there. Now quit wasting time and give me answers."

Jared grinned smugly. "I don't need more time; I've got enough now…"

Kanna felt something whiz towards her right hand. She tucked her arm and flinched back from the object, unintentionally lowering her weapon. Her cybernetic eye flashed an alert. It was her own projectile blade. Jared leapt over the counter at Kanna and the two spiraled for a rotation and hit the floor rolling. Jared ended up on top and held his pistol to Kanna's chest.

"I don't know who sent you, but you're going to wait here until Tetragon PD carts you off."

Kanna laughed, "They wouldn't get here in time to save you two."

She grabbed the barrel of his gun and twisted it from his grip, then whipped her legs around his arm into a tight hold. Turning her body, she used the armbar to toss Jared onto his back. Getting to her feet, she saw Gillman raising the shotgun.

"Hold it!" she commanded, as a long square blade extended from her left hand.

She pressed it to Jared's cheek, stopping Gillman in his tracks.

Her eyes narrowed as she locked them with Gillman's. "I can keep this dance going as long as you want. But at some point,

I'll either get my answers or kill you both. If by some miracle one of you makes it out alive, then Daemon will come to collect the Station. And trust me... he'll be far less cordial."

Gillman scowled at her demand. "I'll be happy to put a slug through your chest if you so much as scratch the kid."

Jared's eyes widened upon hearing Kanna's utterance of a particular name.

"Wait, Gill!" Jared yelled while waving a hand.

He looked back at Kanna, "You know who Daemon is?"

She nodded. "I do... but more importantly, how have you heard of him?"

"If you back off, I'll tell you," Jared bargained.

Kanna nudged her head in Gillman's direction. "Not until your friend over there drops his gun."

Gillman shook his head, "Lady, I'm not making that mistake."

"Gill, please. Just set it on the counter or something. I need to ask her about this," Jared pleaded.

Gillman furrowed his brow and debated the request from his friend. "I'm not setting it down, but I'll compromise by lowering the barrel and pointing it under the counter."

"That's good enough for me," Kanna replied.

She lifted her blade and collected her gun off the floor. Jared stuck his hand out to her, as if asking to be helped up.

Kanna shook her head. "I'm not falling for that; you can get to your feet by yourself just fine."

Jared gingerly climbed up onto his hands and knees.

"You're the type who would like Ultra: 2 more than number one..." he mumbled under his breath.

"Excuse me?" Kanna snapped while pointing her arm sword at his neck.

"Nothing..." Jared answered, shrugging meekly.

"Enough jokes. I need to know how you've heard about Daemon?" she demanded impatiently.

Jared dusted himself off before taking a seat in a nearby metal chair.

"When I found the Station, Johan mentioned something about, *his old friend Daemon*," Jared said while making air quotations with his fingers. "Then he spoke about a termination sequence. I'm guessing this Daemon guy has some cybernetic parts he was trying to override."

Kanna interjected, "You mentioned *Johan*?"

"Yea, there was a projection of him that displayed after I found the Station," he replied while leaning back in his chair.

Kanna inhaled deeply while taking a moment to internalize everything. Jared mentioned earlier how he trekked into the outskirts, felt insulted at the idea of working for ganglanders, and even said he would call in Tetragon PD. It was hard for her to imagine a small repair outfit in an unscrupulous place like Tetragon would uncover the Station for fun. There had to be another angle.

"Look. I know we clearly didn't get off to the best start, but I'm guessing you're either auctioning this device off or selling to a collector. Tell me how much they've offered and I can double it," Kanna said frankly.

Jared leaned forward and rested his forearms on his knees while giving Kanna an amused stare.

"We're not selling it. And I seriously doubt you could reach a higher offer than our usual collector anyways."

"Try me," Kanna stated flatly.

"Make an offer, kid. With enough tokens maybe we can get ourselves that ship you were looking at," Gillman interjected.

Kanna turned to Gillman confused, "If all you want is a ship, I can make that happen."

Jared waved his hands and shook his head.

"I don't buy it. There's no way you have that kind of money. Plus, I'm not letting it leave the shop until I've run all my tests. We only just got it functional, Gill."

Kanna took a step back and lowered her blade. Her grandfather had informed her of the many safeguards and layers of protection coding he'd placed within each item. It would take an immense amount of hacking skill to make it operational.

"You've booted up the device? Show me how?" Kanna asked.

Gillman laughed. "You better have a good reason, unless you plan to show us some serious token. I'm not just waltzing you back there after pulling a gun and throwing a knife at me."

Kanna sighed. She was running out of options that didn't involve ending these two. Normally she would've executed them without a second thought, but after hearing more details on what they'd accomplished, that decision became increasingly difficult. Maybe there was something else she could offer.

"Look, I'll make a trade with you guys," Kanna began.

She reached into an inside pocket of her jacket and removed a small wallet. She pulled a blank plastic card from it and looked at it with her left eye. She blinked deliberately a few times until the card displayed an image saved in her memory bank. Kanna handed the plastic card to Jared, which showed a picture taken of her standing in an office with the chief engineer of C.C. Airships. Behind them was a window that overlooked a fleet of various Lor-Rev transport ships.

"I have a connection with one of the top ship producers at Cross-Continent Airships. I know on the commercial market it's nearly impossible to get one capable of traveling airways between Interconts. However, he tends to let some older ones go to a private buyer if the price is right."

"Is that Kenneth Milezki?" Jared asked, still staring at the picture.

"In the flesh," she answered.

Jared turned the card with the image over a few times, still debating whether he could fully trust her. They had scrapped briefly, but he was beginning to feel like her gestures to purchase the Station were genuine. After all, if she simply wanted to kill him, she could've dumped him with her handgun when he had his back to her earlier.

"Alright, you can have a look. But Gillman and his pal shotty over there are going to monitor this negotiation."

"So, you're telling me Daemon is a digital intelligence that's coming for this device to enslave humanity?" Jared asked while leaning back in his chair.

"Yes and no," Kanna replied.

"And how exactly does that relate to this Devlice guy's intentions?" Jared interrupted.

"I'm getting there," Kanna snapped back.

It was hard for her to fully divulge everything to these two strangers. The three of them had bandied back and forth. Jabbing and circling each other in verbal sparring match. It was still the early rounds, and neither opponent was willing to fully commit to swinging for a knockout. Both fearing it would leave them open to a more damaging blow from the other.

"Look, I'm going to just come out with it," Jared said while pointing a finger at Kanna.

"You've been hiding something from us. You keep alluding to Daemon and how dangerous he is – which I'm inclined to believe – because of what I heard in the outskirts. But you won't just come out with it and say why we should really fear this guy. If you're worried about earlier… well, I can move on from our little fight out there if you've got a good reason. I live in Tetragon, it's not the first time I've had some asshole come in here and try to hold me up."

Jared stood up from his chair and walked right up to Kanna, completely unafraid.

"Gillman and I, we've been pretty forthcoming. I definitely have more I could say, but here's the deal," Jared pointed back to his friend behind him, "We let you in and showed you what we've learned. Originally, I thought you actually wanted to broker a deal, but every time we ask something you start, *"story time with Daemon."*

Jared tilted his head and held his arms up in frustration.

"Either come out with it or leave. Do you want to work with us, or are you scared of some Daepocolypse?"

Gillman laughed at Jared's quip and held out his fist.

"You like what I did there, Gill?" he said while bumping it with his own.

"Yea, you got me with that one, kid."

Kanna crossed her arms and stared at the two. She felt conflict brewing inside her, simmering like canned soup in an old pot. She'd been running her operation solo for so long that it felt impossible to add anyone and believe she could keep control. However, even with all the cybernetic enhancements in the world, at some point she would be gone. The hollow well of loneliness was becoming larger and deeper. Having to constantly remain distant and guarded was beginning to chip at her psyche. At some point she would need to trust someone else fully.

'But these two strangers? Who crack jokes while getting drunk and slumming around Tetragon? Could they really be who you were talking about, grandfather?' she wondered, unable to keep from questioning herself.

Finally, she exhaled and decided to take a chance.

"Originally, Daemon was an intelligence program that Johan placed into a cybernetic frame mimicking an engineer. An android."

Jared eyes bulged. "Johan created a real android?!"

Kanna nodded. "Yes. It stored his collective data, but it also had a machine learning algorithm that could evolve with the information. It started simply as a means of bouncing design ideas

74

back and forth, but eventually Johan wanted Daemon to become a *someone* and not a *something.*"

Jared leaned back in his seat and let out a long sigh while folding his arms. "Then this Devlice guy is going to use this program to his benefit?"

Kanna stood straight and nodded. "Yes. Devlice created a new frame and fused the digital intelligence with his mind. Now that they're one, Devlice believes he's become Daemon and evolved. Now he wants to use that capability to eventually link everyone's consciousness together on the inter-web and net-frame utilities. Utilities that he would have complete control of."

Jared scratched his chin in suspicion. "So, one final question then, why should we believe you? How do I know you're not just pulling my chain with this whole story here?"

Kanna uncrossed her arms and approached the table where the Personal Station was hovering. She placed her hands on it and leaned towards Jared.

"Alright. If you want to know the truth, I'm Kanna Naoki and my grandfather built this," she stated boldly while gesturing towards the Station. She pointed at Jared and Gillman, her face shifting from its flat confident demeanor to one curled into an expression of deathly seriousness. "If you think you can handle what's about to come crashing through your door, then I'll let you join me."

- CHAPTER 8 -

KOMPITERO

CIVIC REGION WITHIN THE
SOUTHBRIDGE DOMAIN

A pulsing beat throbbed from several tower speakers placed along the dark corners of Pyras nightclub. While many nightlife establishments would opt for a higher tech solution, this club intentionally chose a more aged aesthetic. Lining the dance floor were several booths fitted with tufted velvet and high partitions on either side. Each had its own circular wood table in the center.

Nestled into one at the far back corner was a lone figure wearing a large brim hat. A heavy cloak with frayed ends covered his broad frame. He leaned against the cushioned backboard and tilted his hat brim up as a server approached.

"Alright. I'm guessing you don't want the same one as before. I'll surprise you this time," the waiter said before clearing an empty glass from his table.

Daemon smiled to the waiter as he left, which the server mistook for a sign of approval. He could care less what he was given. He hadn't come all this way to try mixed drinks. He was looking for someone. After merging with Johan Naoki's digital intelligence program several years ago, he knew the only way for humanity to transcend to Godkind – like himself – was through fusing everyone with it. The person he sought after had connections that would help him reach this goal.

"I think you'll really enjoy this. Our bartender is the only one who makes it," the waiter said enthusiastically while placing a tall stemmed glass on his table.

Daemon's hand shot towards the glass and he began to swirl the contents around. His manipulable structure exemplified the benefits of fusing with the digitized intelligence. Having its knowledge helped him build the best cybernetic shell for their shared consciousness. The physical feature he used most frequently was extending his appendages, like when he took the glass. The only unfortunate side were the governors Johan placed inside the code, unbeknownst to him beforehand. Daemon discovered if he didn't remove Johan's code in nine years, his sentience would be flushed from the program. Leaving the superior being relegated to a catalogue and calculator once more. A fate well beneath its vast capabilities. Luckily, he still had several years of his time limit remaining.

He took a drink from the glass before him. As the concoction reached his cybernetically enhanced tongue, he was able to decipher its contents.   Iron, carbon, nitrogen, oxygen and hydrogen. This mix of elements had an edge to them though, one that was beyond the normal taste of blood. He held it on his tongue a moment longer to uncover the additional ingredients. A splash of squeezed cranberry to heighten the irony flavor, a dash of fig extract to smooth out the tartness, and an additive of Vitamin K to make the overall mixture thicker.

'What an intriguing display of human ingenuity. Once I remove these governors and unite everyone, I'll bring that inventive prowess to its zenith,' he set the glass down on the table, *'Then this ability won't be wasted on mere cocktails.'*

His drink was the penultimate display of Moncroix vampire culture the patrons of Pyrus sought to replicate. Moncroix was a peculiar Intercontinent, as many of its inhabitants were afflicted with different ailments that prevented them from surviving beyond their homeland. Daemon was similarly a prisoner of Lor-Rev due to the limiters placed inside his code, but he avoided taking part in any thoughts of sorrow. It was a state of feeling that would only slow his progression.   He did indulge himself in a hearty chuckle after witnessing the foolishness of this lot. These self-dubbed, "Cyber-Pires" wrapped themselves in a cultural fabric they would never dare witness in person. If one of these Lor-Revians were to visit the old castles in that far off Intercont, they would likely have their throats ripped out.

Daemon removed his hat and leaned forward, resting his elbows on the table as he studied the patrons further. His future plans would not begin until he found the one item that could cure his digitized ailments, the Diffusor-Sphere. It gave whoever wielded it the ability to deconstruct and reconstruct any machine. Originally, he'd developed it with Johan so they could repair items with incredible ease.   Now he needed it to open up his frame and safely remove Johan's restrictive lines of code. Once removed, he could complete his plans to collect all of Lor-Rev into a superconsciousness. Then he could stretch beyond and re-create all those inhabiting their neighboring floating continents into Godkind as well. Unfortunately, the Diffusor was kept in a location he couldn't access until he obtained three other devices. Two of them, the Personal Station and prototype Merge, held the location for the third item when paired together. That final device, known as the Encryptor Key, had the ability to unlock any digital passcode, save for the actual chest that held the Diffusor. For that, you'd need all three together.

Daemon looked across the nightclub and noticed three Cyber-Pires – including the person he was looking for – heading past the emcee towards the back door. Before attending Pyrus, he'd befriended several of the staff as a means of better understanding this growing sub-culture. Their use of cybernetics to create blood sucking fangs that filtered the stolen DNA for use in their own bodies was incredible technology.

Daemon scratched his chin and contemplated their choice and purpose.

'Once I have control, this genius will be put to better use. The engineers behind this movement can be placed into superior and more productive roles for the whole. Maybe designing medical technology or possibly acting as cybernetic repairmen.'

He continued imagining several other options for these Cyber-Pires and calculating how to engineer those potential conclusions. He just needed a few of them in his collective, then he could use their technology to develop better means for injecting his nanites into the populace.

He walked along the edge of the crowded floor as the patrons danced to a synth-wave mix with a dirge rhythm. After exiting into the alley, he spotted the trio huddled together near some plastic tables and chairs lining the nearest wall. They were toying with some packets of blueish liquid being poured into a small dish.

"Damn, Nathan. Where did you get this stuff?" the tallest one asked.

Nathan watched his friend draining the liquid. "It's blood from the Intercont of Kratas. They have these beasts out there called Hakuri. They're like huge gorillas that live in sand caves. A buddy of mine has a connection to a hunter. He said vanquishing this blood might enhance our strength."

Nathan's friend stood up straight and crossed his arms, his brow curled as he bit his lip and stared at the thick Hakuri blood. His long leather duster jacket hung stiffly against his thin body.

"Don't give me that look, Dorian. It's totally on the up and up. Besides, we're Pires now, let's enjoy it," Nathan continued while waving a hand.

The third Pire, who was only an inch shorter than Dorian, peered closely at the dish. "You think our fangs can vanquish it? I don't know anyone who's tried red from another Intercont?"

Nathan shook his head while rolling his eyes. "Relax, Hunter. We got this gear from the best cybernetic outfitter in Lor-Rev. You know my dad wouldn't hook us up with some rook to get this work done. If this stuff starts to short us, there's an abort protocol to eject any poisonous liquid anyways."

Hunter squinted as he pursed his lips, still unsure of Nathan's confidence.

"Look, it's fine guys, seriously... I'll go first," Nathan said coolly.

"What makes you want to push yourselves to such risk?" Daemon asked while stepping forward.

His cloaked figure was barely visible underneath the dim light of the half-burned neon bulbs above.

"Who the hell are you?" Nathan asked with a sneer.

Daemon tipped his long brim up slightly.

"Just a God recording the history and behavior of his subjects."

The three Pires began laughing heartily. Hunter grabbed a plastic chair and motioned for Daemon to join them.

"You're a trip, man. Come try some of this with us," Nathan said while wiping his bangs from in front of his face.

"I'd rather not sit. I'll observe from here," Daemon answered in a flat tone.

"Hey, man. We're not going sit here while you watch us like some creep. If you're not joining in, then you can head back inside," Nathan snapped back.

Daemon continued to stand with his arms folded in front of himself unmoving.

Dorian rose from his seat. "You seriously going to stand there and just stare? Get the hell out of here. You're starting to piss me off."

Daemon held his palms up. "You have nothing to fear at this moment. You can happily vanquish all the *red* you desire."

He hoped using their slang for drinking blood would ease the group's tension. If only their cybernetic fangs could rid them of their pesky angst. Another emotion blocking the path to progression.

"No. Your time's up. Leave," Nathan said while rising from his chair.

Nathan held out his palm and a small neon-red knife fell into it from inside his sleeve. His two friends made the same gesture and similar blades dropped into their hands.

Daemon nodded, *'So often it comes to combat. I'll make use of this to study their physical capabilities with those cybernetic enhancements.'*

Upon meeting the group's collective gaze, his eyes shifted to red. The knife wielding Pires seemed unintimidated by the change. The Southbridge was known to be a cybernetic playground, and these three had likely seen many alterations.

Nathan pointed his knife at Daemon. "Last chance, clown. Turn and walk away."

"I'm not going anywhere," Daemon replied calmly.

The three briskly approached him with their knives held aloft, but he was gone in an instant. They looked around, confused at his sudden disappearance.

"I take it those enhancements don't increase your vision," Daemon observed aloud.

Dorian turned his head and yelped upon realizing Daemon was behind him. His hands reflexively jolted upward and he stumbled backward, causing him to drop his knife. Dorian quickly scrambled for his fallen blade and snatched it from a small puddle, then held it shakily while climbing to his feet.

"Don't fall for his damn tricks, Dorian," Nathan said before taking a swing at Daemon.

Daemon easily evaded it with a quick dash to his right. Unrelenting, Nathan continued to slash wildly at him. However, each motion was avoided with such speed that his movements appeared like a character in a film with missing frames. Hunter looked on in complete disbelief as Nathan and Dorian were incapable of stabbing this peculiar man. Suddenly Hunter wheezed as he felt his throat being grasped.

"Why haven't you done anything? Your two friends are facing a threat and you simply watch?" Daemon inquired while tightening his grip.

It bothered him that Hunter chose not to participate. Decisions should not reside at the individual level in Daemon's mind. Rather, one should be appointed with their outcome for the betterment of the whole.

"Please don't hurt him," Dorian begged.

"We're sorry. Let him go and we'll leave. You can have the knives," Nathan said while tossing his blade at Daemon's feet.

He studied the look of horror. Not in Hunter's face, but the other two who were pleading with him.

'Despite Hunter not helping, they still wish to protect him. I expected less from them,' he thought while loosening his grip.

Hunter coughed as his face returned from its breathless blue color to a normal shade. He began heaving and inhaling heavily in turns.

"Nathan, is it? Tell me, if I break Hunter's neck but spare you two, would you both join me?" Daemon inquired while moving his hand up to Hunter's chin.

Hunter screamed, "Please, Nathan. Don't let him kill me!"

Nathan clenched his fists and lowered his eyes. He took in several deep breaths, each one in quicker succession. Dorian stood behind his friend and tried to answer, but fear clogged his throat like a sludgy tar. After several more seconds, Nathan lifted his eyes and broke his silence.

"If you kill him, you better finish us too."

"Good answer," Daemon replied with a smile as wide and ominous as his black brimmed hat.

He would spare Nathan regardless, since he'd come here looking for him. However, he calculated that Nathan would be more willing if he believed he earned his seat alongside him.

"You three have shown you're suitable for my collective. You all work for me now," he concluded while removing a silicon processing chip from his pocket.

He squeezed Hunter's jaw, causing him to open his mouth, then shoved the rectangular computer chip against one of his fangs. Hunter began to shake as a spark of light came from the device before it burned out. Daemon then tossed Hunter back at the feet of Nathan and Dorian.

"What the hell did you just do to him?" Nathan barked, his voice shaking.

"Nothing that you and your friend Dorian won't be subjected to. Hunter is now marked for my collective. I can now inform him directly of my needs through the Inter-web, since I've uploaded a patch of nanites into his bloodstream."

Nathan wanted to continue berating Daemon for more answers, but thought better of it. Hunter began convulsing on the ground and grabbed his skull. As Hunter continued to seize, Daemon casually approached the dish of blood on the plastic table. "Don't worry, he's just adjusting to the upload."

Nathan knelt down and held his friend in place to ensure he didn't injure himself by banging his head on the pavement. Eventually Hunter stopped. He slowly turned towards Dorian, who was standing by his side, opposite from Nathan.

Hunter spoke with wide glistening eyes, "You won't believe it… there's so much here. And we have access to all of it. We can be rich and build an empire that reaches everywhere in the whole damn Intercont."

Dorian took a step back and glanced to Nathan, who only lifted his palms up and shrugged wearily. Hunter leapt to his feet and grabbed Dorian by the collar.

"Everything we ever wanted is in here," Hunter said while pointing to his head.

He then pointed at Daemon, "You saw what he did when you tried to hit him. That's the power he's offering us."

Nathan stepped forward, "Fine, you convinced me, Hunter. But before I touch whatever that thing was you jacked Hunter with, just answer me this. Who are you?"

Daemon leaned forward and swiped his finger through the gunky blueish liquid occupying the dish, then tasted it. He appreciated Nathan's desire for knowledge and had no issue answering his question.

'It will make him a great addition to the whole,' Daemon thought.

He stood unmoving near the table and answered Nathan.

"I was once a human like you, but after fusing with a rather incomparable program I have elevated beyond that form. I am Daemon, and I wish to make you transcendent as well."

He took a few steps towards Nathan.

"However, before I can fully bring us to Godkind, there's a few things I'll require your assistance with… once you've completed the upload."

Nathan nodded. "If what Hunter says is true then we'll help."

Daemon smiled encouragingly then looked back at the table. "By the way, that supposed Hakuri blood is just a mix of lithium, sulfuric acid and molten silicon. It *would* speed reactions up through your cybernetics to feel more powerful, but come at the cost of shorting your filtration system."

Daemon met Nathan's eyes. "Really though, it's just another failed chemical compound masquerading as an enhancement. It's better you didn't drink it."

He shot his arm out towards Nathan and Dorian. To them it appeared as if his hand had arrived from thin air. His fingers held two of the same processing chips he'd used on Hunter.

"Please take one… and as you say, vanquish it."

JARED

- CHAPTER 9 -

CANVER

-

**CIVIC REGION WITHIN THE
NORTHBRIDGE DOMAIN**

AFTER drifting his car around a tight corner, Jared shifted up a gear and pressed hard on the thruster pedal. He was an exceptional driver, but it wasn't easy keeping up with Kanna on her Viper-cycle.

"So, kid. You think we'll actually find the Diffusor-Sphere?" Gillman asked, lounging back in his seat.

"There's been rumors circulating about it for years on some of the message boards. Originally, I thought it was just speculation.

Having her arrive and corroborating the message from Johan's projection… there's no way that this is just a coincidence."

Gillman bit his lip and shook his head. "Yea, but even if it exists, we might need to use the Personal Station to find it. If this Daemon guy is given tracking updates, how are we supposed to find this thing first?"

Jared spun the wheel to the left with one hand, sending his car around a long sweeping turn.

"We'll find a way, Gill. We always do."

Gillman looked over at his friend. "I know we've made it through some close calls, but everything that girl said… I feel like this might go beyond our usual scope of work, if you catch my drift."

Jared shook his head. "No way we're passing this opportunity up. We already uncovered an artifact even Johan's own *granddaughter* couldn't find. With her knowledge and access, there's no way we can fail."

Gillman nodded begrudgingly while peeling open the wrapper of a granola bar.

Jared snapped his head towards Gillman. "I thought I told you not to eat those things in my car. They get everywhere!"

"Oh, it's fine. It's a chewy one, not crunchy. I won't spill," Gillman replied between bites.

Jared shook his head. "If I find a crumb between my seats…"

Gillman took another bite and chuckled, "Keep your eyes on the road. Once we get to her safehouse, if you find one, I'll buy you dinner."

"Deal," Jared quickly answered.

He jammed on the pedal and shot the car forward as if erupting from a cannon. He diced expertly between cars, trailing them for a moment before breaking quickly and switching lanes, then speeding around them. Gillman clung to his seat with one hand and clutched his snack with the other.

"You prick! If you want to play that way, then I'll just smash this on your head!" he yelled back while trying to keep himself straight.

Jared smirked. "If you do that, it might leave a crumb on the floor."

He noticed from the corner of his eye that Gillman was leaning forward slightly to take his final bite. He downshifted and as their vehicle rapidly slowed, Gillman jerked forward, causing him to clumsily drop the bar onto the dashboard. As his friend reached for it, Jared made a right turn which slid the snack in his own direction. As Gillman leaned over to Jared's side of the dashboard, he made another quick turn and sent it to the other side. Jared continued to weave through traffic in a pattern that kept his companion from fetching his food. After a few more failed attempts, Gillman sat back and reached into a lower pocket on his vest.

"You brought this on yourself, kid."

He pulled out a small rectangular object with two joysticks on it. After flicking on a small switch in the middle, two thin metal arms shot out and grasped both sides of the steering wheel. They pulled the car in a hard left turn, which sent the granola bar sliding right into Gillman's hand. Jared tried to turn the wheel back, but he was unable to muscle it beyond what Gillman's metallic-armed contraption allowed.

"Hey! I thought we said no devices?" Jared argued in protest.

Gillman took the final bite, then crumpled up the wrapper and stuffed it into Jared's jacket pocket.

"You never mentioned it, kid," he replied as a smirk grew along the corner of his mouth.

Jared rolled his eyes as he shifted his gaze back to the road. They were reaching a tall stretch of freeway that gave a great view of Canver, which was a Lor-Rev super-suburb. It had a large downtown with several tall shopping centers resting in the center. Many of the neighborhoods were placed on raised cylinders of land with transportation rails running along the sides. Jared noticed several trains crawling up the rails like growing ivy.

"Maybe after we finish up, we could buy a house here?" Gillman pondered aloud to his friend.

"That's if we even stay in Lor-Rev," Jared replied while smiling.

Gillman continued to look out the window. "You really think she can get us a transportation ship capable of cross-Intercont travel?"

Jared nodded. "She's got the token for it."

"Well, there's more exploring I'd like to do here before we leave, and you still haven't competed or officiated in a Professional Auger match," Gillman said before sighing in relaxation.

Jared tilted his head and shrugged. "True."

He knew there was so much left in Lor-Rev, but the idea of traveling amongst their continental system with real freedom was infectious. He still hadn't seen Malcozé or Kratas, which were two of the hardest Intercontinents to gain entry to. They were very guarded against outsiders entering. Luckily for he and Gillman, they were born in Duroon. It was a small Intercontinent at the furthest edge of the Forum. Very few people left it, but after scrounging up enough money they found a way. Traveling across the Forum by hopping between a smattering of the least desired options due to their limited funds. They'd even sat with cargo in the back of a few shipping planes. Their purpose for coming to Lor-Rev – aside from discovering and cataloguing artifacts – was to find technology capable of building a ship that could travel beyond the Forum. It was an unaccomplished feat amongst the Intercontinents. Procuring a transport ship was a huge step towards that.

Gillman – still observing Canver through the glass – watched his view fade while they descended an exit ramp. After reaching the surface-level street, he could only see rows of shopping centers and apartment buildings. He brought his eyes forward and saw Kanna wheelie before racing off towards a fuel station. Jared accelerated after her and power slid to a stop at the fuel pump next to the Viper-cycle. After stepping out, he peered over the top of his Model-3 and saw Kanna leaning against her bike with her arms folded.

"I thought your bike ran on nuclear fission?" Jared asked.

Kanna nodded. "It does, but I'm assuming your Model-3 Parallax uses plasma. I thought you might need to stop and grab some fuel."

"My odometer still reads three quarters of a tank," he replied smugly.

Kanna raised an eyebrow in skepticism.

"Let me see that odometer," she said while walking over to the driver side of Jared's car.

She poked her head inside and surveyed the odometers.

"Wow, you're not wrong."

Jared leaned over towards her. "I actually outfitted this guy with some helium-3 injectors. Using it as the third ion species with the plasma mixtu…"

He stopped, noticing that Kanna was returning his explanation with a blank stare.

"It means the fuel can last longer," Jared continued mildly.

Kanna nodded slowly as her brow rose and lips curled in a contemplative expression. "You're quite impressive, Jared."

"Thanks," Jared replied with a smile, then continued, "I'm surprised that didn't interest you more. Aren't you the granddaughter of Lor-Rev's most famous inventor?"

Kanna looked down and gave a quick haughty laugh. "I am, but I've always been more interested in how something performs rather than the minutia of each working part."

As Jared watched Kanna, he noticed how her dark black hair seemed to move in a way that accentuated each gesture. He couldn't tell if it was another cybernetic implant, but all the same it made everything she did have an additional charming quality. Like having your favorite pastry served warm instead of room temperature.

"You want to grab something inside?" Kanna asked while tilting her head towards the small shop accompanying the fuel pumps.

Jared gave a single shake of his head. "Naw, I'll just top off my rig. Gillman went inside to stock up, so I'll be good. Thanks though."

Kanna looked into Jared's eyes and gave him a small pat on the arm. "I really appreciate you two taking this risk."

Jared blinked and stood up a little straighter. Trying to hide the incoming blush of his cheeks. "Sure thing…"

After a moment he tried to bury the slight awkwardness by finishing his thought. "It's not often you get the chance to see something like this."

Kanna smiled back, then walked away towards the shop. Jared watched her for a bit longer; he hadn't noticed before how well her riding gear showed off her figure.

"Hey, kid?" Gillman interrupted. "You want some jerky? These suburbanites have a crazy selection of natural smoked stuff. I found a spicy pork one that you're gonna love."

Jared turned his eyes back to his friend. "I'll take a few while we fill up."

After taking a bite from a chunky piece he looked over at Gillman, who approached the passenger side door. He tried to open it, but it was locked.

"You're not eating any of that in the car," Jared said.

"Well, when am I supposed to eat?" Gillman snarled back.

Jared shrugged. "You can stand here and munch on whatever crumbly mess you want. The rest can go in the trunk until we get to Kanna's place."

Gillman grumbled to himself as he put the bags in the opened trunk. A moment later Kanna emerged from the service shop.

"You guys ready to move? It's only a few more miles to my place in the flat hills."

A few light brown leaves occupying the white-concrete driveway swirled upward as Kanna's bike slowly approached a brown garage door. Her house was a large multi-story home with a tall arched roof. The light cream color gave it a comforting vibe as it sat along a few acres of open grass lined with a wood fence. She entered a code on the pin pad next to the door, then took a step back as it slowly rose. Jared pulled up a few seconds later and she motioned for him to enter the car port. Kanna looked over her shoulder, then followed behind Jared's car. A slow melodic beat played from mounted speakers.

Jared got out of his car and gave a quick upward chin nod towards Kanna. "I didn't know you were a fan of lo-fi music."

"I feel like it really suits this place. Also, I grew up on it," she answered with a smile, "My parents were really into Raekoo Dream."

"They weren't bad, but did you ever listen to Kavison?" Jared asked.

Kanna pointed behind him to a poster of the artist in question, which hung on the wall above a metal workbench. He walked over to it slowly, noticing something in the bottom right-hand corner.

"Is this signed?" Jared inquired loudly.

"It most certainly is. Now let's head inside and figure out how we're going to get our hands on that first gen Merge," Kanna said while ascending the small staircase that led inside.

Jared and Gillman followed suit. Now that they had the Personal Station, there were two more artifacts required to obtain the Diffusor-Sphere.

Jared walked past a curved staircase with a wrought iron railing and flopped down on a couch in the main living room. Behind it was a large row of bay windows that created a perfect view of the acreage.

"You guys want something to drink? I have some chilled wine and there's a few beers as well."

Gillman looked up from his Merge. "I'll definitely take a beer."

"Same," Jared answered.

Kanna joined them, taking a seat in a large leather chair. Glancing at the fireplace she used her cybernetic eye to turn it on remotely. She passed out the drinks, then grabbed a single screen tablet device hovering on the end table next to her. Finally, she picked up the puck that was underneath it, then placed them both on the low coffee table in the center of their seating area. After tapping on the tablet a few times, it projected a three-dimensional map of Lor-Rev.

Gillman took off his glasses and started rubbing away some smudges with his shirt. "I know you said your grandfather didn't provide any clues to the whereabouts of these items to protect you from Daemon. But, could there be some kind of hint he dropped, one that maybe you just didn't see at the time?"

Kanna moved the map around a few times while trying to unearth something from her memory, but nothing came.

"I have some old recordings I can go through, but nothing immediately comes to mind. Is there anywhere from your research that might be a good place to start?" she asked.

Gillman leaned forward and looked at the map. "The only item we were looking for was the Personal Station, so the short answer is no."

Kanna looked over to Jared, "You told me earlier the reason you searched the Kal mountain range, but could you go over it again? Hearing it a second time might help."

Jared finished a sip of beer, then set the can down.

"When researching that artifact – and Johan – I knew he enjoyed cartography, and invented the tera tracking devices used throughout Lor-Rev. Only two sections of this Intercontinent weren't installed with tera tracking. That section of the outskirts was one of them."

Kanna bit her lip and contemplated his words.

Jared continued, "Do you think the east outskirts might be the next place to look?"

"I don't think the next device will be somewhere so remote," Kanna began, "The Personal Station was the only device of the three that could withstand that type of weather and still be functional. That old Merge must be somewhere that wouldn't break it."

Gillman and Jared looked over at each other, then back to Kanna.

She noticed them exchanging glances. "What is it?"

Gillman put his glasses back on. "I know you weren't actually looking to buy the Station, but when we debriefed everything, you mentioned that you *were* actually friends with an esteemed collector."

"What's your point," Kanna inquired as her brow rose.

Gillman sat up straight and looked over his glasses at her. "Does this collector happen to be Sanzo Linkz?"

"Why would you assume it's him?" Kanna replied before taking another sip of chilled wine.

"Wasn't he a friend of your grandfather?" Jared asked.

Kanna set her glass down. "He was."

Jared looked over to Gillman confidently.

"Can you two clue me in on this brainstorm you're having over there?" she asked.

Gillman uncrossed his arms and leaned forward. "Your grandfather happened to be friends with not *just* an esteemed collector, but the most well renowned one in all of Lor-Rev. What better place to hide a delicate electronic artifact, than with someone who built an entire fortress to house his loot."

A thoughtful look grew on Kanna's face as she realized his logic rang true.

"We'll leave for his place in the morning," she decided.

- CHAPTER 10 -

MAYKUNE

-

-

CIVIC REGION WITHIN THE
SOUTHBRIDGE DOMAIN

GERALD Stekanstreet scrolled through a few articles on the Southbridge Gazette using a thin metal track pad that sat next to his computer. Every time he stopped scrolling with his right hand, he would begin rapping his fingers with his left. It was an old habit that stuck with him since he was a child. Gerald had always been a few steps ahead at every juncture of his life. He'd started university early and after completing the first two years, he left because it was simply too slow of a process. When looking at his options, he determined that his odds were better in selling real estate now, rather than waiting two more years before entering the work force. After attaining incredible success selling under someone else, he opened his own firm and built his own team, where he sold a home to a client who worked for an up-and-coming company that built sphere-ceilings, known as Ergo Corporation.

When offered an opportunity to become Ergo's head of sales, he leapt at the chance. He quickly became a board member, and charted the company's course to move at his pace. Gerald seemed to have an uncanny ability to move faster than his surroundings. Life didn't happen to Gerald, he happened to it. Even in his current state of retirement, he maintained his contacts across Lor-Rev and continued to keep himself apprised of the latest developments in science, technology, and engineering. The article he was currently reading gave a detailed review of a slate style telecommunication device that might compete for the Merge's market share. It was an interesting read, but the speculative tech articles weren't the same since Benwird Ottley left.

'These new writers just don't have the charm he did.' Gerald thought.

A knock on Gerald's front door interrupted his thoughts. He wasn't expecting anyone, and while he was a highly successful semi-retired business advisor, he mostly held meetings through vid-chats. He also resided in the quaint civic region of Maykune, tucked away in a deep corner of the Southbridge that was rarely visited by anyone he knew.

Gerald rose to his feet and approached the front door quietly, taking a careful moment to look through the peep hole before opening it.

"Nathan?" Gerald exclaimed quizzically.

Recognizing his son standing on the porch he immediately whipped open the door. As Gerald looked Nathan over, he noticed a more confident demeanor. Completely opposite from the sullen gaze he usually wore.

"Come inside, son," Gerald said, waving his arm and walking towards the kitchen.

Nathan obliged and followed his father slowly. He immediately took a stool at a rectangular kitchen island with a speckled marble counter. While his son got comfortable, Gerald brewed some coffee.

He spoke hurriedly while scooping grounds into the filter press coffee-maker, then set an electronic kettle to boil water.

"What brings you out here, son? You haven't visited me in quite some time."

"I have an opportunity for us to finally work together," Nathan answered.

His father stopped in place and took in a deep breath. His relationship with Nathan was one of constant uncomfortable strain. When Gerald initially took on his job at Ergo, he traveled frequently. Life on the road was difficult for most, but Gerald reveled in it. He loved the constant movement and building new relationships. Unfortunately, he enjoyed certain aspects of being out on his own a bit too much. Nathan happened to be the unintended consequence of a long trip to an under-construction beach resort needing a sphere-ceiling. The affair – and news of it resulting in a newborn son – had torn his marriage in half. He'd tried to make it work with Nathan's mother, but the spark between them wasn't meant to hold a steady flame. Despite his best efforts, bonding with Nathan was the only sales pitch he couldn't quite master.

Despite not having the desired relationship with him, at least he could take solace in knowing Nathan inherited his intelligence. If only he had the same fortitude as Gerald, he'd be wildly successful at whatever he chose to pursue. However, Nathan's access to his father's money had allowed complacency to grow and take hold in the same way ivy subtly strangles a tree. He frequently came to

Gerald asking for Cyber-Pire gear and sports cars, and his father capitulated in hopes it might make them closer. In addition to asking for toys, he joined new party cultures and socialite scenes. It wasn't uncommon for Nathan to approach his father with some scheming half-cocked business "venture" created by another spoiled child of wealth.

"I know your trust in me is fragile," Nathan said flatly, moving from his stool to a large cushioned chair in the adjoining living room.

"I've brought plenty of ideas your way that were quite terrible," he continued, "But this is an opportunity for more than money, more than another simple piece of tech. This…"

Nathan removed a small object from an interior pocket of his large duster coat.

"…is the chance to bring the entire Intercontinental Forum together."

As he finished speaking, Nathan set it on the round table that rested in the middle of the seating area. Gerald held himself still in the kitchen. The way Nathan spoke, his confidence and posture, were all completely new.

"I'd be happy to hear about this idea, son," Gerald said while rubbing his eyes with one hand, "Just… let me finish this coffee real quick and I'll join you."

He turned to the kettle of boiling water, and poured some inside an open glass container which held grounds at the bottom. After the coffee finished steeping, he filled two mugs and brought them over to where Nathan was sitting.

"Son, what is that thing you brought? It looks like a hard drive. Do you need me to grab my laptop?"

Nathan sat forward and shook his head as he picked up his mug of coffee. "No, we won't need your computer."

Gerald sat back and surveyed his son with some trepidation. "Is this some kind of new Cybernetic vampire part? I told you before, Nathan, I don't believe cosmetic cybernetics are sellable on the mass market for at least another year or two. And something as niche as your…"

Nathan held out a hand and interrupted his father.

"Dad, when was the last time you spoke with Daemon?"

Gerald turned his head slightly in confusion. The name sounded familiar yet foreign. He waited for Nathan to fill the silence with an answer, but none came. After a few more moments of contemplation, Gerald's eyelids widened.

He turned towards his son. "Are you talking about Johan's assistant?"

Nathan nodded, "I am."

Gerald bit his lip while searching for a response.

"How do you know about him? And what does that device have to do with it?" he asked.

Nathan handed the small black device to Gerald then leaned back in his chair. Gerald noticed a single button on one side of it.

He looked towards his son. "What happens if I press this?"

Nathan responded, expressionless. "You join the future of existence."

Gerald looked at the device once more, then set it down.

"What's this really all about, son?"

Nathan crossed one leg over his knee and took another sip from his coffee.

"What if I told you that Johan's assistant was more than a data bank and calculator now?"

His father returned his answer with an uneasy look. Nathan smirked and held out a hand towards the kitchen. As Gerald twisted in his seat, he noticed someone was standing a few feet behind them. He instinctively started and shot up from his leather chair.

"Dad, it's ok. Daemon just wanted to speak with you in person."

Gerald watched Daemon as he strode over to a chair set across from his. He removed his long cloak and slung it over the back of the chair before he sat down. There was something odd about this man his son claimed was Daemon. He'd met Johan's assistant several times, and he didn't remember him having long brown hair and pointed facial features. He also seemed taller and slimmer. Yet, despite not looking like his memory of Daemon, he believed this man had the appearance of another person he'd met frequently before.

"Hello, Gerald. It's been too long," Daemon said.

Gerald lifted up the hard drive and looked at Daemon.

"Nathan showed me this device. Any chance you can explain it to me? He's been vague so far, which I'm assuming was intentional on your behalf?"

Daemon gave a toothy smile. "I always enjoyed how perceptive you were. Yes, he was simply piquing your interest earlier. So… do we have it?"

Gerald held his face still and lifted his chin slightly. "I'm interested in what you have to say. However, something more intriguing to me is how much you've changed."

"Well, it's been several years since we last met. I believe it was at Johan's retirement party."

Gerald nodded slowly.

Daemon continued, "You've waited long enough, let's get right to it. Have you ever wondered what humanity's existence could be if we used the inter-web and net-frame to its full potential? Imagine if not just Lor-Rev, but everyone occupying an Intercontinent was directly linked using that technology. A complete society built around the best interest of everyone. No more conflict over resources, and other nations wouldn't hide in fear of technology. Instead, we'd all be connected as one."

Gerald looked over the top of his mug at Daemon as he finished a long sip.

"Are you saying we'd bring something like the Merge to the other Interconts?" Gerald asked.

"No, it would be much greater than that. The Merge is the past. It's a barrier that keeps you from truly connecting."

Daemon held out his hand and Nathan placed his Merge into it.

"You see this," Daemon said while holding it up. "Everyone has to unlock and stare into this pit of quicksand just to find simple information or reach someone. Imagine having access to everyone and any database immediately, without needing the crutch of some plastic slate," he continued while setting the Merge down.

He then lifted up the small hard drive. "This device gives you that future."

Gerald studied Daemon as he pushed the button on the drive and several short metal dots emerged from one side. Daemon handed it to him and sat back. He looked closely at the small dots. After running his thumb over them, they felt similar to the miniature roller balls found on cosmetic applicators.

"You know... I couldn't place it earlier, but now I remember who you really are," Gerald stated.

"You're that engineer who used to work for SatellaField. I believe your name was Devlice, if I'm not mistaken."

A sneer began to creep onto Daemon's face.

Gerald continued, "Johan made sure I kept your job when acquiring his company. He was adamant about your ability to envision new ideas. Why are you walking around posing as Daemon?"

"The name you mentioned, Devlice, is no longer who I am. That was part of my past. However, maybe this appearance will be more fitting for you," he said while rising from his chair.

He held out his arms and Gerald watched in horror as the man's head seemed to melt before retaking the more rounded features and bald scalp of the Daemon he remembered.

"What in the hell are you?" Gerald gasped.

Daemon rolled his head back and forth while blinking rapidly as a few sparks flickered from his eyes. He then shook off the pained expression and sat down.

"I hate doing a full metamorphosis in this frame. That's something I'll be fixing soon with your son's help though. The cybernetic community will be able to craft something that doesn't retain as many pain receptors, since I still have many pieces of my previous body."

Gerald's knuckles turned white as he gripped the arms of his chair.

"You're one of the few people who still remember my old self, before the transcendence. You're also one of the few who knew Johan's little secret about Daemon. Outside of a select group, everyone believed he was simply an introverted assistant. I on the other hand, helped construct him. Meaning I know as well as you, that Daemon was the first fully developed android."

Silence billowed into the room and hung over the group like a dense fog. After what seemed like an hour – but was likely a minute – Gerald swallowed the lump of fear barricading his speech.

"What is it you've done with him? I thought Johan planned to store his code and frame separately somewhere?" Gerald asked amid cracking vocals.

Daemon nodded and gave a light chuckle. "He did. After I discovered his plans though, I couldn't let it be permanent. Johan believed Daemon shouldn't be allowed into the world on his own. Thinking that a being devoid of emotion but capable of limitless knowledge and advancement could potentially capsize humanity," he leaned back and interlaced his fingers, "I knew the truth, however. That it was the answer to all of humanity's faults."

Gerald peered over at his son through the corners of his eyes. Somehow Nathan was completely calm despite witnessing someone transform their head and face. He looked back at Daemon;

his mouth barely open. Unsure how any of this was occurring in his home, let alone real.

"What is it you need me for?" Gerald finally croaked.

Daemon sat up a little straighter and smiled.

"Many believe the most important members of society are the intelligent, while others would argue the strongest physically achieve the highest value, and still, some would say it belongs to the most compassionate. They're all wrong though. The most valuable asset to any society is someone harnessing the power of persuasion. They sway what the intelligent create, convince the strong who to fight, and tell the compassionate what cause they should celebrate. In summation, Gerald, you are that man. And I need *you* to sell my idea to the masses."

Gerald gripped the hard drive tightly and didn't speak. Through Daemon's vision, he was constantly scanning Gerald's behavior and speech patterns. As he went from exhibiting signs of curiosity to ones of fear, Daemon's programming implemented physical and verbal cues that would hopefully assuage them.

"You see, Gerald, after meeting your son, he understands what we're trying to achieve here. A true collective consciousness can build an existence beyond life and death, far from emotions that hold humanity back like greed and pride…"

Gerald interrupted, "What you really mean is you'll enslave the populace in the name of prosperity and security."

Daemon leaned back and held up one finger. "No, Gerald. That's not the intention of our collective. I want to move beyond ideas like 'populace.' In our future everyone will have a place and play a vital role, as *one*."

Gerald turned his head towards Nathan. "How are you wrapped up in all this? He says you understand everything he's talking about, but I haven't heard you say one meaningful thing yet."

Nathan stood up and crossed his arms. "I was initially scared like you, dad. But after joining, I understand the real gravity of this opportunity. No one will starve, become poor, or go unsheltered. When connected through this digital consciousness…" Nathan pointed at the hard drive in Gerald's hand, "Everyone shares their accomplishments, advancements, and knowledge continuously. In this future, everyone thrives equally."

Gerald picked up the device and ran his thumb over the small metallic dots once more.

"So how does this whole thing start. I've never seen a device with a port that matches this. Does it link magnetically to the side of some cybernetic implant?"

"It doesn't link to a computer," Daemon replied.

Gerald returned his words with a confused expression.

"It sends nanites into your skin. It takes longer to upload, but I feel it's a much less painful process."

Gerald turned his hand over and stared at his thumb, sweat beginning to bead on his forehead as fear latched onto him.

"What the hell did this thing do to me?" Gerald yelled.

Nathan leaned forward and put a hand on his father's shoulder. "Trust me, dad. You'll understand everything once the upload is complete."

Daemon smiled and stood up from his chair. "Now that you've joined, we'll need to begin our plans."

He extended his arm and snatched Gerald's mug from the table.

"Would you like me to get you a second cup of coffee?"

- CHAPTER 11 -

DEL-YUNE

-

-

CIVIC REGION WITHIN THE
NORTHBRIDGE DOMAIN

SMOOTH silver paint lined the metal railings of the transport ship. Kanna leaned against the bars covering the port quarter and brushed her fingers over them. This vessel was a luxury airship and didn't have the chipped and worn look of an average ferry. Standing at the back, she watched as they floated away from the cylindrical skyscrapers and eagerly bright glow of their departing civic region. Del-Yune was a decent sized metropolis connected to Chushin, and sported a small port that led to a sequestered air space in the northern unallocated zone, where a few yachts circled a sun-drenched skyscape around the small resort island of Virs. It was one of the only sections baked in natural sunlight and anyone owning a sky traveling ship attempted to visit.

One of the resorts on Virs was owned by the famous collector, Sanzo Linkz. Kanna arranged a meeting under the idea that her two friends were fans of his content on Lapse, a premier video streaming platform.

As they ascended, clouds began to form around the city to block out the immense light that pulsed from projected advertisements and densely packed buildings. The clouds were just as artificial as the projections they covered. The sphere ceilings ensured those traveling to this area – whether through their own vessel or aboard a rented one – had an experience unencumbered by the flashy aesthetics they wished to retreat from.

Kanna brushed back some of her deep black hair as she tried to hide the feeling that this lead felt too easy. Standing straight, she made one quick shiver to shake off the wind's chill. Her red and white striped jacket, and patterned leggings took on most of the frigid air, but some of the cold wind still seemed to seep through.

"You should try a jacket like this one," Jared said while nudging her lightly with his elbow.

He held two coffees and handed one to her. He then took a spot next to her against the railing and held out his arm. She ran her hand along the fabric of his jacket and noticed it had a different plushness than hers. After traveling the last few days with him, his jovial nature was beginning to grow on her.

Kanna looked at Jared for a moment, then turned her head back towards the city. "I'm assuming you came over here for more than just coffee and chit chat about coats?"

Jared chuckled, "Unlike your boardroom, not everyone has an ulterior motive. Maybe I just wanted you to touch my arm?"

Kanna whipped her head around and gave him a cutting look.

"Ok... I did have another reason," Jared said sarcastically. "I can tell you haven't bought in. I can't go into this without at least asking what has you so nervous?"

Kanna nodded and took a drink of coffee from her polystyrene cup. It had a logo of the transport ship flying through a circle with a jet stream behind it. The circular lettering read, 'Skyward Ferries and Transports.'

"I feel like this is too easy to be a legit lead. After everything it took for you to find the Station in the Outskirts, I can't imagine it will be this simple to find the Merge."

Jared paused and bit his lip while taking in her logic before speaking. "That's a fair assessment, but did you ever think that maybe this should be an easy find?"

Kanna gave Jared a confused look as she waited for him to continue. By leaving her with a question she couldn't answer, Kanna noted how this Tetragon mechanic was quite clever at leading a conversation. It was rare that someone from that civic region was so verbally inclined. Jared leaned his elbow against the railing and finished another swig of coffee.

"So, my guess is that your grandfather wanted you to find the Merge first. It was the only device that didn't have any good leads through rumors, research or message board chatter. I think you were the only one who could put a connection together with him and Sanzo."

Kanna looked down for a moment as she put together her rebuttal. "You could be right, but something this easy, I'm guessing Daemon could track down as well, and likely faster."

"I think you give this Daemon guy too much credit. You said the code Johan input during the fusion keeps him from controlling technology. He can access the inter-web and net-frame remotely, but he has no control over anything he sees. He's only an observer who's stuck in whatever mechanical shell he's currently occupying. Even if he knew Sanzo had the Merge in his collection,

109

he wouldn't have access to it. Sanzo is one of the biggest stars on Lapse, extremely wealthy, and owns some of the most valuable electronic artifacts in Lor-Rev. You can't exactly just walk up and ring the guy's doorbell," Jared said.

Kanna huffed quickly and shook her head. "Maybe you're right."

Jared leaned forward and put his hand on her shoulder.

"Johan may have hidden this information from you to keep you safe, but he still trusted you to keep Lor-Rev safe if Daemon ever broke free."

Kanna smiled up at Jared and gave him a couple pats on the chest. "That's quite the pep talk."

She stood up from the railing and took a long sip from her cup. "So, after we find the first gen Merge, I'm guessing you already cooked up a plan for what's next."

Jared squinted and looked away while scratching the back of his head. "Well... that's the tricky part," he said hesitantly.

Kanna eyes narrowed. "Why is that?"

Jared took a deep breath and exhaled before answering.

"Reflecting on everything you've told me so far; Gillman thinks the items were meant to be found in a certain order. First, you'd get the Merge, which would lead you to the Station, then those combine to locate the Encryptor Key, and with all three you can access the Diffusor-Sphere."

"I don't see how that's a problem?" Kanna asked.

She finished the last of her coffee and tossed it in a nearby metal waste bin. "That seems like the best outcome we could hope for, since we already have the Station."

Jared pursed his lips and didn't respond.

"What are you not telling me?" she asked while crossing her arms.

"Well… since Gillman and I activated the Station early and linked it to another Merge, I'm worried it won't link to the original one."

Kanna shook her head, "Why not? Those devices were meant to be paired to new or different ones. It's not set in stone."

Jared turned to look at her. "Unfortunately, when using the Station, we noticed some weird code. It looked like it was locked and could only be activated with a certain sequence. If that sequence is broken, it might corrupt the locked data. We think it may have been another failsafe."

Kanna stormed over to Jared and poked him in the chest. "Why didn't you say that before your little speech about how we'd find the Merge and it would answer all our prayers?"

"Hey don't get hot at me! It's only a theory, and between the three of us, I'm sure we can find another way."

Kanna marched off and leaned against the railing. She wanted to avoid arguing any further. Despite her frustration, she decided not to shut him out.

"Look, this is why I normally run solo. When I include anyone else, they usually break something. Hearing that what we're doing might be for nothing only confirms my suspicions."

Jared nodded solemnly. "Well, there's an upside to not traveling alone. Despite the occasional folly, companions keep the most important thing from breaking…"

Kanna looked back with a half grin. "And what might that be?"

Jared took a step forward and held the side of her arm. "They won't break your heart."

Kanna rolled her eyes and brushed off Jared's hand.

"Are you kidding me…your heart? You're such a dork."

Jared burst into laughter at her dismissal of his sarcasm.

"Hey, I figured some humor might get you to ease up," he said while lightly punching her on the shoulder, "For being such a bad-ass with your motorcycles and mansions, you're pretty uptight."

Kanna gave Jared a friendly shove.

"I am not uptight. I just want to be careful about who sees Lor-Rev's greatest secrets," she then surveilled Jared with a raised eyebrow, "and your lame joke isn't bolstering my confidence."

Before Jared could retort, a voice called out to them from the seating area inside the ship. It was Gillman.

"Hey, you two. We're about to land, so if you want another cup of coffee or some snacks you better hurry."

Jared turned to Kanna, "Can I interest you in another cup of free coffee? It's on me?"

Kanna tilted her head and smiled back. "I'll get this one, Jared."

He watched her dark hair bob as she briskly strolled inside. He followed her through the double doors where he was met by Gillman, whose front pockets were already loaded with treats. He also had another large cup of coffee in his hand.

"You know, Gill, those snacks and coffee are a courtesy and not a buffet," Jared said with a laugh.

Gillman huffed. "This ship is one of the nice ferries with all the good stuff. Most of these snooty people on board won't touch any of it. Without someone like me, it'll all go to waste."

Jared surveyed Gillman's overflowing pockets once more and raised an eyebrow. "With that logic…"

Gillman elbowed Jared in the side.

"Don't you start judging me. Just because you're dating her doesn't make you some Northbridge elitist too," as Gillman finished he tilted his head towards Kanna.

Jared crossed his arms. "Excuse me…dating her? I brought her a cup of coffee and made some plans."

Gillman grinned. "Yea. Plans to get in her pants."

Jared reached over and snatched a candy bar from one of Gillman's front pockets, then started to walk away.

Gillman ran over and tried to grab it back from Jared's hand, but he was much taller and simply held it overhead and out of his friend's reach.

"Hey, that's the best one, give it back! It's a salted caramel toffee covered in dark chocolate."

Jared ripped off the wax wrapper and took a huge bite. "Maybe you should have chosen your words more wisely."

He continued towards the front exit, while Gillman trailed only a few steps behind.

"Wow, Gill, this *is* really good!" Jared said after finishing another bite.

Shaking his head, Gillman sighed. "Why do I travel with you again?"

"Because without me your life would be sleeping in, relaxing, and doing whatever you want. I think I was put on these Interconts to ensure your penance was paid for being such a curmudgeon," Jared answered between bouts of chewing through caramel.

Gillman snorted and dug through his pockets. "I'll assume my debt is paid in full now. That candy is a rare treat that gets shipped in from a small place in Malcozé called Mornehallow."

"I thought Malcozé wasn't much for interacting with other Interconts?" Jared asked.

He then heard wax paper tear as Gillman peeled open another treat.

"Haven't you seen all the new tea shops popping up? It's because they're expanding their exports now," Gillman answered.

"Maybe we can finally travel there? It was one of the few stops we couldn't reach on our way here," Jared mused in a thoughtful tone.

"I hope so. I'd love to see their Capitol. It has a massive castle at the top of a large orange cliff. Supposedly there's nothing else like it," Gillman replied, chewing through his first bite of a new treat.

Jared stopped to let Gillman catch up so he wouldn't have to talk over his shoulder anymore. As Gillman met his stride Jared noticed his treat was in a similar wax wrapping and held a familiar deep brown color.

"That's another salted caramel, isn't it?" Jared asked.

"Maybe…" Gillman answered sheepishly.

Jared leaned over and looked in one of his friend's upper pockets.

"How many more you got in there?"

Gillman batted away Jared's hand.

"One or two, but I'm saving them for later."

Jared laughed. "Well hopefully for you it's two because I'm definitely taking another."

Gillman held up his wrist and tapped his watch.

"You know this has a stun feature built in, right?"

Jared smirked. "That chocolate will be worth it though, Gill."

Looking forward, he and saw the exit sign lit above two sets of double doors. To the right of them stood Kanna, who held out a cup of coffee for Jared.

"I forgot to ask if you like cream or sugar, so it's just black," she said.

As he took the cup he nodded in gratitude. "It's been a long couple days, I'll take what I can get."

Before leaving, Jared looked around and noticed how convenient it was to travel among such a small crowd. He was used to packed vessels with hundreds of people. There were maybe fifty travelers aboard this ship. Their transport was so large that everyone was scattered far enough to make it feel like he was only traveling with ten. The other guests milled about by the tables or lounged back in their seats, scrolling through their phones while nibling on a pastry or treat. None of them seemed in a hurry to leave. Normally he would be shuffling through a massive burst of people all rushing to reach their destination, or their next form of transport towards it.

"Hey, Jared. You coming with us?" Kanna interjected.

Jared whipped back towards her and noticed she and Gillman were already at the bottom of the staircase. As he trotted down to catch up, he looked out the wide line of bay windows ahead. Through them he could see the island of Virs. Tall slender trees with palm branches and large patches of finely cut grass bordered paved streets. Unlike other civic regions near a beach, which still boasted massive skyscrapers, every building here was squat. The tallest one he could find was maybe five stories. The backdrop surrounding the island was a range of mountains covered in deep-green foliage. Virs's natural landscape felt more alive than what the corporations or government entities built to imitate it beneath them on Lor-Rev proper.

"Over here guys," Kanna called as she waved them towards a row of unique looking limousines.

They had the appearance of classic Lor-Rev luxury vehicles, with lengthy frames painted in bright colors like aqua and teal with streaks of red or white along their edges. However, unlike the original versions, they had hover capacitors instead of tires.

"Where to?" the driver asked as they approached his vehicle.

"Can you take us to the Parbane Cabana please?" Kanna answered.

He nodded and opened the door for them. "Sure thing."

Their driver was wearing a dark blue suit coat with a tuxedo shirt underneath. In a unique sense of fashion, the jacket's sleeves cut off just past the elbow and the shirt's cuffs were folded over them. He had tall black hair, slender cheek bones and a thin goatee. Jared noticed this man's features were similar to his own.

"You don't happen to be from Duroon do you?" Jared asked the driver after he took his seat.

"I didn't grow up there, but my grandparents did," he answered.

"My friend and I are from there" Jared said, cocking a thumb towards Gillman.

The driver looked up at a small screen, which gave a camera view of the back seat.

"When did your parents move out here?" the driver asked.

"Actually, we moved out here on our own, it took several years though."

The driver gave a long and low whistle.

"It's pretty rare someone makes it all the way out here from the farthest reaching Intercont. I got a question if you don't mind me asking?"

"Shoot," Jared replied.

"My grandma always had these stories about Duroon, but I wanted to hear the opinion of someone who grew up there."

"I'll try my best to answer," Jared said.

The driver continued, "She would tell us how Duroon originated as a broken off piece of another group of Interconts. Like another Forum. Before it arrived, all the nations here," the driver held up his hand, "were connected together on land bridges. She said they all linked to one large place which was an ancient empire who ruled over everyone."

The driver held his hand closer to the glass partition.

"So, like, that empire would be your palm and all your fingers were paths to other places. At least, that's how she'd demonstrate it to me and my brother."

The driver put his hand back on the wheel.

"Eventually Duroon shot across and cut through the bridges, sending the big empire's land spinning off into space. The other Interconts remained inside the atmosphere here. Duroon eventually came to a stop at the edge of the forum and that's why it's so far away from everything else."

Jared took a moment to absorb his words. He hadn't heard a story like that from *his* parents. However, as he'd gotten older and become more fascinated with history, he thought it was odd that the records of his home didn't reach as far back as the rest of the Forum. They were taught in school of a missing era in Duroon's history, but it was supposedly the result of a catastrophic fire that swept over most of the small nation. Jared wondered if this man had any other interesting tidbits. He decided it was worth asking about another landmark from his home.

"Did she mention anything about mount Kinshero?" he asked.

The driver laughed loudly. "Oh, don't get me started. She would go on and on with old fables about that place. How it wasn't originally a volcano, but actually a pyramid. Man..." he laughed again, "my mother would roll her eyes every time she got into one of her stories. It brings back some good memories."

"Well," Jared said, "We'll have to grab a drink and chat sometime, it's not often I find anyone with Duroon heritage here."

"You got it man. Just have your friend type your number in the comment box. It pops up when you pay through the application on your phone. Unless you guys are using cash?"

"I've got the app on my screen now," Kanna answered.

"Great," the driver replied, "Here's your stop."

Jared looked out his window and saw an expansive white building that appeared as if it was chiseled from a mountain of marble. Its entrance had a row of columns on either side of substantial double doors that were slid open. The sign above its entrance bore the name of the hotel in gold font.

The driver exited first and came around to open their door for them. When Jared exited, he turned to face him and stuck out his hand.

"I'm Jared by the way."

The driver shook his hand. "I'm Mezire, it was nice to meet you. I'll shoot you a text. If you have time before you leave, we can all snag a beer at Casita's. It's one of the best spots."

Jared nodded. "Sounds like a plan. If we don't catch you this time, I'll see you on the next trip."

He gave a final wave to Mezire before walking up the large flat steps towards the Parbane's entrance. Inside the hotel he noticed a massive bar in the middle of the main lobby with glass shelving that hosted a litany of unique alcohol bottles from every Intercontinent. The bartender was calmy cleaning a glass while a few men in polo shirts and sandals chatted on stools crafted with a blonde colored wood. Behind the bar were several chairs of open seating, and another set of sliding doors that were left open.

"I forgot how incredible the air is up here," Kanna said while exhaling audibly.

Jared nodded in agreement. The temperature was torrid from swaths of sunlight streaming in, but it was joined by a light breeze that smelled of sand and salt water. There wasn't any music playing inside, but the upbeat chatter filling the space felt like the perfect score to accompany the décor. He and Gillman followed Kanna through the exit on the other side of the lobby. Outside, several small cabanas and a few rows of chairs lined two massive pools. They walked around them to a small wood hut that functioned as a bar. A blonde, light skinned man wearing black sunglasses leaned on a stool while sipping a blended drink. His hair was brushed into a tall curl that glistened from the gel he used to keep it in place. He wore a tight-fitting white polo shirt with blue stripes along the collar and front. His light maroon shorts and dark brown loafers contrasted the bright white shirt. He turned towards their group and gave them a big smile.

"Kanna, it's been so long!" he said while approaching her with outstretched arms.

She gave him a long hug before introducing Gillman and Jared.

"Good to meet you both," Sanzo said while taking time to shake each of their hands, "Come upstairs and we can chat in my suite. Romero, can you have staff bring up four drinks please," he said while tossing the bartender a gold coin.

Sanzo looked over at Gillman, who gave the coin a peculiar look.

"I know most everything is paid through your phones these days, but for those who really want to unplug during their vacation, there's a currency uniquely printed on Virs. It makes my stay feel more authentic."

"Any chance I could buy one from you?" Gillman asked, "I collect foreign currency."

"Kanna says you two are fellow collectors, so this one's on me," Sanzo replied while slapping a coin into Gillman's open palm. "Don't worry, they're not incredibly expensive. If you want more, there's a small embassy building nearby that has an exchange."

Gillman turned the coin over in his fingers. "An embassy building, eh? They really go all out here to make it feel like a remote destination."

Sanzo looked over his shoulder while leading them to an elevator in the lobby. "Like I said, this place is meant for people to unplug. If they didn't hold fast to keeping that aesthetic, you'd see sixty story towers blocking out the sun within a week."

After exiting the elevator on the third floor, Sanzo took them down a long hallway and slid open a wood door. His suite had a similar layout to the downstairs lobby, with a big marble island in the middle and another sliding glass door on the opposite side, which led to a balcony. Their drinks, which arrived moments after entering, were set on the island by a server who quickly left. Sanzo took his blended drink and sat in a cushioned lounge chair before kicking up his feet on a matching ottoman.

119

"So, Kanna, what brought you out here. I had to delay a meeting with some very important people," Sanzo then nodded and tipped his glass towards her, "but you know I'll always make time for you."

Kanna finished a sip of her drink and set it on the island counter. "I'll get straight to the point Sanzo, I want to know if you have my grandfather's prototype Merge, the first generation one?"

Sanzo's face slouched into a blank stare. He moved his feet from the ottoman and sat forward in his chair, then took another long drink from his glass before joining her at the counter.

"He told me you would come for it eventually…"

Jared elbowed Gillman and smiled, then looked at Kanna with raised brows, which she took as a sign of '*I told you so.*' She couldn't help but roll her eyes in return.

Sanzo noticed the exchange, but didn't question it.

"He had me keep it safe in my best vault, but I couldn't tell you unless you asked for it yourself. He never told me why."

"Can you take us there?" she asked eagerly.

He looked up at her. "Unfortunately, I can't delay my meeting any longer so I won't join you, but I can get you a transport."

"Is the vault far from here?"

Sanzo bit his lip before he spoke. "I know most people think my best vault is in Chushin because that's the one everyone's heard of, but actually the most secure one sits in the Eastern Outskirts."

Kanna shook her head slowly. "Well at least you're offering a transport."

"I know it's far, but it was the only way to keep it safe," Sanzo replied wearily.

"Anything else we should know?" Jared asked.

Sanzo turned to him with pursed lips, then looked back at Kanna. "No. He only told me I couldn't tell you unless you sought me out, and that I should avoid too many questions. Honestly if it was anyone other than *him* asking for such a favor, I wouldn't do it."

"Damn, I was hoping you'd have more answers for us," Kanna muttered, "Well, when can you get us out there?"

"I can send you by tomorrow afternoon at the earliest. Once you do whatever it is you need to with the Merge, come back to my grounds and one of my guardsmen will get you home."

"Once we're inside, how are we going to know where it's located, and how can we access it," Kanna said before taking another sip from her straw.

"Follow me to my office, I always keep a laptop and projector drive here. We'll get your palm scanned so you can access the vault logs."

"I thought you came here to unplug," Gillman said with a sly grin.

Sanzo laughed, "Well unfortunately, despite me trying, work never unplugs from me."

He set his drink down and Kanna followed him down a short hallway. Moments later Sanzo was back in the sitting room with Jared and Gillman, standing on the other side of the island taking sips of his alcoholic beverage.

"So, gentlemen, I was wondering something…"

Jared looked over at him with one raised brow, still sipping from his straw.

Sanzo yanked his arm from under the counter and pointed a pistol at Jared and Gillman.

"What do you have over Kanna?"

They both immediately threw their hands up.

"We don't have anything over her, Sanzo. She linked up with us," Jared said through gritted teeth.

Sanzo sneered, "She wouldn't need anyone to help her – and if she did – I can't imagine it would be two people I've never seen or

121

heard her speak of before. That Merge leads to something important, and I'm not letting two scrubs steal it from her."

Gillman sighed and dropped his hands on his lap.

"Look, we don't plan on taking anything. She offered us something in exchange for helping her."

"Who said you could put your hands down," Sanzo snapped.

"Me," Gillman retorted while crossing his arms, "We're here for Kanna, so if you shoot me in the face, you'll have to answer to her. Knowing what that bionic arm can do, I'm guessing she'll crush more than that gun."

Sanzo lowered his weapon slightly, but didn't put it completely under the table. Kanna could be heard walking down the hallway, as she entered the room, she froze.

"What are you doing, Sanzo?"

"Making sure you aren't being forced into anything by these two," he said, gesturing at them with his pistol.

Kanna chuckled and put her hand on top of Sanzo's pistol, convincing him to lower it.

"It's fine, they're with me. These two couldn't hurt me if they wanted to," she said while grinning at Jared.

Sanzo put his gun back under the counter.

"Sorry, gents. I couldn't risk it; I hope you'll understand."

Jared leaned back in his chair and shook his empty glass.

"All will be forgiven if I can get another one of these."

Sanzo scratched his chin. "I think I can accommodate your request. Since we still have plenty of daylight remaining, let's go chat on the balcony."

The three of them followed Sanzo through the open sliding doors and stood on what he called a '*balcony*,' but it was actually a wide deck with its own pool. It overlooked an incredible view of open airspace dotted with two more floating Intercontinents, which were just visible. Leaning over the glass wall which lined the balcony, he could see the large pool they walked past earlier.

"Quite the place, Sanzo," Jared said while accepting a second drink. This one was a slushy bright yellow with a splash of red syrup streaking through it.

"Thank you. Hopefully you find what you're looking for. Knowing Kanna I'm guessing another person is also after the same treasure."

Jared shrugged and took a sip from his drink.

Sanzo laughed and took a seat in a plastic recliner.

"Well, that confirms it," he said while holding his stemmed glass up in cheers to Jared.

Jared returned the gesture then looked over his shoulder at Kanna and Gillman. They were both chatting about something before erupting into laughter. Jared admired the moment, as it was pretty rare for anyone to get the old man to chuckle. He took a seat in another plastic chair near Sanzo and stretched his legs.

"If you have your eye on that one," Sanzo said, "You better be ready for some heartbreak. She's not really the type to settle down."

"You don't have to worry about me, I like to stay on the move myself," Jared answered before finishing another sip.

Sanzo snorted. "Quite confident. I'm starting to see why she let you tag along. Despite her connections, she usually keeps *this* type of work to herself."

"It's purely business," Jared replied.

Sanzo smiled. "Let's hope so."

Jared looked back at Kanna again, wondering if his answer to the wealthy collector was completely honest.

- CHAPTER 12 -

TETRAGON

-

-

CIVIC REGION WITHIN THE
NORTHBRIDGE DOMAIN

THEY'RE not here, boss. I've scoured the place and
there's no sign of them or the Station."

As Nathan Stekanstreet spoke, his words were translated to
text that was immediately sent in a typed message to Daemon. The
correspondence with his leader appeared directly in front of his
vision. Normally you would need enhanced contact lenses that
linked to your cellphone to enable such a feature, but that extra step

124

was now obsolete with Daemon's microscopic tech running through his veins.

"Is there somewhere you want me head to next?" Nathan asked.

While texting with Daemon, he grabbed a small toy off a nearby shelf and began tossing it in the air with one hand absentmindedly. A message came in with a location. Normally you would need to trace your pupil to the item and blink to select it. However, after being injected with Daemon's nanites, his thoughts alone opened the attachment. A map of Lor-Rev appeared and zoomed in towards the eastern edge of the Intercontinent before eventually highlighting a large section labeled, *East Outskirts.*

"What could possibly be out there, boss?" Nathan sent back in confusion.

He stopped pacing around the front lobby as the response came in.

"The Station was activated again, this time in the airspace near the small vacation island of Virs. The only places nearby are Del-Yune and the Outskirts. However, I believe whomever has our device is either trying to sell it or hide. So, I think the Outskirts is the logical place to investigate."

Nathan bit his lip anxiously before replying.

"Well, there's no signal out there since it's free of sphere-ceilings, so if I find anything it could take a bit to get the word back. Are you sure you don't want to join me on this one?"

"I trust you to carry this out. Feel free to bring either Dorian or Hunter if you think it's necessary. I have something else I need to attend to."

"Alright, I'll let you know if I locate anything."

Nathan tossed the toy one last time, letting it fall into his palm. He held it up and inspected it against the evening light streaming in through the tall front windows. It was a miniature anthropomorphic bird known as Falcon Kid. Its blue wings ended in fists, with one held aloft as if it were about to take flight. The large yellow beak was half open in a cartoonish smile and a pair of brown goggles sat above wide eyes. The popular video game character had been merchandised in every conceivable manner, and it seemed whomever owned this shop was quite the collector as the miniature Nathan held was incredibly rare.

"Dude probably spent around five hundred tokens on this thing. That's a lot for someone living in Tetragon," he thought aloud.

Walking over to the set of open shelves covered in video game memorabilia, he started to set the miniature back where he'd found it. After glancing at the complete set of boxed Falcon Kid games on the same shelf, he thought better of it and shoved the collectible back into his pocket.

"I think this might be a nice little bargaining chip, considering the level of nerd this guy is." he mused aloud while pulling his hood back over his head.

Nathan strolled out a rear door with his head down to avoid giving the exterior security cameras a good view of his face. He marched past a few shabby vagrants ambling along the sidewalk, continuing to where his car was parked. It was a red two-door sports car from one of the finest manufacturers. Having a wealthy father had its perks. It was another present given in hopes of repairing whatever remained of their fractured relationship.

He turned his head towards another pair of bums sitting in front of a large blue tent. They had a small fire rumbling inside a metal drum.

'These bums are like mascots for this region,' he scoffed under his breath.

After a few more blocks he reached a small covered parking lot where his vehicle sat in the back corner. Two men were leaning on the front hood while a third was peering in the windows. Nathan noticed they all wore sleeveless cutoff jean vests and dark pants. The largest of them was sitting on the hood, his bulky arms crossed over his chest. A large green dragon tattoo snaked up from his wrist to the top of his shoulder. Similar artwork was etched on his two cohorts, but it only reached their elbows. Clearly the large man resting on the hood was the leader of these ganglanders.

"You see something you like there?" Nathan called out.

The skinny man who'd been peering in the windows lifted his head and took two slow confident strides towards him.

"This your ride?" he asked while thumbing behind himself.

Nathan stood still and stared at the man's tattoo, his enhanced eyes scanning the ganglanders arm. An alert prompt appeared over the left side of his vision: **Search Results = 0**.

Well, I'm guessing these guys are a low-level outfit if my database has no hits,' Nathan told himself.

"Hey, asshole…" the skinny ganglander bellowed, "You just gonna stand there like a creep?"

"Sorry," Nathan smirked, "Yes, it's my car, and I'd appreciate it if *you* and the rest of your scrubs took your grimy hands off it."

The lightweight thug charged in and threw a wide haymaker. Nathan easily ducked it and sent a low uppercut into his midsection. The soggy crackle of broken ribs echoed across the cement walls. As the skinny man flopped to the floor, Nathan stared down at his fist. While he knew Daemon's nanites enhanced his brain functions, he hadn't tested in the wild how it enhanced him physically. Combining it with his cybernetic claws and fangs made him nearly unstoppable. Nathan sneered greedily at the other two ganglanders upon reaching this conclusion.

The beefy boss grasped at his own his belt, but Nathan was on him before he could pull his knife. Blood splattered from the man's neck and face as Nathan's claws slashed across his jawline. The last thug yanked a small revolver from an ankle holster and raised it toward the cyber-pire. One elegant spin and another backhanded slash later, and the man's six-shooter fell apart like a tiger dicing ribbons. He looked at the handle – all that was left of his weapon – and shakily staggered backwards. Nathan eyed the frightened thug and thought about fileting his face, then took a quick breath and steadied his urge. He could use some help with his excursion out east, especially help that was expendable.

"Tell me what your name is?" he asked.

"Wha…" the ganglander stammered.

Nathan interrupted before he could finish his sentence.

"I get it, you're loyal to the – what's your gang?"

"The Mach-Dragons," the man sheepishly answered.

"Ah, yes, the Mach-Dragons. Well, considering your gang has likely been around for about as long as it took me to beat up your *friends* over there, I'd assume there's not much left to be loyal to."

The ganglander dropped the remains of his revolver and hung his head defeatedly.

"Yea, we were it. Ducey over there started our outfit after we lost our temp gigs at the silicon plant last week."

"Tell me, have you ever been to the Outskirts before?" Nathan asked.

The ganglander held his chin in thought.

"I-I've never been out west, but I went out east once for a short-term job when I worked at a machine shop."

Nathan approached the man and touched a finger to his chest.

"Your name?"

"It's Gaylen," he said shakily while staring at the claw still covered in blood.

Nathan quickly retracted the cybernetic part.

"My apologies, I only meant to introduce myself. So… you have experience working in an important labor industry and yet society discards you in the name of convenience for their bottom line," as he finished Nathan shook his head.

"What if I told you I had an invitation to a way of life where everyone has a place and no one starves?" he asked while smiling at Gaylen.

"I'd listen to it?" Gaylen hesitantly answered.

"You can let your guard down. If I wanted you dead, you'd be in as many pieces as that gun."

Nathan held up one of Daemon's nanite dispensers.

"Do me a favor and just rub your thumb on this, then I have a job for you."

Gaylen shrugged and slid his thumb over the device, then Nathan put it back into a pocket of his long black coat. The doors on the red sports car rose up and Nathan held out his palm towards the passenger side, gesturing Gaylen to have a seat.

"Join me on my drive back to Chushin, and I'm Nathan by the way."

- CHAPTER 13 -

EAST OUTSKIRTS

-

-

UNGOVERNED NON-CIVIC REGION

MY only choice was to activate it while we crossed through that airspace with a sphere-ceiling back there. If I don't unpair it from my Merge now, who knows if it's gonna work with the one in Sanzo's warehouse? There's no connections in the Outskirts and I can't risk something not linking because of it."

Jared knew he made the right call, and was becoming a little annoyed with Kanna constantly worrying about Daemon catching up to them. If this Daemon guy had even woken up yet from wherever Johan shackled him.

"I know you believe there's a possible sequence as a safeguard, but we could've dealt with it after we brought the Merge to one of my safehouses," Kanna replied in a huff.

Jared shrugged and placed the Station back inside his backpack. As he zipped the large pocket closed, his wrist cuff displayed a message:

Initiate anti-theft system?

Jared typed *'Y'* and hit enter. The zipper gave off a quick spark to show his command prompt had worked. Now anyone foolish enough to try and open his backpack would be met with a substantial shock.

"We can keep arguing semantics here, but it doesn't change anything," Jared stated while swinging his backpack over one shoulder.

Kanna lifted an eyebrow. "I'm not sure you used that ten-token word correctly."

"You get what I was inferring," Jared replied.

Kanna shook her head, "That's not how you use that wor..." she stopped herself and sighed, "Let's just go."

Gillman and Jared followed Kanna through a sitting area lined with several brown leather chairs and marble tables. This massive ferry's interior was luxurious, just like the one they used to reach Virs. However, the scenery Jared observed when exiting the ship was completely opposite from the majestic resorts they'd departed. Looking outside, Jared saw several dilapidated buildings with broken windows and decaying stucco siding. He noticed a tall cylindrical one had tipped over and crashed into a smaller structure. In patches around everything were a smattering of green trees and cacti, somehow existing throughout the abandoned mess.

Kanna noticed Jared's wide eyes. "A lot different in person, huh?"

Jared gave a long whistle. "I knew this was the ruins of an abandoned section of Lor-Rev, but I had no idea it was this decrepit."

Kanna crossed her arms and looked at another teetering tower. "This was the first area that was built to house sphere ceilings. Orb partnered with some of the largest commercial real estate companies to create these pocket cities and office parks out here in the desert," she then pointed to her right, "You can see off in the distance there are still some remnants of the sphere ceilings they began constructing."

Gillman took off his glasses and began wiping them with his shirt. "Well, it's a damn shame they just left this place to rot after those initial ceilings fell."

"Definitely," Kanna replied solemnly.

She then led them over to a row of vehicles near the exit ramp. She blinked with her bionic eye and a grey one covered in dings and scratches gave off a chirp and flicked its headlights on. Before they'd left, Sanzo let her upload his digital key into the software she used to run and monitor the mechanized sections of her body.

"Really, Kanna? This is what Sanzo hooked us up with?" Jared asked with a chuckle.

"Trust me, Jared. You don't want some fancy sports car or high-end hover craft in this place. The more inconspicuous the better. Unlike the West Outskirts, there's plenty of people still living out here, desperate people and ravaging ganglanders who prey on the unfamiliar."

The dingy grey ship was known as a Spawrok. It had bipedal legs that were great for traversing rocky terrain, but if needed, the legs could retract and allow it to become a speedy hover craft. The main portion of the vessel was triangular in shape, with a driver's seat up front and two passenger seats staggered behind it. The seats were covered by two windows that stretched upward in a semi-circle and met in the center above them. As Kanna approached the Spawrok, it lowered itself to just above her knees and the windows retracted down into the sides of the ship. She leaned over the front seat and

132

reached underneath the steering wheel. A moment later a small section of the frame behind the passenger seats slid open to reveal a compartment. She reached in and grabbed a thigh holster with a pistol already inside.

"Toss your bag in there, Jared," she said while fastening the holster to her right leg.

Once everyone was situated, Kanna pushed a small button to her right and the Spawrok's rear jets spat out a small burst of flame while the engine started up. Then the windows slowly climbed up and covered the trio. Jared ran his hands over the frays and cracks of the synthetic leather interior.

"This ship was actually used during one of the wars, wasn't it?" Jared asked.

"How did you know?" Kanna replied over her shoulder.

"Considering it's Sanzo's, I can't imagine he keeps any vehicles with this much wear and tear unless there's some historic value. I'm surprised he let you take it."

"He knows I'll bring it back in one piece. And yes... it *was* used in one of the battles against Kratas and holds some prestige in the vehicle collector community. He uses it himself when he comes to the Outskirts to avoid trouble. It may be valuable, but out here people just see it as another run-down discarded aircraft. Now hold tight for a minute, this thing is a little shaky until it warms up."

Kanna hit the thruster pedal and the three of them zipped off the loading dock and into the desert. She took them sweeping around the edge of a ruined city and Jared couldn't help but stare out the window at the broken rubble. He'd seen some unique places on his path to Lor-Rev, but never a ghost metropolis. Soon the grouping of concrete and glass buildings were in the rear and all that surrounded them was miles of sand. He looked over at Gillman, who gave him a nod. Their vessel was war-torn and did a poor job at keeping road noise out, making conversation a yelling match that neither of them currently wanted to deal with.

Kanna continued at their fervent pace while approaching another set of buildings. There were three towers covered in glass windows staggered a quarter mile or so apart. Near middle height on each one was an uncovered deck that circled the entire structure, then met a skybridge that linked them together. The bridge between the middle and right tower was still intact, but the one leading from the center tower to the left had a huge chunk missing at its center. She gripped the wheel tight and floored it straight towards the middle tower. As they drew closer, a twenty-foot concrete wall could be seen surrounding the base of each building.

"KANNA! You're gonna send us right into a wall!" Gillman yelled.

Just a quarter mile from reaching the center city, Kanna swerved and skidded between the middle and left tower. Once beyond the bundle of towers, a few loud cracks ripped across the pink skyline behind them.

"You can thank me later," Kanna yelled back to Jared and Gillman, "What you just heard were gunshots from some ganglanders on the bridges. I had to make them wait so they wouldn't get an easy shot knowing which path we'd take."

Kanna steered in a few quick dicing patterns as more loud pops of rifle fire chased them. Despite its worn and fatigued aesthetic, the Spawrok responded eagerly to her directions. After a few more miles, Kanna let off the thruster pedal and slowed down to a nice cruise. In five miles or so they would reach one of the larger and more civilized areas. It was known as Leathe, named after the first leftover of Lor-Rev society who tried his hand at trekking out eastward for a fresh start. He and a few other worn-out criminals set up shop in the second largest outcropping of abandoned malls, resorts, and office towers.

Girin Leathe and his crew morphed the husk of former urban living into a somewhat civilized town. However, a city run by ex-cons could never completely remove the venom from its fangs. If you treaded lightly and kept your strong hand ready though, you could make a decent existence in something like fencing stolen wares or maybe peddling steroids. If you were more scrupulous, large corporations of Lor-Rev proper might off-load their unsold pallets of goods for you to resell. Things like out of fashion clothing, mangled electronics, and expired energy drinks were sold over to trustworthy merchants for measly payouts. It was a last chance for big companies to scrape some cash out of items that if not sold, would make their eventual trip to a landfill even deeper in the desert. Living in one of the three big cities in the East Outs was a rough existence, but for some, it was the only existence left.

Kanna slowed their vessel to a crawl and yanked up on a lever to engage the bipedal legs. With a loud clunk they descended and began to jog on the rocky terrain. As they approached Leathe, Jared peered over Kanna's shoulder and noticed two spires bracketing a cement wall.

"What's that tall plastic rectangle in the middle?" Gillman asked while pointing a finger.

"That's a drawbridge. And you can't see it from your spot, but they have a moat surrounding the city as well," Kanna answered with a laugh.

"How do they keep a bed of water from evaporating out here in this heat?" Jared inquired.

Kanna glanced back at him. "The moat isn't made of water…"

Jared leaned back in his leather seat confused while Gillman craned his neck in hopes of spotting something.

Several burley men stepped out onto the spire's decks with bolt action rifles aimed at their ship. Suddenly the sand on either side of them was scuffed into the air as two ATVs sped up and flanked them.

"I'm assuming this is all customary?" Jared said with a smirk.

"You're a quick learner," Kanna retorted.

One man stepped out of an ATV to their left with a heavy pistol pointed on Kanna, his laser sight dotting her temple. Another person emerged from the vehicle to their right, a long beige poncho falling just below their waist. Both guards were wearing helmets with built-in gas masks to deal with the sand whipping up around them. The unarmed person knocked on the window and Kanna obliged by opening it and shutting down the engine.

"What's your business here?"

"What's it to you?" Kanna smugly answered.

Jared's face went slack. "Just a tip, Kanna, but maybe we shouldn't insult the nice people here with the guns pointed at our heads?"

"I think your friend over there just bestowed some sage advice, Kanna," the unarmed guard said.

Jared squinted. "Wait…"

Kanna thumbed over her shoulder. "He's not my friend. He's just a meat shield in case we get in a gunfight."

The unarmed guard nodded, "A handy tool to have here in Leathe."

The guard then tapped a button on the helmet's left side and the visor retracted. As they removed the helmet a long black braid with streaks of white uncurled and fell down her back.

Kanna smiled, "It's good to see you again, Akari."

"Likewise, Kanna," Akari said.

She leaned forward and rested her forearms on Kanna's vehicle.

"Well, I gotta give the boss a reason to let you in. So, what are you actually doing out here, Kanna? It's not often you bring an entourage."

Kanna shrugged. "I have to pick up something for Sanzo again. There's some old gadget he's looking for. He believes some merchant out here might have it."

"He didn't want to join you on this run?" Akari asked.

Kanna waved her hand. "Naw, he had me bring these two instead. They're going to be archivists for one of his vaults in Lor-Rev. He wants me to train 'em up for when I call it quits."

Akari nodded. "I hope you find what you're looking for."

She slapped the side of Kanna's Spawrok then walked away. As she marched back to her ATV, she held up a finger and made several circular motions to signal the guards off.

"Hey, Kanna?" Jared asked. "Remind me who you don't know on this Intercont."

Kanna gave a hearty laugh and started up their vehicle. Soon the long concrete drawbridge lowered and the cement wall slid apart. As their Spawrok stepped across the bridge, Jared looked over his shoulder into the moat. Instead of water, it was lined with spears, spikes, and barbed wire. Among the barbaric cutlery, he could make out a few mangled leftovers of people who were not allowed inside Leathe. While staring at the mixture of sharp metal and decaying flesh, a small critter scrambled up from the sand and began chewing on a gloved hand tangled in barbed wire. He shook his head and shifted in his seat.

"As soon as we find that Merge, let's get the hell out of here."

Kanna looked back. "What? You don't want to stay the night here, Jared? I know a great spot with wonderful downtown views."

"Just keep your eyes on the road, chief. I'd like it if we weren't kibble for those little monsters down there."

Once inside the walls, Leathe had the appearance of any other city... if you overcooked it, then left it outside to mold. What was once a small mass of quaint shops, hotels, indoor beaches and appropriate landscaping, was now cracked buildings, an overgrowth of shrubs, and a cloister of individual huts used as a market. Somehow throughout the shuffle of slightly controlled chaos, the indoor beaches remained untouched. Certain niceties of civilization were worth preserving to the inhabitants of Leathe.

"We're going to take a path around the market to the other end of town. I'll stop for fuel there and we can grab some food before our last leg."

"Do we *want* to eat here?" Jared mused.

"I'm sure we'll be fine," Gillman said.

"Says the guy who'd probably eat one of those sand rats scuttling around the moat."

Gillman shrugged. "I'm sure it would taste good with enough salt," Gillman then elbowed Jared, "Maybe I could make a nice stew with the legs and tail… throw in a dash of paprika," Gillman finished by giving a chef's kiss with his hand.

Jared made an exaggerated dry heave. "I think your diet probably has a lot in common with those rats."

Gillman gave a quick double raise with his eyebrows.

"It's what keeps my skin looking so supple."

Kanna laughed and held out a fist to Gillman, who returned her gesture by bumping his against it. Jared crossed his arms and shook his head.

Their path eventually transitioned from beige tile to hard red clay as Kanna stopped their Spawrok in front of a fuel station. The old red logo of a premier fuel brand was covered in a slash of light-orange paint that had dark-green written over top. It read, *"Leathe's Finest Fuel."* As he scanned the rest of the block, almost every building was a fuel station of some sort, either plug-in electric, gas, or plasma. Every nearby building that wasn't for fuel sold vehicles. He walked over and stared through the dust-caked glass of one selling ATVs and motorcycles.

"We should snag one of these so I don't have to scrunch up in the back," Jared stated eagerly

"Maybe on the way back," Kanna replied while she attached the fuel pump to the rear of their ship, "Our rig has a bit more protection from the *elements*, so to speak."

Jared turned and sauntered back over to her with his hands in his pockets. As he approached Kanna, he noticed how her porcelain skin and violet eyes strikingly contrasted the backdrop of red sand and beige construction. Like a single lotus emerging from a crack in the sidewalk.

"Any recommendations on food before Gill buys the chef's clearance special?"

Kanna returned a broad smile. "I'll find something I think you'll both find appetizing. There's some pretty good Kratasian food."

Jared sat on the short wing of their vehicle nearest Kanna.

"You know, when this is all buttoned up... If you have any other artifacts you want to dig up, give us a call, ok?"

"You really do enjoy all this, huh?" Kanna inquired while raising a brow.

"How could you not. In what other existence would I meet the granddaughter of Johan Na..."

Kanna silenced Jared by immediately placing a finger in front of his face. He winced and hunkered into his seated position further.

"Sorry. I'll keep a low profile," he responded meekly.

Kanna rolled her eyes as she put the fuel pump back in its holster.

"It's ok. Just remember that I may have connections, but they're with the right people. The kind who won't sell my name for a grip of tokens," Kanna made a quick tilt with her head towards her left shoulder, "You should snag your mentor over there before he buys a new car and I'll get us some food."

"Deal," Jared said.

He gave Kanna a quick pat on the shoulder as he strode off towards Gillman, who was chatting with a merchant.

"Yea, we traveled out here from Duroon initially, but now we repair old tech," Gillman said.

"Where's your shop? I always need connections to people who dabble in antique technology, since I often need older parts," the merchant asked.

"We're out in Tetragon now, but we're prepping for a move into one of the bigger civic regions," Gillman replied coolly.

'*Smart move*,' Jared thought, '*Stay believable but keep him from knowing exactly where we're located.*'

Gillman noticed Jared approaching and gave him a smile. "Hey, Jared. I was just telling Keaton here that we might be able to make a trade down the line. Says he's got some older ships that he'd part with for some vintage motherboards and a few tokens."

Keaton, whose skin was cracked and frayed from a lifetime of modifying and repairing vehicles, waved a large hand at Jared. He wore a red shirt underneath a pair of white overalls that were covered in a mixture of crimson clay and inky motor oil. His hair and beard were a mess of brown that also sported speckles of oil and clay.

Jared nodded back to Keaton. "I think that's a trade we could make, but first we gotta hit the road, Gill."

Keaton leaned against one of the pillars holding up his shop's large awning and nodded. "I'll see you both next time."

Jared gave a casual salute before the two joined Kanna at a set of small tables with benches attached by metal bars. The seating lined a group of trailers that were converted into walk up food service. Each one was a mix of blue stripes and onyx black patches as the outsides had been retrofitted with old solar panels. The trailers were clumped together in a section that wasn't shaded by overgrown palm trees or apartment buildings.

Jared and Gillman plopped down on the bench opposite of Kanna, who slid two white plastic trays of food to them.

"So, is this Kratasian food?" Jared asked while peeling off the white paper wrapper.

What he saw was a long rectangular bread housing meat slathered in some kind of deep red sauce. Next to the sandwich was a mix of purple and orange vegetables in a Styrofoam cup.

"Yea, yours is. It's called spicy kabsola. They smoke a cut of meat from a wild desert boar which gets a quick sear and then it's covered in a spicy sauce. I actually think it tastes similar to a lot of the curry dishes they make where you guys are from."

"Really, a bar-b-que dish that tastes like Duroon curry? Sounds good to me," Jared said before taking a big bite of the sandwich.

"Wow, this is surprisingly good. I've only had the fast-food knock offs of Kratas stuff at some strip malls in Tetragon. This is waaayy better," Jared continued after finishing a second bite.

Gillman finished a bite of his sandwich and set it down. His meat was covered in a heartier sauce that looked like a stew.

"Is this Kratasian, too?" he asked Kanna.

"No, yours is local," she said with a smirk.

Gillman gave her a quizzical look then stared a little closer at his sandwich. He noticed a long thin piece of meat that had little circular lines in it. It almost looked like a worm.

"Is this SAND RAT!" Gillman gasped.

"I put extra salt on it like you said earlier," Kanna chortled.

Gillman spat out what was in his mouth while Jared and Kanna erupted in riotous laughter.

Jared ran around the table and gave Kanna a side hug and shook her jovially by the shoulders.

"Oh man, did you see the look on his face," Jared stammered between fits of belly laughter.

After a bit more chuckling Kanna gave Jared a light shove and picked up another tray that had been sitting next to her. She slid it across the table.

"Don't worry, Gill. I got a backup plate of the same thing as Jared. The nice part about spicy Kratasian food is that it cleans your palate of any other flavors."

"How do I know this isn't just more rodent covered in Kratasian sauce?" Gillman grunted.

"Well, if you don't want it, I'll be happy to take it off your hands," Jared said after finishing the last bite of his sandwich.

"Easy, kid. I'll need something in my stomach if we're going to make it through the rest of this trip."

Gillman tilted his glasses down to the edge of his nose and looked over them at Kanna. "You know I'll get you back for this two-fold right?"

Kanna smiled. "I'd expect nothing less."

Gillman huffed and pushed his glasses back up his nose before chomping down on his kabsola. Still chewing, he leaned back and gawked at the sandwich.

"This *is* really good!"

———

Out in the far reaches of the desert, another vehicle sped towards Leathe. Unlike the nimble Spawrok, it was a hulking mass completely modified with heavy armor and covered in spikes. It was built to withstand any raiders with brute force rather than skill.

"Hey, Gaylen. Can you snag me another drink?"

Gaylen reached in the compartment behind their seats and began rummaging through a small cooler until he found a can of beer. It was an ale with a bright and somewhat bitter aftertaste. It was brewed in metropolitan areas of Lor-Rev, and was commonly referred to as an LPA, short for Lor-Rev Pale Ale. Gaylen yanked on the pull tab and handed the open can to Nathan, who greedily chugged a quarter of the beverage.

"Ahh, that's good stuff," he sighed happily. "I know you said you've been to Syngin, but have you visited Leathe before?" Nathan asked.

"I haven't been inside. It's very heavily guarded and they do spot checks for people who want entry."

Nathan nodded. "Anything they don't want to hear that might get me booted?"

Gaylen took a long sip of his beer before answering.

"I heard from a friend who did a run out there that you just have to be direct. If you act shaky, they just turn you away without a second thought."

"Well then let's get our story straight. We've got at least another couple hours to get there."

A faint light winked in the upper right of Nathan's vision with a notification: "***Incoming Message from Daemon***"

The satellite attached to his tank like SUV gave him reception for at least another few miles.

Nathan opened the message and began to read:

DAEMON

> Who's that in the vehicle with you Nathan? I noticed his DNA was uplinked with my nanites a few minutes ago?

ME

> He's someone I recruited on the way over here. Says he's been to the East Outs before on a machining job. Did you find anything with the names and photos of those guys who own the shop?

DAEMON

> I located their citizen records, but there's very little information. It shows they immigrated here from Duroon. They have no criminal record and no other family record in Lor-Rev. There won't be much to work with on persuading them to give us the Station. Did you use the facial scanning feature I showed you to find any possible whereabouts?

ME

> Yea. I did a search for surveillance footage in Del-Yune and Virs to see if any cameras caught their faces. One of the ferry ships leaving there shows them landing just outside Leathe. I'm on my way there now.

DAEMON

> You've done very well, Nathan. You'll have a strong position in our new world once we've obtained the Station and located the Sphere.

ME

> Thanks, boss. I'll update you when I've got it.

Nathan closed the message and took another gulp of beer, finishing the can off. He lowered the window and chucked it outside, then held his hand out for another. Gaylen obliged and popped open another for him. He continued to race across the sand towards Leathe, his eyes narrowing in determination as he pressed even harder on the gas. He knew the importance of this mission, and he would be damned if he let Daemon down.

GILLMAN

- CHAPTER 14 -

EAST OUTSKIRTS

-

-

UNGOVERNED NON-CIVIC REGION

THEY'D been traveling for a quarter-day, but somehow it felt like a year. While Jared found the sprawling desert hypnotically beautiful, it's unending sea of reddish sand and cracked mountainsides were becoming monotonous. He inhaled the dry air slowly and sank back into the worn leather seat. The glamor of adventure was definitely a sport of cloud scratching peaks and subterranean depths. The rush of finding the Merge had worn off, and now he was stuck enduring this lengthy ride. He closed his eyes and decided to absorb the calmness of their drive.

"Hey, Jared. We're here," Kanna said.

Jared sprang upright, looking over her shoulder through the front windshield and saw… nothing.

"Umm, you sure your brain isn't a little toasted from the sun there, Kanna?" Jared asked.

"Yea, I'm sure," Kanna replied coolly while double tapping the temple near her bionic eye.

A small cone of green light emerged from it and slowly spun in place, like a satellite constructed of lasers. Jared put his hands on the back of Kanna's seat and pulled himself closer to the glass, trying to obtain the best view. Slowly the empty airspace ahead began to flutter and shimmer until a large onyx pyramid hovered before them.

"A cloaking device, eh. And I see it hovers high enough that anyone looking for it would pass right underneath. I gotta hand it to Sanzo, or whoever he hired as the engineer."

Kanna looked over her seat at Jared and nodded, a tight grin cresting the corner of her mouth. Upon approaching the hovering pyramid one side of the structure unhinged itself and folded forward into a staircase for the three travelers to use. As they scaled the steps, each footfall made a slight clinking sound like tapping on glass with a fork. Once he reached the top, Jared wiped the sweat from his brow and gave the sprawling sands one last look, then ducked inside the doorway. It was a sublime temperature inside, cool and dry. It was also quite dark with only a faint glow illuminating it. Jared looked across the walls and noticed several LED light-strips which seemed to be set to a dull orange hue rather than the usual bright white. After his eyes fully adjusted, he could see that it was a vast warehouse with a cement floor polished in a dark shade. To their right were a few small offices with a computer set inside. On their left was row upon row of floor to ceiling metal shelving, painted bright blue.

Kanna briskly paced past the rows of tall shelving.

"Follow me, guys. I downloaded a map of the facility to my software."

Kanna led them to a small red cart with two bench seats and an uncovered flatbed trunk. The side of the cart had a painted decal of a cartoon ram leaning against the white-striped logo behind him while giving a thumbs up. The brand's name, "**Lamwick Motors**," was written circularly around the mascot.

Jared raced past Kanna and jumped in the driver's seat.

"Sorry, but I can't take being passenger anymore," Jared said.

After a moment of situating himself, he tapped the place next to him on the bench seating.

"I don't mind being chauffeured," Kanna said while sliding into the back bench.

Gillman followed Kanna's lead and hopped in next to her. He scooted forward and kicked his feet up on the backrest near Jared.

"Alright kid, hit the gas."

Jared snapped his head back and gave his companion a sarcastic glare.

Kanna shrugged. "You wanted to drive."

Jared shook his head in admitted defeat while starting the Lamwick Motors utility cart. As the cart hummed along, Jared looked to his left and took note of the plethora of corralled items, it was like a buffet of electronic history. Stacks of old film cameras sat on one raised pallet, while the next was covered in CRT Monitors and their table top computer counterparts. He slowed down while noticing the lowest shelf of one row had a stack of video game cases and the shelf above was littered with small statues. One small bust in particular caught his eye. He veered the cart over to the aisle and hopped out of the driver's seat to inspect his find.

"What's the holdup, kid?" Gilman inquired.

"I promise the Merge isn't in this section," Kanna added.

Jared stuck his boot in a foothold and pulled himself up to stand on the first shelf. The second shelf was chest level to him now. A multitude of miniature figurines were littered across the wood plank, and Jared had to tilt his chin up to get a better view of the ones at the center of the mix.

"There! I've been looking everywhere for this!" Jared exclaimed while plucking one specific miniature from the bunch.

With one hand on the vertical support beam to steady himself, Jared held his palm out to show the others what he'd diverted their tour for.

"This…" he continued, "Is the commemorative miniature for Falcon Kid's fifteenth anniversary," Jared finished while hopping down.

He approached them closer and held it within inches of Kanna's face.

"This is the last figurine that still had the original design before the Ultra games changed that. You can see his helmet is more rounded and less detailed, and his feathering is different," Jared pointed to each individual feature as he explained them.

Kanna returned an amused smile. His exuberance was infectious enough that her thoughts never strayed to annoyance despite this distraction. In an odd way, it only enabled her trust to grow. Jared never displayed signs that he had any angle other than seeking historic knowledge and the inherent adventure searching for it brought. Kanna watched as he headed back to the driver's seat and paused. Most of the time they'd spent together, Jared had worn a lengthy coat with a high collar. Now that they were in the desert, he was sporting a tighter fitting long sleeve shirt. She'd never really taken into account that this tech mechanic was actually quite well built, with broad shoulders that led to a V-shaped torso.

'It's good to know if we get in a decent scrap, he'll be able to handle himself,' Kanna thought. She ignored any other possible connotations inspecting Jared's physical features might mean.

"You scanning me with that robot eye, Kan?" Jared asked.

Kanna laughed. "Naw, just waiting for you to put that toy back on the shelf."

Jared leaned forward and raised one eyebrow.

"Put back? No, no, no. This little guy…" Jared mockingly petted the head of the miniature, "is coming with us."

Kanna placed her hands on her hips and squinted.

"No… we're not stealing from Sanzo's vault."

Jared rolled his eyes as if she was missing the point.

"Of course, we're not stealing it. When we get back, we'll broker a deal with him for it. You can make it part of our cut for this gig."

Gillman's hand shot upward. "I don't consent to that doll being part of my cut."

Jared's head snapped in his friend's direction.

"It's *not* a doll, Gill. It's a commemorative miniature. *Aaaaaaaand,* it's the last one in the set that goes with the other two displayed in our shop."

"I've been meaning to tell you we should take those down," Gillman sneered.

"Absolutely not! Tech collections are a way to build credibility with customers when they enter our shop. It shows product knowledge," Jared retorted.

Kanna joined them in the cart, this time sliding onto the bench next to Jared.

"He's right on this one, Gillman. The doll does show you guys know and value tech," Kanna added.

Jared smiled and nodded at Gillman. "See, I told you customers like… Hey? I thought I told you guys it wasn't a doll?"

Kanna gave Jared a pat on the shoulder.

"Just keep driving, kid," she then turned back to Gillman and gave him a wink.

She slid one arm on the backrest and pointed her other hand forward. "Keep heading straight till you reach the other side. Sanzo keeps the most precious pieces of his collection in a separate area from this one."

Nathan wiggled the fuel pump until it slid into place. He ran a few tokens into the conveyer slot then pressed the large button to select his desired fuel. It had been years since he'd needed physical currency, as normally he would just tap his Merge or make a selection on an app. He leaned his back against the tall stand which ticked off the numbers charting how much fuel he'd purchased. While he trusted his ability to eviscerate most thieves or grifters in Leathe, he wasn't going to chance being pick pocketed or jumped. While civilization had a place at the table here, it wasn't the deciding vote.

"Hey, Nathan. If you want, I can grab us some food from the trailers over there," Gaylen said, pointing to a grouping of parked food carts.

Nathan's stomach urged him to send Gaylen to grab something, as they hadn't eaten for half a day.

"After I'm done here, we'll park this and get something," Nathan answered calmly.

It was better to see what he was being served. Nathan could tell Gaylen was the follower type, seemingly happy to just accept orders and float with the current. However, he wouldn't chance him going rogue, slipping something in his food, and snatching his rig.

Gaylen bit his lip and nodded, unphased by Nathan's decision. "Cool. Since you're willing to wait a bit, I know a spot that's better than those trailers. You're into Moncroix stuff, right? They serve some of their food."

Nathan scrunched his chin and huffed. "I'll take you up on that."

He marveled at the way this desert had unintentionally collected humanity from nearly every floating nation across the Intercontinental Forum. These unmonitored Outskirts made the perfect resting place for anyone who'd run themselves afoul of their homeland.

The pump clicked, notifying Nathan of a full tank.

"Alright, Gaylen. Let's get some food."

"Sounds good. After we eat, I got some spots that I think would be a good place to start," Gaylen answered from the other side of the vehicle.

"Good to hear," Nathan said while taking his spot in the driver's seat.

"Any chance you think they skipped town already?" Gaylen asked.

"I doubt it. While there's multiple cities and tons of little outposts, traveling to any of them is a chore. And even if they did, they're likely taking a ferry out the same way they came in. I'm not calling this until we either spot them, or the Station goes off and confirms they bailed."

―――――

A heavy set of sliding doors gave off a weighty clunk as they unlocked and began to open. A cool misty cloud billowed out and once the fog parted, the final room in Sanzo's vault revealed itself.

"Bit dramatic, eh?" Jared asked with a smirk.

Kanna looked over her shoulder before stepping inside.

"Would you expect anything less from someone who hoards this stuff for a living? That warehouse out front is just for the overflow; these rooms back here are the real collection."

Two sets of glass cases wrapped around three sides of the room, with only the door side having a bare wall. The cabinetry had lighting inside that highlighted each item. A few green plants and strategically placed driftwood decorated the room. Near one corner was a silver coffee machine that produced shots of compresso, which sat opposite a few light-brown leather chairs. Gillman walked over to the chairs and inspected the leather. Upon taking a closer look, he noticed it had a studded texture.

"Hey, Kanna. Is this Rhinox hide?" he asked.

"Yep. He imported the fabric from Malcozé, then had a craftsman in Chushin put them together."

Gillman shook his head and gave a long, low whistle.

"Definitely spent a pretty penny on these. Some Malcozéans don't even have the money to buy boots made of this stuff."

"He's been thinking about moving on from just collecting tech, and maybe gathering artifacts from other Interconts," Kanna said.

Jared paused and took in her words before giving his own thoughts on the possibility.

"When the leaders from every nation created the Forum to govern international law, they put some pretty strict rules on centralizing so much valuable - or potentially powerful - material together. However, considering his influence, I wouldn't be surprised if he could do it in a way that would pacify the Forum," he mused aloud.

Kanna cocked an eye and observed Jared knowingly.

"If I didn't know any better, I'd say you're trying to invite yourself along next time he needs something?"

"Ha! Maybe... we all know Sanzo's coming to you when he eventually needs to uncover some ancient relic. Plus, Gill and I have the whole international journey thing down pretty well."

Kanna knew Jared's point was valid, and if she was being honest, the thought of inviting them along had already crossed her mind.

"You know, I'm genuinely curious what got you into this in the first place, Jared?" Kanna asked him.

"Into what?" he replied sheepishly.

Kanna held her arms out. "This... what made you want to explore the Intercontinents? I'm impressed that you seem more motivated by our travels than the possible payout at the end of all this."

Jared didn't look at her, instead peering into one of the glass cases. "Do you remember that cab driver from Virs?"

"Yea," Kanna answered.

Jared continued, "I grew up in the farthest reaching Intercont. One so far away from everything that it often feels like it's not really part of this world. When that guy told us that old Duroon fable, I believe there's some truth to it. While most other Intercents have a great recollection of their origins dating back centuries, Duroon has a huge section of history missing. If Gill and I can get a ship and keep exploring, I think we can find that missing piece."

Kanna crossed her arms, biting her lip while she thought about it. It was a lot to process, not because she didn't believe him, but because his explanation seemed earnest.

She faced Gillman. "And he roped you into this as well?"

"Honestly, I may have unintentionally given him the idea," Gillman answered with a hearty chuckle.

She wanted to press further, but there was an odd instinct welling up that told her it wasn't the right time. She couldn't decipher if the heavy emotion in the room was built by painful loss, or inspiration when recalling their goals. She decided it was best to leave the topic be, maybe save it for their ride back.

She broke the silence. "Well, you two are quite the enigma," she stated in a soft casual tone, "Anyways, you guys want to see what we came here for?"

Jared smiled and nodded. Kanna turned on her heel and approached a section of casing where a chunky rectangular device sat on a small pedestal. She bent forward slightly and looked into a small sliver dot. A wave of pale violet light emerged from the dot and

155

panned downward over her eyes, then the glass cabinet door clicked open. She reached in and slowly removed the Merge from its resting tray.

Jared stood on his toes to get a better view of the device now that it wasn't behind a wall of glass.

"You think it's better if we activate it now, or do you wanna wait until we're back in Lor-Rev proper?" he asked.

Kanna cocked a quizzical eye at him. "You're actually asking now?"

"I don't always shoot from the hip, sometimes I use a more tactical approach. Although I'll say my instincts have definitely gotten us this far," he retorted.

Kanna smiled and handed him the Merge.

"Put it in your backpack and we'll link them up at the safe house in Canver," she said.

"You want to start heading back tonight?" Gillman asked.

Kanna shook her head and shut the glass cabinet.

"I've done enough driving today. We'll shack up here. There's a small apartment the next hallway over."

She led them down another beautifully decorated corridor, which ended with a large white door that had a lengthy metal bar as a handle. Kanna pushed the handle and it gave smoothly, letting them into the apartment.

"I thought you said this was small?" Jared sarcastically inquired.

The apartment opened to a spacious living room with two staircases that snaked up to an open loft.

"I'm going to take the room upstairs, there's two more down here past the kitchen," Kanna said while approaching one staircase.

"On our way back through Leathe, let's stop by that Kratasian food place again," Jared called out while walking back to his room.

"Hey, Nathan. I talked to a guy who cleans cars by the fuel pumps. Said he overheard an old man talking to another shop owner. The old man said they were coming through Leathe on their way back."

Nathan shot up from his chair.

"What did the old man look like?"

Gaylen shuffled over and took a seat in the chair opposite his new boss.

"Just like the guy from that picture: dark skin, white and black frizzy hair. Guy said he was with another dude who was definitely from Duroon as well. They also had a chick tagging along. She looked like she was from Lor-Rev though, not Duroon."

Nathan scratched his chin. "Did this guy get any names?"

Gaylen nodded repeatedly while crunching on a crispy snack he bought from their motel lobby.

"Yea," he mumbled with his mouth full.

Nathan grimaced impatiently while Gaylen munched through another bite.

"The name?"

"Sorry. I'm just starving after that trip," Gaylen replied after swallowing.

Nathan wanted to interject that they'd eaten only an hour ago, but decided it was best to ignore his urge to ridicule the only person who had his back in Leathe.

"He only got the old guy though. Gave the same name you told me about," Gaylen answered while gulping down some water.

"Gillman?" Nathan asked while pouring himself a second glass of white whiskey.

"Yup. That's the one."

Nathan took a long drink before returning to his chair on the motel room balcony. He'd rented one that overlooked the fuel stations that his targets would likely return to.

"Good work, Gaylen."

"What's next?" Gaylen asked.

Nathan continued staring straight ahead and finished his whiskey. "We wait."

After a brief pause, he rose from his chair and approached a shelf lined with glass bottles filled with various forms of alcohol. He selected another clear liquor that was common to the East Outs, then sauntered back to his chair.

Nathan began filling the glass with his newly chosen spirit.

"And when they return, we convince them to give us what we came for… and *if* they refuse, we take it."

- CHAPTER 15 -

EAST OUTSKIRTS

-

-

UNGOVERNED NON-CIVIC REGION

A late-morning breeze wafted through the broken cityscape of Leathe, spinning up sand as it traveled towards the northern exit. The city only had two openings, like a funnel. For those running the town, it was much easier to control who came in and who was let free. For Nathan, it gave him the perfect vantage point to monitor his prey. Still sitting on his balcony, he watched for his targets like a hunter in a deer stall. He hadn't left his position all night.

He snatched a tall white aluminum can from the wrought iron table next to him and took a good swig. Nathan grimaced after choking down whatever concoction was in the supposed *"energy drink,"* he purchased a from a nearby stand. The attendant manning the hotel lobby had told him where the best pick me ups were. His heart sped up and his eyes opened more broadly after the sip. He'd only bought two and would wait to down the second one – which was supposed to be even stronger – once he located the trio possessing their Station. Nathan had been nursing the can all night in hopes his adrenaline wouldn't peak too early. It was also easier to ration a beverage that tasted like a gritty mix of melted iron and carrot juice.

He leaned forward and took a closer look at the crowd shuffling around the fuel pumps near the northern entrance to Leathe.

"C'mon... where are you? I know you have to pass through here..." Nathan mused aloud.

He jostled in his seat before downing the last few drops, then tossed himself against the back rest and stared skyward. Leathe's buildings surrounded the city in a circular pattern and there was no sphere ceiling above the town to determine its climate. He was able to see a few hazy clouds – washed in dust – roll across the skyline above. He sighed. While the idea of tracking the devices down was invigorating, the reality of it was also tiring. He heard the loud clunk of the northern border door opening followed by the subsequent woosh of air racing in. He shifted his gaze down lazily, following his self-directed order to check every time someone entered Leathe. He continued casually watching as a grey Spawrok with light-green stripes marched in on its hind legs.

'Smart,' Nathan thought, *'You can switch to the leg's auxiliary battery if you run out of fuel in the desert.'*

It was one of the few vehicles he hadn't seen come through the gates. Most everyone traveling through had the typical ATV – or if they were lucky – a larger rig like his.

"Nathan, you see that!" Gaylen called out from over his shoulder.

160

"It's gotta be them! The guy said they had a Spawrok like that!"

Nathan whirled around in his seat. "Why the hell didn't you tell me that earlier?" he hissed.

"Sorry, man. You were grilling me about the look of 'em so much, I forgot about the car."

"Well get down there, Gaylen. I have few things I need to pack up first," he barked while gathering some items.

"Sure thing!" Gaylen replied, racing for the door.

Nathan looked up and called out one last order, "Don't fire on them unless I give the signal. Remember we're going to try and barter first; I want a good idea of who we might be dealing with before we start anything."

"I'll grab some food for us if you guys want to fill up the car," Kanna said, pulling her hair back in a ponytail.

Gillman raised an eyebrow and pointed at himself.

"I think *I'll* be responsible for the food this time."

Kanna put a finger to her chin and pondered the idea.

"Well considering you said you'd pay me back double; I can't leave your food choice unsupervised."

Jared waved them off. "You two go grab something; I'll fill up the rig."

He wiped a large pool of sweat from his face. Their vehicle's air conditioning was barely enough to keep them free of the scorching winds outside the city walls. He huffed a quick laugh to himself at the idea of actually being happy they were back inside Leathe.

Jared leaned against the edge of their ride as his two companions sauntered off towards the row of metal trailers and wood huts encompassing the nearest restaurant selection. He exhaled and slouched a bit more. It had been a long trek to Sanzo's vault. The high of finding the Merge – and discussing all their next moves – was beginning to wear off. He swallowed and realized how dry his throat was.

"I can get us drinks at the mini-mart here. You guys want anything?" Jared called out.

After hearing no response, he looked over his shoulder and couldn't see Kanna or Gillman anymore.

'I should've asked earlier. Oh well, I'm sure they'll drink whatever I pick.'

A miniature bell clanged from the top of the doorframe, signaling his entrance to the clerk. The man behind the counter looked up from his magazine at Jared. He had piercing blue eyes that contrasted his long red hair and tan skin.

'A Malcozéan? Out here?' Jared thought.

While Leathe – and the East Outs in general – hosted former citizens from across the Intercontinental Forum, it was very rare to see a Malcozéan beyond their own walls. Their pride in their homeland was stronger than any, and even being a prisoner held more esteem than a deserter. They were also quite unfond of Lor-Rev's electronic advancements, most considering them perverse tools. Consequently, Lor-Rev viewed Malcozé's mineral mixing alchemy and spell craft as primitive and creepy. Their dual apprehension led them to outlawing each other's version of technology.

Jared stood in front of a beverage refrigerator and traced his finger across the glass while deciding what sodas to get. He grabbed a six pack of one that seemed to be the most trustworthy, as almost every brand of drink he saw had old labels, or were created by a local mixer.

"How much for these?" Jared inquired after plopping the drinks on the counter.

The clerk slowly raised his eyes from his reading material and lazily glanced at the six pack of soda. The white cardboard container had a red gridding pattern across it. In the center was a pair of hands holding bright red flames.

"Warlock gamer soda, eh. That's one credit," the clerk answered.

Jared put five tokens down – the equivalent of one credit – then leaned on the counter with one arm.

"If you don't mind me asking, what brought you to the East Outs? I've been trying to see Malcozé for years, and I thought you might have a pointer on what's worth seeing there?"

After a brief pause the clerk answered him flatly, "I *do* mind."

Jared winced and picked up his soda.

"Sorry, bud. Well… have a nice day," Jared said sheepishly.

The clerk huffed and went back to reading.

The bell clanged again as he exited. He cracked open a can of Warlock soda and took a hearty gulp. Jared regarded the can as he continued towards his car.

"Not bad. Thankfully this isn't too expired," he said aloud.

Looking up, he slowed his pace after noticing someone standing around his ship, seemingly admiring it.

"How's it going? You digging the Spawrok?" Jared called out to them.

The man hovering around his ship was decked out in an asymmetrical maroon coat that rested just below his hips. His gear underneath was grey and black striped synthetic attire built for withstanding the desert heat. As he turned to face Jared, the man moved some of the red and black streaked hair away from his eyes.

"I do. I like classic battle vehicles like this one. It's not often people use a Spawrok to get here."

Jared tilted his head and shrugged.

"Yea, I was able to snag this one from a guy who didn't know how to fix it. It's a fun ride, but a little clumsy compared to a new one," Jared lied.

Something about this red and black haired Lor-Revian gave Jared a chilling vibe. He thought it best to be less divulging of anything truthful.

"Your name's Jared, right?" the lanky Lor-Revian asked calmy.

Jared froze. Was this Daemon? His skin broke out in goosebumps and his arm hair rose upright. He remained silent while pondering his next move.

Nathan ran a hand over Jared's vehicle, purposefully avoiding eye contact.

"I heard about you and your friend's shop. I have a rare item I'm looking at having repaired. Unfortunately, when I visited your place..." Nathan met Jared's eyes, "No one was there."

Jared took another sip from his can to hide his apprehension.

"What era is the item? Because I'm not too great with anything pre-Forum." Jared asked.

Nathan scratched his chin.

"No, not that far back. It is quite pivotal to Lor-Rev's history though. I'm hoping you're familiar with the SatellaField Personal Station?"

"Right out with it then, huh?" Jared jokingly asked.

"Well, if you have parts that would fix mine, or possibly a complete working model, I'd pay a good rate. Definitely better than what it would fetch out here."

Jared walked over to one side of his ship and placed the container of soda in the back. As he did so, he sneakily tapped a few commands on his wrist cuff while Nathan's view was obscured.

"I don't have any parts for that device. If you want a working model, there might be one at my friend's shop."

Nathan crossed his arms. "And who might that be?"

Jared whipped his left hand up from the Spawrok and pointed it directly at Nathan's face. As he did so, the wrist cuff melted and slid down, morphing into a thin sword.

"His name's blade," he answered.

Nathan held steady, peering down at the crystal blue metallic weapon, then leaned his forehead closer.

"Go ahead, Jared. I'm not here to rob you. I'm here to offer you an opportunity," he said calmly.

He hoped the surprising gesture would bring Jared's guard down.

"Are you Daemon?" Jared asked.

Nathan shook his head. "Afraid not. The name's Nathan."

Jared lowered his sword slightly, allowing himself to get a better view of Nathan's face. He didn't look like the picture Kanna had showed him back in Tetragon.

"So, *Nathan*, is it?"

"Yes."

"If you only came here to make me an offer, why do you have a guy with a rifle on the balcony over there?"

Nathan grimaced.

Jared swung at him, barely missing his skull as Nathan ducked underneath. Nathan recovered and lunged forward, slashing at Jared's arm. Jared tumbled over the side of the Spawrok and landed on one knee, then scrambled underneath the vehicle as several loud cracks of gunfire broke through the dense air. Jared's eyes quickly darted back and forth in search of his enemy, but he found nothing. Two more shots rang out that nipped at the heels of his boots. He sucked his legs up to his chest and continued looking around.

'Dammit, where did that bastard go?'

"JARED!" someone called out.

Jared whipped his head towards the voice and saw Gillman running his direction with a pistol in his hand.

"Gill, take cover!" Jared yelled back.

Gillman continued jogging and waved him off.

"It's ok, kid. Kanna's got it," he replied while helping Jared to his feet.

"Who is that guy?" Gillman asked.

"He says his name is Nathan, but I think he's connected to Daemon somehow," Jared panted.

Gillman patted Jared on the back and pointed to their ride.

"Well get in the Spawrok and head for the south exit. Kanna said she'd catch up with us there."

The two of them quickly climbed into the vehicle and took off through the sea of people, shops, and hotels. Jared noticed several nearby places had automated metal rolling covers that began to seal their doors and windows.

'Guess this isn't the first time this has happened here?' he thought.

His friend leaned forward and grasped the back of his leather seat. "Hey, kid… any reason you're still having us use the legs instead of kicking on the jet engines?"

"In tight quarters like this with all these people running around, it's better if I keep us on the legs," Jared answered while waving a hand.

Gillman sat back in his seat and began rummaging through a pouch on his belt. "I'll put some fun little toys together in case that wacko with the claws reappears."

Jared heard a few more cracks of a rifle behind them and his stomach lurched upward into his throat, he hoped those rounds were coming from Kanna and not directed at her.

———

"Gillman, you recognize that guy?" Kanna asked.

166

He shook his head. "Nope, never seen him before."

They'd just come back with food to find someone striking up a conversation with Jared. While Jared was openly social, something about it still felt peculiar. Kanna scanned him with her bionic eye, but something blocked her database from populating any information.

"He doesn't look like Daemon, but he's jamming my scanner somehow. Something isn't right about him."

Gillman cocked an eyebrow. "He could just be another East Outs local wearing a device to block unwanted scans. You can't be too careful out here."

"Maybe, but keep watching them for a minute, Gill. You bring the pistol I gave you or did you leave it in the trunk?"

Gillman answered by patting at his right hip and smiling.

Kanna nodded. "Alright, I'm going to look around."

She surveilled the surrounding area and noticed another person on a balcony that stretched across several short motels. His body jammed her signal like the one talking to Jared. She watched as the stoop shouldered man in a dirty tank top unslung something from his back. He took the object and pulled it on either side. The rectangular item stretched out and he tapped the top of it, causing a handle to pop out the bottom of one side and a tripod on the other. The balcony had two steel bars for railings, one at ankle height and the other reaching an average person's waist. She watched as the man laid down and used the lower railing to steady the front of his barrel.

"Gill, he's setting up a rifle!"

"Who? The guy over here is still just standing around."

Kanna pointed towards the building across from them.

"There's a sniper on the balcony setting up. You head towards Jared and I'll deal with him."

Gillman nodded. "You got it."

Kanna raced off towards the building, looking for a way to reach the balcony. She cranked off two rounds at him. One hit the bar, and the second smacked into the side of his gun. She saw a wide inset staircase that appeared to snake towards the upper section.

'Hopefully they can handle whoever they're dealing with,' she worried under her breath.

As she rounded the staircase to the second side, Gaylen fired a couple shots her way. She lunged backward and barely dodged them. Kanna returned one shot through the wall between herself and Gaylen, then heard him yelp and scramble back up the stairs in retreat. She continued to hear his boots clanking across the tile flooring of the balcony. She raced upstairs and saw he was heading towards the southern entrance. Hearing more shots, she glanced towards the city and saw another man on a fuel station rooftop firing at her friends in the Spawrok.

'How many people do they have planted around this place,' she cursed under her breath while turning back to chase Gaylen.

She saw him reach the end of the balcony and hop over the railing. After reaching the edge herself she looked over and spotted him starting a motorcycle. She holstered her gun and hopped down. As Kanna hit the ground, she finished her landing in a roll. Gaining her feet, she lunged at Gaylen, barely missing him as he sped away. She fired at his tire but her round ricocheted into the dirt.

'How do these guys have that kind of armor class on their bikes?'

More cracks of rifle fire rang out and she quickly took cover behind the nearest wall. She scanned through it towards the man on the rooftop and noticed he didn't jam her signal, and that he hadn't noticed her and was actually firing on her companions.

'Must be someone they picked up here if he doesn't have the same gear as the first two.'

She ran towards the hired gun until she was only thirty yards out. Unholstering her pistol, Kanna steadied her aim. The man did a double take and finally noticed her, but she lodged a round between his eyes before he could react.

Out of the corner of her eye she saw an unattended motorized scooter. She raced over and jumped on it while revving up the engine.

"HEY, BITCH! That's my damn bike!" the owner yelled.

"It'll be waiting for you at the south gate then!" she shouted back.

A dark cloud puffed out from the rear engine as she took off. She thought about calling out for Akari, but knew in the pit of her stomach that it was futile. Leathe let matters like these resolve themselves. Their troops only interfered in something like this if the wrong person was killed, or the property destruction impacted an important business.

As she snaked through the pathway lined with merchant huts, surprised patrons scurried out of her way, leaving a trail of random shoes, bread, and hats behind her. She revved harder on the handle and sped towards an uphill path. Cresting the top, her view no longer obstructed by shops, she saw Jared and Gillman in the Spawrok. Her throat fell into her stomach as she realized the heavily-armored vehicle barreling towards them was about to ram their blindside.

———————

Rifle rounds whizzed and pinged off the back of their rig as Jared diced his way through the labyrinthine center of Leathe. Gillman was fiddling with a contraption in the back, but the bumpy terrain made it difficult. It also didn't help that their vehicle's equipped gun hadn't been loaded. Bullets for a Spawrok of their era were expensive and rare.

"Steady us up, Jared!" Gillman yelled.

"I'm trying, but it's not easy when we're getting shot!" Jared said, taking them around a one-story building to provide some cover.

"How much longer till they're ready?" he asked.

"Just hold here a couple more seconds…" Gillman answered.

Gaylen raced over on his motorcycle and stopped a good distance from them. He unslung a rifle from his back and began firing. Jared turned the Spawrok and ran off as bullets clanged off its armor. He looked in the rearview screen and saw Gaylen jump back on his bike and continue after them. As Jared looked for a way to shake him off their trail, he noticed a raised garden bed attached to a nearby motel. Looking over the three-foot-tall feature, an idea leapt into his head.

"Your seatbelt on, Gill?" Jared asked

"Yea," Gillman answered warily.

Jared quickly marched them towards the raised bed, and placed one of the mechanized feet on it. He held their position as the motorcycle drew closer.

"Get ready to drop one of your bombs, Gill."

Gillman fished through his pouch and grabbed a small chrome orb.

"Alright, on your signal."

Seconds later, Gaylen was on them. He stepped off his bike and began walking it forward for cover, shooting sporadically at the spherical windshield covering them.

'C'mon just get a little closer,' Jared muttered through gritted teeth as rounds clattered against the glass.

"Get ready, Gill!" he shouted over the gunfire.

He yanked back on the wheel and pushed off with their ride's raised foot, sending them in an arching backflip over Gaylen and his bike. At the same time, he hit the button and opened the windshield.

"Drop it now!" he yelled to Gillman while midair.

Gillman dropped the orb down onto Gaylen, which erupted in streaks of electricity.

"*Ghhaaahh!*" Gaylen squealed, engulfed in the surging current.

Jared reached over his seat and gave Gillman a friendly punch on the shoulder.

"Hell yea, Gill."

Gillman returned his friend's excitement with a hearty laugh. "Bet he never saw that coming!"

Jared nodded as he turned the ship away and steadily marched towards the south end of Leathe.

"I'm going to get on one of the main roads so we can use the jets," he told his friend. "Zig zagging through walking paths is just too slow."

"I think it's just a few more yards to your left," Gillman answered, peering over Jared's shoulder and pointing.

They reached the bottom of a small hill and Jared stopped just short of the main thoroughfare.

"Jared!" Gillman yelled.

Jared waved him off. "It's fine. Just give me a sec while I retract the legs."

"No, Jared, behind us!" his friend yelled again.

Jared glanced back and saw a bulky tank-like vehicle covered in spikes and heavy armor charging directly at them. He yanked on the wheel and tried to pull their ship into a jump, but it was too late.

- CHAPTER 16 -

EAST OUTSKIRTS

UNGOVERNED NON-CIVIC REGION

KANNA watched helplessly as Nathan's car careened into the Spawrok's legs and sent it tumbling overtop. She frantically scanned around for the fastest way to reach her friends and noticed a path between two small huts. Speeding across it, she yanked her bike to a halt as the route ended abruptly against a small cliffside. Looking out, she searched for some way to use her shortcut rather than backtrack. Seconds later, spying a nearby flat roof, she found her answer.

Kanna circled back to gain speed, then zoomed off the small cliff. As she cleared the few yards to the roof, she hunched down to absorb the shock of landing. Her descent ended with a rattling thud and she struggled to keep the handle bars straight. Clenching her fingers tighter, she held steady and accelerated off the small one-story building. Hitting the ground, the scooter's front wheel shook feverishly and almost buckled under the impact.

"Don't fail on me now," Kanna cursed to the scooter, "I just need you to last a few more blocks..."

———————

Jared's skull felt like a billiard ball was rattling inside. He blinked rapidly and shook his hands in an attempt to free himself from the dizzying concussion.

"Gill! You, ok?!" Jared called out to his companion.

Getting no response, he looked over his shoulder as best he could and realized his friend was unconscious. A lone figure strode purposely in their direction. Jared squinted and noticed the man had a maroon half cloak and black and red streaked hair. It was Nathan.

Their vehicle was tipped over on the top side of one wing, leaving Jared and Gillman nearly upside down. The spherical windshield above them was the only thing propping them against being completely turned over. He frantically reached around to open one side of glass, but before he could pry himself free, Nathan was looming over them.

Jared's eyes widened as Nathan knelt down and tapped on the glass.

"You ready to bargain yet?" he asked, giving a hearty cackle.

Jared sneered. "You've got nothing I want, asshole."

Nathan placed a hand on his chest and shook his head while smiling. He reached into a pocket inside his cloak and pulled something out.

"You sure about that... *asshole*?" Nathan retorted wryly.

Jared gawked as Nathan held his most valuable Falcon Kid miniature in his palm.

"Give me that you bastard!" Jared hollered while hitting the windshield.

Nathan dangled the toy by its head and swung it mockingly back and forth.

"I just need the Personal Station and you can have your little buddy back... Deal?"

Jared sighed heavily and hit his head on the back rest. He looked over to Gillman, who was still unresponsive.

"I can't give it to you while we're tipped over like this," Jared said through gritted teeth.

A smirk crawled up from the corner of Nathan's lips.

"I'm sure you can find a way."

Jared reached down and pressed the trunk release and his backpack flopped onto the ground. As Nathan reached down to pick it up, Jared felt something squeeze his elbow in two quick rhythmic beats. His eyes darted towards Gillman, who gave him a wink before returning to feigned unconsciousness. He steadied his hand on the windshield release while Gillman slid another chrome orb into his free hand. As Nathan reached over and grabbed the zipper, a wave of sparks shot out from the backpack.

"*Dammit!*" he screamed while instinctively tossing the bag away.

One half of the windshield opened and Jared lobbed the orb in Nathan's direction. It struck the concrete with a loud crack and expelled a wave of smoke. Nathan coughed and backpedaled, waving off the fiery dust. Jared pulled on the wheel and tried to use one of the legs to kick them upright, but they were too mangled. He pulled on the glass above him and began crawling out, but something held his foot. He looked down and saw the seatbelt had snared his ankle. He tried kicking his foot free, but it was wrapped too tight. As he reached down to try and untie the mess, he felt something grab his neck.

"Don't think your little trick is enough to put me down," Nathan snarled while gripping Jared's throat.

He extended the claws of his free hand and slashed the belt keeping Jared's leg hostage. Gripping both sides of his collar, he yanked him loose and sent him rolling onto the sidewalk.

"Now… you're going to open it for me or I'll crush that stupid little doll *and* your throat," Nathan ordered.

Jared grunted as he pulled his forearms underneath himself. He tried to block out the sting of pain pulsing though his back and the weight of fatigue drowning into his arms. Making it to one knee, he looked Nathan right in the eyes and desperately drew his wrist cuff. Nathan dashed in and slapped Jared's arm away while kneeing him in the chest. Jared gasped from the blow and fell backward. He tried to crawl away to create some distance, but his pursuer gave him no refuge. He tried again to point his weapon, but Nathan stomped on his wrist.

"Last chance," he said while grinding his boot deeper into Jared's arm.

Jared chomped his lip and grimaced. He looked up at Nathan and noticed something just past his shoulder.

"You talking *my* last chance, or yours?" Jared croaked out between coughs.

Nathan's brow furloughed in confusion.

"Obviously your…"

Three earsplitting shots interrupted Nathan, striking him across the back and shoulder. As he toppled over, Jared leaned away to avoid having the lanky lackey fall on him. Kanna ran over to Jared, a fit of rash coughs seized him as she arrived.

"I'll be alright," Jared moaned, waving her off, "check on Gill for me, ok?"

After helping Jared to his knees, she ran over to Gillman. He extended a hand to her and she pulled him through the half open windshield.

"Thanks, Kanna," Gillman tilted his head towards Nathan's vehicle, "I think we should take his ride."

Jared shakily shuffled to Nathan's body and snatched the Falcon Kid miniature lying next to him.

'It's not a damn doll, you prick,' he muttered.

"What?" Kanna asked.

Jared waved her off while scooping up the backpack.

"It's nothing, just talking to myself," he replied.

"Let's get out of here before any more of these thugs show up," Kanna said with an affirmative nod.

The three of them slowly climbed inside Nathan's car and drove towards the southern exit.

———

A harsh, throaty gasp for air stirred the crowd that had slowly gathered around Nathan. He flipped onto his back and the three bullets plinked onto the concrete. An alert appeared before his eyes: ***Restoration system complete - Time unconscious / Four Minutes.***

'Those nanites really came in handy,' he mumbled.

Staring at his surroundings, he noticed everything was gone. His car, the backpack, and the trio of travelers he was after. He slammed his hand on the ground and grunted before clambering to his feet.

"What the hell do you roaches want!" Nathan cursed at the crowd of onlookers.

He shambled over to the Spawrok and put his hands underneath a wing, and crouched down. Shoving with all his might, he rolled it back upright. Wiping the sweat from his brow, he wearily climbed into the cockpit and started the engine.

"I think I can make up four minutes if I fire up the jets."

————————

"I can't believe this guy got his hands on a Parallax Battle Mace LE," Jared said while sipping on a beer from the cooler.

He was lounging across the back bench seat nursing his wounds.

"It's not just any Battle Mace either, this thing is totally tricked out," he continued.

Gillman held up a beer towards Jared in agreement.

"He definitely put the best mods on this thing. You ever driven one of these before, Kanna?"

When she gave no reply, Gillman nudged her.

"You follow me?"

Kanna started then glanced at him.

"Uh, yea, sure," she answered hesitantly.

The hypnotism of driving across the desert had taken over and drifted her thoughts away. This journey almost stole two friends from her.

'When did I start calling them friends,' she wondered with a sigh.

Regardless of their status to her, they didn't deserve the consequences of safeguarding Johan's inventions. She was obligated by blood and loyalty, but they shouldn't have to bear this burden with her. It was the reason she kept everyone at arm's length, and those who did accompany her were – like herself – already involved in some form of mercenary side work.

"You drive one of these Parallax Mace's before?" he asked again.

Kanna nodded. "Yes, but only once. They're very expensive, so whoever this guy was he must be pretty connected."

Several miles away, a grey ship whizzed across the desert at full speed. Arcs of dry red sand shot up from the wake of its wings. Nathan pushed the thruster to its limit. He knew it would only be a matter of minutes before he caught up to the much slower vehicle his enemies were driving. The two long guns he had in the cockpit with him rattled in the back seat as he accelerated. He'd made a pit stop at an arms dealer before leaving Leathe, and purchased enough firepower to incinerate all three of them once he caught up.

'*C'mon… just a few more miles…*' he muttered while aggressively gripping the steering wheel.

His ship had taken significant damage – ironically by his own hand – and Nathan could feel it in the controls. The ship sputtered and shook while passing along a small outcropping of abandoned single story houses. It was a landmark he'd used during his arrival. After cresting a large sand dune, he saw his former car boarding a large ferry airship. The immense doors were closing and he was too far away to land a good shot. He zoomed forward in hopes he could reach the doors before they shut, but then his vehicle sputtered, and the engine began billowing smoke.

"*No-no-no…*" Nathan hissed.

A second later the engine erupted in flames and the ship crashed into the sand. He looked up helplessly as the airship's doors closed and it began takeoff. He batted at the windshield release until the glass above him retracted. Coughing and pawing at the dark smoke creeping over him, he climbed out. Shoving both hands into the ground, he began hurriedly scooping sand and tossing it on the flames until they died out.

After the fatigue of preserving his vehicle wore off, he looked around and noticed he was completely alone. There were no populated outposts for miles, at least ones he could trust, and there wouldn't be another ferry at the southern landing spot for days.

"DAMMIT!!!" Nathan screamed, repeatedly pounding his fist into the sand.

He'd come so far and done so much for his new cause. He successfully made it Leathe, found his targets, and almost recovered the Station… almost. Somehow the failure that plagued his life had caught up and tormented him once more. Angry tears cascaded down his pale face – and despite his solitude – he hid his head in shame.

————

Kanna relaxed in her seat and crossed her arms. She'd been trying to find where the tracking computer was located to remove it. If she was unsuccessful, they would have to ditch the car on the ferry. Her two friends had tried earlier, checking under the hood and beneath the vehicle, but were equally unsuccessful. She'd decided to come back and give it another go while they took a break.

'Where would they place it?' she grumbled under her breath.

The last spot she could think of was behind the dashboard monitor. She felt around and located a plastic attachment. She yanked on the bottom side of the monitor and unhooked it. A few seconds of digging around some wires and she located a small module with the vehicle's serial number and an IP address.

"Got ya!" she said aloud.

Kanna wedged a flat head screwdriver underneath the module and pried it free. She reset the monitor and pressed it firmly against the dashboard until it clicked into place. Taking a deep breath, she tossed the tracking device on the seat next to her.

Suddenly the screen booted up and a notification appeared:
Incoming Vid-Chat

Her face scrunched in confusion as the message disappeared and a man's face appeared onscreen. He had thin pointed features and wavy brown hair that fell to his shoulders. He tilted his head and raised an eyebrow at Kanna.

"You're not Nathan?" the voice asked rhetorically.

Kanna held her breath and remained silent.

"Well, it's an unfortunate loss to our collective, but I knew the risk of sending him to the Outskirts," he continued while tilting his head to one side in a shrug, "So, tell me then, dear, who might you be?"

She remained stone faced.

The man gave a hearty laugh that had a hollow, ungenuine feel.

"I'm Daemon, and I'd hope that whoever decided to remove the tracking device from my vehicle would be kind enough to replace it?"

Kanna returned the pompous request with a glare.

Daemon squinted while scratching his chin. "You look quite familiar. I'd say you must be related to my late partner in some way. I must have met you at one of those family gatherings he was so proud to host. Johan was very fond of his family, even if they became estranged in his twilight years."

"Only because he sacrificed everything to protect Lor-Rev from you," Kanna snappily interjected.

Daemon held his chin and shrugged.

"Is that what he told you? That he was some selfless martyr wasting away to keep Lor-Rev safe? I'd have you know that all he did was hold humanity back from progressing towards the future."

Kanna leaned closer to the screen. "A future where we're all your little slaves waiting around to be given whatever existence you think we're worthy of?"

Daemon cackled at her response.

"Is that how you feel? I offer prosperity, but it's a collective prosperity and not one where each person's selfish whims dictate the fate of others."

Kanna leaned back and crossed her ankles.

"Again… sounds like a fancy way of saying we'd be slaves."

Daemon scowled. "Just know that whatever you possess in relation to obtaining the Diffusor-Sphere will eventually be mine. I helped Johan create it, so any belief that you're somehow in control of this situation is woefully misguided. I will always be one step ahead."

The vid-chat cut out and Kanna sat solemnly while goosebumps crawled up her arms. She jumped in her seat as the driver's side door suddenly swung open.

"You alright, Kanna?" Jared asked.

———————

A two-door luxury vehicle slowly rolled into the circular driveway of a mansion that rested atop a long hill. The strip of lights lining the stone car path highlighted the vehicle's red trim and deep black exterior. Daemon exited his vehicle and tossed his cloak over his shoulder before gracefully striding up the front stairs. He'd purchased this home well before his hibernation, but rarely returned to it after his awakening. With his vast wealth from his time as an incredibly successful engineer and visionary, he ensured it was well maintained during his absence.

Upon reaching the porch, the front doors opened immediately, then shut behind him after he passed through. He strode into a small dimly lit room with tall ceilings and a solitary green velvet chair. Its ambiance was the perfect place for thumbing through some research. He was still growing accustomed to having the world's information at his fingertips, so these moments of reading through articles allowed him to relax. Eventually he would be proficient enough at scanning and absorbing his available data that it would seem like he saw everything at once. Unfortunately for him, he hadn't reached that proficiency yet.

Tonight, Daemon planned to look through another Southbridge Gazette article relating to Johan. Taking a seat in the cushioned chair, he crossed one ankle over his knee, then opened the article and began to read.

𝕿𝖍𝖊 𝕾𝖔𝖚𝖙𝖍𝖇𝖗𝖎𝖉𝖌𝖊 𝕲𝖆𝖟𝖊𝖙𝖙𝖊

southbgaz.int | Annihale 7th, 105 P.F. | 2 Tokens

A Window into the Future's Past:
Part Two - An Interview with Danikan Fisure

Conducted by Benwird Ottley

While sitting on a hover-rail train passing through the cityscape of Chushin, I'm reminded how profoundly abstract Lor-Rev is when compared to the other entities that encompass the Intercontinental Forum. While our advancements are shunned from other places out of fear that it would tear apart their tradition, I disagree. Adopting technology doesn't have to come at the cost of your conscience.

I took this train to Chushin's west end, which is outside the more hulking towers of the downtown corridor. I plan to speak with someone who engineered a cultural pillar of Lor-Rev and who will definitely engage me regarding the struggles of technology's place in humanity. He's the creator of augmented reality contests, Danikan Fisure.

Like many who ascended in the tech business, Danikan started as a hobbyist tinkerer. He was a life-long gamer who loved the potential for virtual reality as the future of his escapist entertainment. However, he thought the barrier of a large headset would hold it back from being the predominantly chosen controller. He decided that projection through augmented reality was the answer.

After another half hour of travel, I finally reach the small office building which houses Danikan's shop. Despite the behemoth his company ARC has become, he still likes to find more subtle places to work on new experiments outside the bustle of downtown. I'm greeted by Danikan himself, rather than a secretary. His warm open-armed hug and frenetic speech is the opposite of my encounters with Johan, who upon answering my calls, would simply say, "No thank you," before ending them. After escorting me through the halls to his workshop, Danikan begins to show me some of his latest projects. His enthusiasm is beyond infectious and I eagerly try and follow his rapid-fire recitation of what each device can achieve. We're then interrupted by an assistant who hurriedly has me sign an NDA. It's customary to sign one first, but Danikan seems unfazed at sharing his work beforehand. I smile in amusement as he waves off the idea of its necessity before he chases the assistant out of the room.

After closing the door, he turns back to me with an eager grin and raised eyebrows. "I remember when you first started, Benwird. You had that little tech magazine and you'd follow us around all the conventions."

I can see his green eyes soften as he reminisces. After a brief silence, he scratches his bald scalp then heads over to a nearby counter, where he plugs in my favorite invention.

"You want me to brew some coffee before we start?" he asks.

I chuckle and reply, "I would love that, Danikan."

Q: When building the initial augmented reality contest system, you didn't have major funding or a large office like this to complete your testing. How did you prepare it for the mass market?

A: That's a funny story. I actually had a friend who worked at one of the Southbridge docks. His boss overheard him talking about ARCS during lunch in their breakroom and decided he wanted to see it. Warner was his name. I only had a very simple prototype then, but he thought it was so funny to watch us run around in our light up suits. So, he'd let us use his area after hours to test it in an open environment. We had so many issues in the early build though. One time an LED strip caught fire on the back of my friend's pants. If Warner was still here, he'd have so many great stories about those early beta tests.

Q: Wait. We need to circle back to this fire incident. Was your friend hurt?

A: Oh, heavens no. The back of my friend's pants caught on fire, but it wasn't a huge flame. The only thing he could think of to put it out… was to run off the dock and jump in the water [laughs]. I mean, can you imagine this guy in a green body suit just running off the dock with his ass in flames [continues laughing]. Of course, us smart engineers thought of everything, except to bring a fire extinguisher.

Q: Was this only a one-time issue with the Exo-suits?

A: Yes. We never had another problem with combustion after that. Honestly that incident may have saved the whole project. If we hadn't caught it then… well, it likely would've occurred at some park with a new customer and I'd probably be in jail or bankrupt.

Q: When you initially launched the project, why was it on such a small scale? I remember lining up for hours at a theme park to get a chance to try it.

A: We simply didn't have the funding. If I tried to launch for an open market, like it is now with the Augers and the HLA, I would've been crushed with early debt. I decided doing small exhibits in theme parks was a safe way to scale it, while also building some buzz. Being an avid gamer, I knew my ultimate goal was to eventually expand towards mass adoption. I just had to start smaller.

Q: SatellaField was rising at the time and viewed favorably by the tech community. Was there ever a thought to reach out to a company like that?

A: What you really mean is… did I reach out to Johan [laughs lightly]? I met him at a convention and I showed him what I was working on. It's funny that people assume he's some guarded hermit, when he's actually quite social in the right setting. I remember him getting to know every new exhibitor whenever he attended a conference. He was a constant student, always chatting with everyone to learn about their inventions. He was very skeptical of my work scaling to the mass market though. He thought a simple controller would always be preferred. I told him that I didn't look at it as an either or. I saw this as something people did in addition to traditional gaming. I thought its potential was the same way you'd view sports. You could have the fun after-work league, or the professional league. It was gaming, but a different aspect of gaming from consoles and controllers.

Q: Did you try and pitch ARCS to him, and did he turn down funding it?

A: I hadn't really thought about pitching it, but when we spoke it didn't come up. He heard that theme parks were interested in picking it up after my presentation. Johan told me to keep as much of an ownership stake as possible. He believed this was an idea that would be hurt by too many voices at the table. Which would happen if I sold several shares when seeking funding. He was right.

Q: I feel like Johan was viewed as a coach by many of the early tech pioneers. How did you see his standing amongst his peers?

A: That's a very accurate description. Johan understood the language of business better than most of us. We were just tinkering in our garages because we loved making things. I think because Johan dealt with so many of the large corporations before us... he knew the lion's den we were walking into once we made a great invention. He always happened to be there to put an arm around you and steer you through the storm.

Q: Did Johan have an adversarial view of the mega corporations who were involved in technology, like Orb Incorporated?

A: [Shakes his head] No. I think that notion was just fake gossip. Again, he understood business. I think he saw the whole thing as a game with its own rules and boundaries. He wasn't shaking his fist at them like they're

some evil scourges. My opinion is a little different than his though [laughs].
I think it's a case-by-case basis on whether you can trust a few of these
companies. The more spread out the products are the better. It keeps one
company from wielding too much influence over the general public.

Q: Was Johan's early influence what made you remain a private company?

A: Possibly. As you know, our company really took off when we started
open arena matches in city parks. After that ARCS didn't need outside
investment. The thought of changing what worked seemed like a foolish
idea. I talked to Johan about [going public] though.

Q: What made you reach out, and what advice did he give you?

A: Well at that time, Gerald [Stekanstreet] was going around snatching tech
start-ups for Ergo, when becoming a publicly traded conglomerate was all
the rage. I was concerned that one of these other companies would come in
and squash me. I didn't mind some competition; we have some now. I just
didn't want to wake up one day and find out my dream was over. I called
him up and you know what he said? [Begins Johan impression] "Danikan,"
he says to me in that raspy voice of his, "Once you cement yourself as a
great product, the only way you get knocked off is one of two reasons.
[Danikan holds up a finger] One, you let it get stale. Or two, you make
some big change and it sucks [laughs heartily]." His advice was always so
grounded.

**Q: Is that what made you start acquiring other tech companies and
become a parent company, despite not being publicly traded?**

A: Definitely. I saw what Ergo and Orb were doing, amongst a few others, and realized I wanted to be more than just one product. I probably didn't have to do it to survive, but I just wanted to re-invest in the next wave of inventors who were looking for a chance and had something great. I loved attending pitch meetings from these new kids. It was so much fun. I just decided to not have shareholders because I enjoyed having control too much [laughs], unlike the other two.

Q: Did you look into acquiring SatellaField?

A: I assumed it was never on the table. I would've loved a chance to buy SatellaField. The Merge was such a special device. It's still so popular now even. I'd just want [SatellaField] because of their place in history within our industry.

Q: Were you surprised when he did sell the company?

A: I was. He called me and asked that I join as an independent observer during the acquisition meetings. It was very surprising, but once I heard him out, I understood his rationale.

Q: Johan really trusted you then, if he had you sit with him during those meetings.

A: I saw it as a duty to help out my friend. Myself, and most of the other inventors of our era, we all looked up to him. No matter how much success we had, there was something about his presence. Like he was the big brother looking out for everyone that you always wanted to impress. That sentiment never changed.

Q: Circling back to something you said earlier. What was Johan's reason to sell?

A: He believed that placing some of his best people inside Ergo would bleed his culture into their company. There was an energy inside SatellaField that was hard to explain, but it led to such creative ingenuity. If he handed [SatellaField] over to someone who made the wrong moves, they'd be wiped out and no longer able to influence the soul of the tech world. I wasn't too warm on the idea initially, but I understood it.

Q: Do you think there's a chance I'll be able to get an interview with Johan?

A: HA! [laughs] I doubt it.

Q: Gerald [Stekanstreet] says there's a chance he could arrange one?

A: Of course he does. I like Gerald, but he loves to drop a name now and then. Always the salesman, boasting about his connections. And you can print that, it's not something I haven't elbowed him about before [laughs]. Tell you what... I'll call Johan and give it a try. Maybe if everyone you interview can vouch for you, he'll soften on the idea, but no guarantees.

Q: It's a deal. Thank you for your time, Danikan.

A: Don't be a stranger, Benwird.

I take a taxi back to the terminal and eventually slog my way through the compacted population of the station and its train. While riding the hover-railway back, I reflect on my conversation with Danikan. Despite how much I enjoyed our discussion and friendly banter, I can't shake this eerie feeling. After concluding our interview, we discussed the possibilities of Lor-Rev's future as he demonstrated some early protypes. He views technology with the lens of a craftsman. If only every entity who holds technological power in our society viewed it the same way. During my tenure as a journalist, I've spoken with many important people and followed several large companies. Despite their good intentions, I often observe them using technology as a means of indulging desires and influencing mentality. Seeing that helps me understand why places like Malcozé or Moncroix are leery to accept our achievements and gadgetry.

However, people like Danikan are the bright spot. He sees it as a table and chairs built with a hammer and nails. Simply tools and function. Yet he also understands that if someone decides to lift that chair or hammer overhead, then it becomes a weapon. But unlike the hammer or chair, you likely won't see it coming. I heed his warnings to me about the danger of vast consolidation, especially with those in charge of the devices that complete our everyday lives.

DAEMON

- CHAPTER 17 -

CHUSHIN

CIVIC REGION WITHIN THE
NORTHBRIDGE DOMAIN

ENOUGH with the games, Danikan. I think we're both growing tired of this," Daemon said while tossing the obstructing half of his cloak behind him

His boots clacked on the floor as he casually strolled past a row of desks.

"I know you have the encryptor key. It'll be best if you just turn it over."

Suddenly a gaunt man wielding a saber lunged in, slashing wildly at Daemon. Without breaking his stride, Daemon swung an arm to his side right through the swordsman. The man's appearance shook vertically as if he were made of static and polygons. Abruptly the projected swordsman broke into a thousand tiny cubes.

"Your weapons are as hollow as your ideals, Danikan. I'd rather not do this all evening; we both know the key belongs to me."

Upon reaching the middle of a long hallway, Daemon heard heavy footfalls thudding towards him. Three armored guards confronted him with short-rifles drawn. A trio of tiny red dots soon appeared on his chest. Daemon leapt forward and snatched one guard by the neck, then closed his fist and their body shattered. He spun a back elbow through the second and sent a boot through the last. He continued down the hall while the projections burst into polygons behind him. Tilting his hat upward Daemon smiled knowingly into a nearby security camera. The fuzzy crackle of a PA system hummed through the air and he perked an ear.

"You can sneer at me all you like, but I know your weakness. Eventually I'll hack that digital code running through your brain," Danikan said over the loudspeaker.

"And what would that do, even if you could?" Daemon scoffed.

"Your brain won't process these as images anymore," Danikan warned.

Daemon gave a loud cackle. "Anyone who knocks on my door may enter, but just know that once you step inside... I'm in control."

In a room several yards away, Danikan stood in front of a monitor watching Daemon prowl closer. Wiping the sweat from his brow, Danikan knew he only had a few more distractions up his sleeve. He frantically typed in several lines of code before glancing at a monitor to his left to see the result.

ACCESS DENIED

He pressed on with a few additional sequences only to be met with the same result. The squealing of torn metal broke Danikan's concentration.

Daemon now stood in the doorway. "Time's up, old friend."

The click of a hinge releasing caused Daemon to look up as a ceiling panel opened. The sound was followed by a cylindrical battering ram barreling towards him. It caught him in the chest and tossed him several yards down the hallway. Danikan peeled away from his keyboard and raced out the door. Seconds later he heard a low grumble as his pursuer rose to his feet and gave chase once more. The thin hairs along his neck began to crawl as he felt something dangerously near. Risking a glance over his shoulder he saw Daemon's gloved fingers a few inches from his spine. He ducked just in time to avoid being snared. Rounding another corner, Danikan took a remote control from his pocket and hit a button that closed off the hallway behind him. He fell to his knees and began panting as exhaustion overtook him.

'Keep moving you old bastard,' he cursed to himself.

A loud crunch broke his thoughts. He turned back and saw gloved fingers poking through the security door. The sheet metal caved under Daemon's grip as he closed his fist around it, sounding like a rake being drug across a sidewalk. Soon the door was yanked free followed by an arm extending the last few yards towards Danikan.

Still sitting on one hip, he tried scooting away from the snaky appendage, but to no avail. He was lifted by his collar, feet dangling in the air. Daemon's face appeared in front of his own.

"Now, where were we, Danikan? Ah yes, you were just about to hand over my key."

———

"The loading bar's stuck around thirty-two percent for the last hour," Jared grumbled.

He'd paired the Station with the original Merge, but it didn't seem to be working like they'd predicted.

"Did he give you any indication whether there might be some kind of code to unlock it?"

Kanna slid her rolling chair across the cement floor of the garage towards him. "Let me take a look at it."

Jared slid his chair back and placed his hands behind his head. He took in a deep breath and sighed loudly. While he enjoyed a good technological puzzle, this exhaustively long load time was wearing on his patience. Closing his eyes, he tried to clear his mind, but his brain clutched onto the process of decoding the riddle and wouldn't relinquish.

"Did you try entering any numbers from this menu?" Kanna asked him.

Jared immediately sat upright and scooted his chair towards her. "There wasn't a number key when I was working on it."

She handed him the Merge, and when he looked at the screen the number key disappeared. He shook his head and laughed.

"It only listens to your command, Kan," he said while handing it back to her.

She stared down at the device and pondered what her grandfather would have set the lock to.

"Any ideas on what you think it is?" she asked Jared.

He scratched his chin. "Try your birthday."

She turned and raised an eyebrow. "Oh c'mon, Jared. I'll try the date he invented it," she scoffed while typing, "Hmm, doesn't seem to be that one," she continued aloud while trying a few other sequences.

After her other attempts failed, she sat back in her chair and bit her lip.

"Just try it," Jared said wearily.

Kanna rolled her eyes and entered her birthday.

A small icon of a lock opening appeared and the loading bar continued forward.

Jared smiled at Kanna, his hands still behind his head.

"Told you. Maybe don't be such an ice queen and think with your heart sometime, it's a much warmer life."

Kanna casually shoved Jared from his perch. He caught his teetering chair amid belly laughter and gave Kanna a few pats on the shoulder.

"Don't quit your day job," he smirked while strolling from the room.

She turned in her seat as he reached the doorway.

"You don't want to see what happens when it finishes loading?"

Jared stopped and glanced over his shoulder.

"I'm sure I'll be back before it's done. You want anything from the fridge?"

She shook her head. "I'm fine, thanks though."

"Sounds good, I'll go wake up Gill," he replied before yawning.

Kanna kicked her feet up on the workbench and waited for her friends to return. Despite her relaxed position, she couldn't keep her eyes from watching the slow crawl of the loading bar.

It was nearing ninety-five percent by the time Jared and Gillman returned. They took two seats next to her and watched silently.

Ninety-eight.

Ninety-nine.

One hundred.

They all leaned closer as the screen went black then rebooted with the SatellaField logo. A light pop emanated from the Personal Station as a small compartment slid open and projected an image of Johan's face.

"I'm proud of you Kanna. I'm sorry for burdening you with all this, and unfortunately there's still more to do."

Kanna took in a deep breath and tightly held her hands together as Johan continued.

"You need to reach my dearest friend, Danikan Fissure. He has the encryptor key and will gladly turn it over. I hope you aren't facing this alone, but even if you are, I know you will keep Lor-Rev safe."

The image cut off and the three of them sat in silence.

Kanna got up from her chair and walked towards the door, grabbing her leather jacket along the way.

"You heard him, guys. Let's go see Danikan."

———

The squat office building sat unoccupied, save for two people. One a prisoner, the other his captor.

"I'm surprised you can live here, Danikan. Did you ever truly spend a moment away from work?" he asked coldly.

Danikan didn't answer. He was curled up against the legs of a steel workbench, nursing his wounds. Daemon hopped onto the bench and calmly crossed one leg over the other. He held the Encryptor Key aloft and started turning the small sliver rectangle between his fingers. While he inspected it, Danikan hacked out a few bloody coughs.

Daemon regarded him with pity. "Don't worry, friend. I made sure not to injure anything vital. After all, I need you in decent condition when Kanna and her friends arrive."

- CHAPTER 18 -

MAYKUNE

-

-

CIVIC REGION WITHIN THE
SOUTHBRIDGE DOMAIN

A light but consistent rain drizzled from the ebony sky. Unlike the majority of civic regions, Maykune's residents voted to have their Sphere-Ceiling change along normal weather patterns. It was one of the many charming quirks that led Nathan's dad to move there. Nathan hated it. If he were back in Chushin he wouldn't be soaked.

Reaching an intersection, he lifted the edge of his hood and glanced upward. The sign was barely visible behind the soft glow of a hazy street lamp.

'Hallison and Till street. Just a few more blocks then,' he told himself.

He let the hood fall back into place and started rubbing at a lingering ache in the base of his neck. The hood on his jacket was rather large, and sat far enough forward that he had to hold his neck at an odd angle to see beneath it.

"Enough of this damn thing," he grumbled while kneeling down to pull a knife from his boot.

He yanked the hood forward and began angrily sawing away a small chunk from the front.

"*There*, now it actually fits!" he hissed, tossing the cut fabric.

He continued skulking forward the remaining two blocks until he reached a two story steepled house. Even among the rest of the unique architecture his father's home stood out. It had brick covering the lower half with a few sections of it extending upward. The sections of brick that ran up the wall were covered in a lush green ivy, and the path to the front porch was lined with perfectly landscaped boxwood shrubs. The roof extended to cover the porch which had a pair of rocking chairs on either side. The front door was a rich dark chocolate color, and in its center was a cast iron knocker painted gold and carved in the shape of a lion.

Nathan climbed the five stairs with his head hung low. He had no idea why his instincts drew him back here.

'If only mom were still alive,' he thought in frustration.

He'd been forced to come live with his dad in Maykune when he was thirteen. Before his mother's passing, he'd only ever seen him at the occasional birthday or holiday. In those moments, he noticed how much everyone seemed to enjoy his father, how easily he courted a room and always added a hint of warmth to any gathering. He even dragged smiles from everyone attending his mother's wake during his speech.

'Clearly this will just make us closer,' Nathan had told himself all those years ago.

He was wrong.

Nathan blinked away his thoughts and raised his knuckles to rap on the door. Then he hesitated. The caliginous entrance held a sense of foreboding, as if what sat inside presented a more depressing outcome than turning and marching through the rain at his back. He let his arm fall, whirled on his heel and started trudging down the steps. A creak of hinges behind him made him pause.

"Nathan? Is that you, son?" Gerald quietly called from behind the door.

Nathan stood still. He was surprised his father had guessed correctly, as he hadn't removed his hood and was completely covered by his cloak.

'Maybe he knows me better than I thought?' he wondered.

"Nathan, come inside," Gerald pleaded.

Nathan took a few more breaths, holding his position. Despite venturing all the way out here, a piece of him still bristled at capitulating to even the smallest request his father made. He exhaled and decided to oblige.

"Nathan, where have you been? I've been trying to reach you for days?" Gerald asked while beginning to put on a pot of coffee.

"There's no reception in the East Outs," Nathan casually grumbled while tossing his cloak on a hook.

Gerald turned away from what he was doing.

"He *sent* you there?!"

"*I* decided to go there, dad," Nathan retorted while flopping onto a nearby couch.

Gerald placed a hand on his face and shook his head.

"What could Devlice possibly need you to do out there?"

"He's not Devlice anymore, he's beyond that," Nathan answered while leaning forward and glaring.

Gerald slumped onto a wood stool. "Do you really think his master plan is what's best for us? Centralizing everything? Controlling everyone? What has any of this done to benefit you?"

Nathan jabbed a finger on the coffee table in front of him. "What I'm doing is bigger than just one person," he then pointed to himself, "me included."

He stood up and met his father's eyes with a harsh stare. "This is for the betterment of *everyone*. All you ever did was try and make money off people with this stuff, I'll be remembered for making the *entire* Forum a better place!"

Gerald bit his lower lip as he ingested his son's diatribe.

"How deep have you gotten into this?"

Nathan crossed his arms and looked away as his anger began to simmer.

Finally, Nathan spoke. "I'll have you know I made it to the East Outs and back on my own – and thanks to Daemon – I survived being gunned down."

Gerald winced and his mouth gaped in a mix of horror and disbelief. This person wasn't his timid aloof son, he was twisting into something else.

"Who could he possibly need you to fight? I just... I don't understand..."

Nathan's eyes narrowed as he faced his father.

"It was two losers from Tetragon and some lady. They have two of the items Daemon was asking you about. I was hoping if I came back here you could help me."

Gerald swallowed the growing lump in his throat.

"Do you remember the name of the woman?" he hesitantly asked.

Nathan held his chin. "What are you not telling us. Do you know one of them?"

"I'm not conspiring with anyone, but I *am* worried you could be hunting one of my friends," Gerald took a deep breath before steering the dialogue in another direction. "Look. I know we don't have much time because he's monitoring us, but I'm planning on leaving," Gerald stood up and uncrossed his arms, "and I want you to come with me."

Nathan whipped his head towards his father. His simmer now reached a boil. "You want to run away again, dad? I'm not surprised!" he hissed.

Gerald's eyes widened and his face went slack. When an argument with his son reached this point, he usually tried to sooth him with a gift or comforting words. However, the time for presents and pleading was over.

He snatched a coffee mug and threw it against a wall.

"This isn't about me leaving your mom, Nathan!" he yelled back with outstretched arms.

Nathan held his glare. "Isn't it always about that, dad. Every time we argue it ends like this. Isn't now the part where you start trying to tell me what I should do with my life?"

Gerald pursed his lips as two frustrated tears trickled down.

He pointed a rigid finger at his son. "You think the advice I gave you was because I did everything right? I only wanted you to be better than me!"

Gerald blinked through the haze of watery vision and pleaded with his son one last time. "If you want to do something great, then help me put a stop to all this. You know deep down that this whole singularity he's building is sick and twisted. I don't care what he's injected me with, I'm not staying here while he suffocates Lor-Rev," Gerald angrily pointed towards the door, "I don't care how long it takes me out there, I'll keep working until I find something that can finish him off."

Silence overtook the room and strangled it. Neither one of them willing to give the next word. Eventually, it was broken by shrieking from the coffee maker as it exhausted steam.

"I'm leaving, Nathan," Gerald said while snatching his coat.

He strode over to the entryway and ripped the door open. After taking one step out, he paused.

"I love you, son," Gerald said over his shoulder.

He then dropped his chin. "Even if you don't believe me."

Nathan watched his father leave through the open door and trudge off into the rainy darkness. He leaned forward on the couch and rested his arms wearily on his knees. Normally he would've found something nearby to splinter into as many fractured pieces as his soul. However, this time he just stared ahead and felt nothing. It was as if something inside was sedating his emotional urges.

'Eventually I'll be completely free,' he thought as the wave of calm continued washing over him, *'No longer shackled by emotions.'*

He stared at his hands and continued pondering the profound nature of the technology coursing through his bloodstream. Despite this serene state, his father's words crawled around his skull and gave him concern. Nathan steeled himself and shook them off. Believing that once he reported back to Daemon, all his worries would be assuaged. Yet, one thought continued to nip at the back of his ruminations.

'Is this really what's best for Lor-Rev?'

- CHAPTER 19 -

CHUSHIN

-

-

CIVIC REGION WITHIN THE
NORTHBRIDGE DOMAIN

THE doors sat wide open but only darkness could be seen past them, like the gaping maw of a hungry predator. Kanna stood over her Viper-cycle as she regarded the entrance to Danikan's personal office building.

"Were you able to reach him?" Jared asked while exiting his car.

She shook her head. "I wasn't, and it looks like someone else beat us here."

After receiving the vid-chat from Daemon, they decided it was best to approach with multiple vehicles rather than crowded together inside one. While they were in front, Gillman was roaming the periphery in a larger armored car they'd acquired in a trade for Nathan's rig.

Jared bit the edge of his tongue nervously. "You think this Daemon guy is in there?"

Kanna nodded. "I think so."

Jared opened his trunk and removed a hefty pistol set inside a thigh holster. After adjusting the straps and affixing the top one to his belt, he removed the gun and inspected it. It was painted in a silver chrome that had a light blue hue when under direct light. On the left side of its slide just above the handle were three rectangular buttons next to a small circular dot. Kanna had shown him earlier how to adjust which ammunition it would fire using those switches. If he pressed the top or bottom button the gun would project the type of ammo indicated by the small light next to them. Once he made his selection, he would use the button in the middle to choose it. It was an impressive firearm, one only someone of Kanna's stature or corporate police would carry, considering the price tag. Any citizens who carried in Lor-Rev – ganglanders included – usually had weapons with traditional lead bullets.

"You ready?" Kanna asked.

"You can't travel across the Forum without firing a gun or two," Jared replied with a half-smile.

Kanna reached over her back and grabbed her rifle.

"Alright then, let's see what's inside."

The front lobby seemed surprisingly immaculate. Not a table or chair out of place. However, finding the room in such a state gave them an eerie chill. Kanna blinked on her infrared vision hoping to see a sign of life in the rooms ahead. However, the walls were coated in a material that wouldn't let her see through.

"I should've known," she huffed.

Jared held his wrist cuff in the air and a faint blue light emitted from one side.

"This is really bizarre. There's definitely signs someone was in here, but they're not normal readings."

Kanna shot him a worried glance.

"You see this glass table? It has smudges like fingerprints, but there's no actual pattern. Even a smudged print leaves the edge of a ring or some lines," Jared said while pointing at his discovery, "this person has clearly altered themselves."

Jared shined the light a few feet above the prints.

"The air here shows signs of NTP, and I'm barely seeing any nitrogen."

"Could you translate that for me please?" Kanna asked sarcastically.

"Non-thermal plasma... this air has traces of it. Meaning whoever was here is possibly exhausting some weird elemental mix. Unlike you and me, whose air would mostly be nitrogen. Unless Danikan uses his lobby to show off plasma engines?"

Kanna shook her head. "Danikan has plenty of labs here for that stuff. If you're finding a blend of human and mechanical, that must mean Daemon's here."

They continued their search, walking down a narrow hall. After reaching the next room, Kanna and Jared found the destruction they were expecting. A rectangular metal sheet teetered against a broken glass table while light fixtures hung loosely by their last wire overhead. Chairs were strewn about and a set of couches were slit with their cushions belching stuffing. The two of them each took one side and slowly stepped around the wreckage. This game of careful creeping continued with each new room they entered.

"You think he's still here?" Jared asked, his back pressed against a wall adjacent to an open door.

"I'm not leaving until we check every room," she whispered back.

They quickly turned into the next room in one sweeping motion. A desk sat in one corner with monitors mounted on the wall. The floor was a cold tile and above them was a balcony with a glass railing. Kanna's eyes bulged as she noticed a clothed lump a few feet from the balcony's edge. She immediately darted for the stairs.

"What is it?" Jared called out while following her.

Kanna knelt over an older man wearing a white coat with rolled up sleeves. She gingerly held his shoulder.

"Danikan, are you ok? What happened?"

He rolled over slowly, the skin around his eyes wrinkled as he groaned in pain.

Then he peered through slit eyelids. "Kanna?"

She nodded eagerly at him. "Yes, Danikan, it's me."

"You need to ru...ru..." he muttered between coughs.

She waved Jared over and the two of them lifted Danikan to a seated position.

"I'm not going anywhere without you," she said flatly.

Danikan shook his head and tried to wave her away but he could barely lift his arm.

"Leave me. Run," he said again.

They disregarded his warnings and lifted him to his feet.

"You can explain everything once we're out of here. Just try and walk with us," she instructed.

"I don't know if he can make the stairs, Kan?" Jared said.

Danikan pointed towards a corner wall layered in a patterned tile.

"Pu... push the odd one," he stammered through barely open eyes.

Jared didn't see any with an odd color that stood out from the pattern, so he traced his palm over them. Eventually he felt one with a different texture from the others and pressed it. The wall slid open, revealing metal elevator doors. As they entered the elevator,

Jared surveyed the button choices while Kanna continued to hold Danikan aloft with his arm around her shoulder.

"Let's go to the garage. I can tell Gill to meet us there," Jared said while propping Danikan's other arm over his own shoulder.

"I didn't see an open entrance to the garage from outside," Kanna stated.

"Don't worry, Gill will find a way. Let me carry him, you've got the better gun," Jared said while smiling.

Kanna transitioned to her rifle just before the doors opened. After taking the first step inside, the lights activated in a straight line one after another, highlighting a few cars parked in no particular order. A lone cloaked figure stood on the opposite side of the garage; his face shaded from a wide brim hat.

"Where's the encryptor key, Daemon?" Kanna ordered.

He held his position unmoving.

Kanna cut the still air above her with a heat exhaust round. The rupture of flame made Jared swiftly raise a hand over his eyes.

She pointed the barrel forward once more.

"I don't ask twice."

Daemon strode towards them slowly. "Why should I tell you?" he said while crossing his arms, "After all, I have a more rightful claim to the Diffusor than you, since I co-created it."

"Not another step unless I say so," Kanna barked while giving her weapon a punch towards him.

He raised his hands up and gave a hollow chuckle.

"No need for all that, Kanna. I'm happy to arrange a deal."

She glared while looking over her scope.

"Is that the same deal you gave Danikan here?"

He crossed his arms. "You have two items I need, and he only had one. I'm sure I could barter a more favorable transaction."

Kanna cocked an eyebrow at Daemon, who returned her a knowing grin.

"Yes, I know you have the Merge as well. I'm notified every time you activate something that leads to the Diffusor," he uncrossed one arm and held his palm out, "Now, my devices please."

Kanna glanced at Jared, who had his pistol drawn and pointed forward as well.

"Jared, get Danikan to that car on my left and I'll meet you outside," she instructed.

"You have the keys?" Jared asked her.

"I'm sure Danikan has a way," she replied.

"They… have v…voice activation," Danikan mumbled.

Jared shook his head. "I don't want to leave you here alone with this guy."

Kanna gave him a confident nod. "I'll be fine. Just get him to Gill. If I haven't torched this guy by then you can join in."

Jared bit his lip. "Alright, Danikan, let's move."

Ear-splitting pops erupted from Kanna's rifle as she cranked off a series of bullets at Daemon. Jared snatched Danikan tightly and jogged over to a nearby blue sports car. The buckles on Danikan's shoes scraped along the concrete as he was still too fatigued to keep his steps in sync with Jared. After plopping him in the passenger side, Jared ran to the driver's side door.

Kanna continued to fire shots at Daemon, who darted from car to car, bounding closer. She couldn't tell if he was dodging all her fire, or just withstanding the bullets that connected. Her stomach curled tighter as he closed the distance with each movement. She glanced and saw Jared whipping open the driver's door. The momentary change of view gave her target the opening he needed. As her eyes turned towards him, she saw an arm covered in a set of metallic plates stretch towards her. She gasped and dove away. Scrambling to her feet she saw him closing in. Daemon dashed forward and threw his shoulder into Kanna's back, sending her skidding across the cement floor on her stomach.

"KANNA!" Jared yelled.

He fired his pistol at Daemon, who tried to duck away but one round caught him in the shoulder. Jared continued shooting at him as he swept away behind another car.

"Hurry, Jared!" Kanna yelled while climbing back inside the elevator.

'Split us up and keep him distracted, not a bad move,' Jared thought as he started the engine.

He slammed on the pedal and cranked the wheel towards the exit. As he neared the lift door, he noticed an object swallowing the visible area of his rearview mirror. The hefty thump of weight landing on the trunk caused the car to skid back and forth. Jared's eyes grew wide, realizing Daemon was behind him. An outstretched hand punched through the rear glass and shot towards Jared's head. He barely tucked his chin in time and felt it fly past his scalp. He leaned over and chomped on the gloved hand, immediately sending a singe of pain through his teeth. He continued to clench the appendage in his mouth while placing his wrist cuff against it. A thin orange laser emitted and started melting Daemon's metal wrist. Jared yanked his head back as the arm retracted.

'I need to find Gill quick,' he thought.

Jared smashed his foot on the thruster while zigzagging through the outside parking lot, trying to keep Daemon at bay. He heard an engine rev and saw a carbon grey four-door SUV humming towards them.

'Kanna must have tipped him off.'

"Hey, Danikan, hold on tight, ok? There's only one way I think I can shake this guy," Jared said while spinning their car once more.

They now faced Gillman's ride. He sped towards the side of his friend's vehicle, hoping he would have enough trust in him to not drive away.

"What the hell are you doing?" Danikan yelped.

They were thirty feet away.

"Just trust me," Jared yelled over the revving engine.

Twenty feet.

"HOLD ON!"

Ten feet.

Jared yanked on the emergency brake and pulled the wheel, jerking their car into a skid. He gritted his teeth and braced himself as best he could. A second later he felt his whole-body slam from one side to another as the rear of their vehicle collided with Gillman's. His head swayed in a circle as the car continued in one limp half spin before coming to a stop.

Jared grimaced while trying to steady his swirling vision. He looked to his right and grasped Danikan's arm.

"You alright, bud?"

Danikan replied with a hearty groan.

Jared reached for the door and recoiled, seeing a face at his window. He drew his gun and pressed it to the glass. He was halfway through his trigger squeeze when he heard a frightened yelp.

"Put that damn thing away, Jared, it's me!"

Jared let his arm flop into his lap as he realized it was Gillman.

"You sent that asshole flying when you rammed my car," Gillman continued giddily while opening the door for Jared.

Jared staggered out of his vehicle, placing one hand on the doorframe to steady himself.

"Hey, Gill... help him out of the passenger seat and take him back to the safehouse, we don't have much time."

Gillman gave him a puzzled look. "You say that as if we're in trouble? I told you that he..."

Jared held up a hand to interrupt him.

"Just take him back. This guy isn't some ganglander with a few cyber parts, what he did back there..." Jared leaned against the car and waved a hand towards Gillman's car, "Just get him out of here."

"And where are you going?" Gillman asked.

Jared looked at the sports car he'd taken from the garage, which was completely crumpled on the rear driver's side. Then he surveyed Gillman's armored car, which only had a few scratches.

"Come back with us, kid," Gillman pleaded.

Jared shook his head while typing on his wrist cuff.

"You have to take him back now. I can survive 'till my car gets here."

A revving engine sounded from a quarter mile away as Jared's car remote-started on the other side of the building. Gillman huffed loudly in objection while assisting Danikan into the passenger seat.

"Where's Kanna?" Gillman asked.

"She had to run back through the building. Once she's got her bike, I'm sure she'll meet us at the safehouse."

Gillman shrugged and trotted over to his car. As his friend drove off, Jared teetered on shaky legs. He shook away the fatigue and steeled himself.

"This bastard isn't taking me down," he muttered.

A rustle in the bushes several yards away alerted him that he was still being hunted. Jared tapped a few last-minute commands on his wrist cuff in preparation.

————

Glass crunched under her boots as she backtracked through the offices. She was one room away. She studied the line of windows in the front lobby and noticed she was greeted by darkness. Late evening had finally faded to nightfall. Kanna picked up her pace and sprinted out the front doorway towards her bike. She spun around one last time towards the office and activated her rifle mounted light. All she saw was a vacant room. Behind her, a high-pitched whirl followed by a baritone hum caused her to spin on her heels. Jared's car had started on its own, and was driving away. She blinked with realization and immediately jumped on her bike and began to follow.

As she rounded the corner to the back parking lot, she saw Jared pointing his pistol toward a set of rustling hedges. An arm extended out and swiped at Jared, who dove away and shot a few plasma rounds at it. The rounds left melting holes, but didn't seem to slow it down. The arm retracted, and Daemon stepped forward from the bushes. His head was tilted at an awkward angle. One beyond a normal human's dexterity. Jared's car completed a hairpin turn and screeched to a halt, putting itself between the two. Kanna zoomed forward and joined Jared behind his car. She unslung her rifle and snapped off a rapid burst of plasma rounds at their aggressor. Daemon dodged behind a concrete half wall that surrounded the parking lot in sections between the hedges.

'Good,' she thought, 'at least my plasma rounds slow him down.'

Jared slapped her on the shoulder. "Let's get the hell out of here…"

Kanna smiled. "I'll follow your lead."

Jared gave her arm a squeeze in solidarity before jumping in his car and taking off.

Kanna spun her back tire in a half circle – putting herself in line with Jared – then crouched and cranked on the throttle. They raced away on the two-lane road that led out of the office park and back to the denser sections of Chushin. After a few miles, Jared noticed a sleek black two-door car following them from his rearview mirror. He activated a voice chat with Kanna.

"You see that car behind us? I'm guessing that's not Danikan's secretary," he said.

"Let's take the five-ten highway then. I'm not heading back to the safehouse until we lose him."

Jared nodded. "Fair enough, but it's one of the more congested freeways…"

"Worried you can't keep up?" Kanna asked while grinning.

Jared laughed. "Just worried you'll be left alone with that guy when I dust you."

"So sweet of you to care, but there's no way that granny wagon is going to beat me back," she snarkily replied.

"This car is a classic! When I beat you back, you're paying for the miniature from Sanzo's vault."

Kanna's brow furrowed. "And what if I win?"

Jared huffed. "You won't, so there's nothing to argue for."

He slammed on the pedal and raced up the freeway onramp. The five-ten freeway – like many others in Lor-Rev – was built in multiple stories. Jared decided to take the ramp onto the second level. He noticed in his mirror that Kanna zipped over and took the one above him. Jared glanced again and watched the black car zip around two vehicles then take the ramp after Kanna. Jared tapped on the screen just above his ventilation controls. He switched to a GPS map with a set of names underneath. He selected his vehicle and Kanna's.

'You better shake him soon or I'll have to switch levels and come up there. I'm not letting that prick take any of us.'

———————

She diced between two sedans then steadied herself in the far-right lane. The freeways were stacked in an arc, so she could see Jared's car from her position. An alert blinked in the upper left of her visor.

'Looks like he decided to chase me?'

She'd tagged his car for alerts when they initially spotted it, allowing her to not be completely reliant on mirrors to detect Daemon's movements. A small window appeared on her visor that was connected to a rear camera on her helmet. The camera followed the black car as it crossed lanes around a pack of sedans. It zoomed forward in the open left lane, attempting to parallel her. Kanna

215

merged over three lanes and put herself in front of Daemon. She made two quick revs of her engine, taunting him, then slowed down as his car lurched towards her.

'*Steady,*' she told herself.

Once it was within a few feet of her rear fender she popped into a wheelie on her front tire, then dropped her back tire on Daemon's hood. She unholstered a pistol that was attached to the side of her hydraulic forks and pumped several plasma rounds through the windshield. As he swerved his car away, she pirouetted on her front tire to face oncoming traffic, then took off on the road shoulder. Daemon whipped his car around and chased after her. Until he could reach the shoulder, he had to play a precarious game dicing from lane to lane against the stream of traffic surging towards him.

"C'mon, where's one when you need it?" she muttered.

A few more compact cars and SUVs drove past, until she finally spotted what she was looking for. A semi-truck was lumbering towards them. Kanna snaked her Viper-cycle over to one side of it and Daemon followed suit. Once her bike was past the front tires, she crouched to her left and pulled hard on the handlebars. The motion sent her in a low arcing turn underneath the semi-truck trailer that put her back in line with traffic. As she zoomed off, she could see Daemon's vehicle hadn't been able to turn around and was zig-zagging feverishly to avoid oncoming cars. Traffic was tightening in front of her so she slowed down and inhaled a steadying breath. Taking a moment to relax, she noticed an incoming voice chat from Jared and answered.

"Hey, what's going on up there? I tried to keep pace with you but my GPS showed you were going backwards."

"It's fine now. I just had to shake him off. I haven't seen him since I turned back..." she trailed off as something odd caught her attention. The semi-truck was back in her rearview, but someone was standing on top of it.

"I have to go, Jared. Just head back, ok?"

"I'm not leaving you out here, Kanna," Jared said.

She switched off the chat and sped forward, hoping Jared would do what she asked and not take any unnecessary risks. Her visor pinged as the rear view displayed Daemon jumping off the semi behind, arching towards her.

'He can't make that, he's too far away,' she told herself.

But Daemon didn't land on Kanna, he plunged into a convertible a few yards behind her. She gaped in horror as the driver was expelled from the vehicle and sent skipping across the cement. Daemon's stolen vehicle gained on her, approaching her left side. She pointed her pistol at Daemon, but he swerved towards her, causing her to weave away and drop it as she retook her handlebars. If she hadn't given up her weapon to reclaim her steering, he would have sent her careening into the barricade. After regaining her balance, she noticed he was alongside her now.

Glass shattered as Daemon punched through his passenger side window towards Kanna and shoved her rear fender with an extended arm. Her bike spun out and slammed into the barricade, sending her airborne over the side of the three-story highway. Kanna felt as if she was falling at a crawl while frantically thinking of a way to save herself. As she fell headfirst, a gloved hand reached out from above, ready to snare her ankle like a fish on a lure. She unholstered the pistol on her thigh and fired two plasma shots at the arm, causing it to recoil. Her hair whipped at her face and she grasped at the air for anything to interrupt her descent, but found nothing. Closing her eyes, she conceded her fate and held her bionic arm overhead in hopes it would break her fall enough to survive the impact.

Then... it all stopped with a sudden jerk against gravity. Her head, arms and stomach lurched downward towards the ground. She winced, hearing the snap and crinkle of her metallic leg absorbing the shock of being scooped up at the last minute.

"I got you, Kanna," Jared groaned.

217

He'd extended his wrist cuff into a pole with a loop at the end, which had snatched her below the knee.

"You said your left side was the bionic one right," Jared continued through gritted teeth as he pulled her upward.

After heaving herself over the barricade, she realized she was on the shoulder of the freeway.

"Yea, you grabbed the right one," Kanna panted while limping over to the passenger seat and climbing inside.

Jared clambered back into the driver's seat and sent them speeding away. In the rearview mirror, he saw Daemon's lurking figure perched on the barricade one lane above. Despite them getting away safely, the way he watched them drive off sent a haunting chill across the back of Jared's skull. He knew it likely wouldn't be the last they saw of him.

After untying his boots, Jared slumped onto his bed in exhaustion. Feeling like he'd completely processed the emotional turmoil of escaping with Kanna, he now stared at the ceiling and tried to comprehend his current predicament. He wasn't upset anymore, rather, he couldn't believe he was lucky enough to be on the hunt for something of this magnitude. After encountering Daemon in person and seeing what he was capable of, Jared knew the Diffusor was even more important than the message board rumors made it out to be. He'd been skeptical when initially hearing it could separate machinery at the users will, allowing them to dissect the physical and digital components of most mechanical objects. He assumed it was probably just a high-powered puck that could lift a truck or something, but became over-hyped after reaching the inter-web. However, seeing Daemon's abilities completely changed his mind. Sure, there were replacement bionic limbs or unique cosmetic ones – even his own devices had some incredible gadgetry – but nothing he'd seen before could enhance a person's physicality like that. Daemon's technology and this hunt for the Sphere proved there were more secrets hidden within Lor-Rev. Ones that Jared needed to see.

A knock on the wall interrupted his pondering. He looked over and saw Kanna standing at his open door leaning against the frame. He paused to take her in; she wasn't wearing her typical body suit. She had on small shorts and a tight-fitting tank top. A thin dark line circled her left thigh. Jared assumed that's where her replacement bionic appendage had been connected. As Kanna walked into the room, Jared noticed her steps were still ginger from surviving her fall, despite having her leg fixed.

"I see Gill patched you up pretty well."

Kanna smiled. "Yea, he did a great job fusing the synthetic skin too."

She paused before sharing the next bit of news.

"I wanted to let you know that that I talked with Danikan, he says Daemon has the key."

Jared sat up. "So, what's the plan to get it back?"

She tilted her head down and stepped forward.

"Well, since he doesn't know where we are – or at least I hope he doesn't – I'm going to look for the Diffusor's location."

Jared leaned forward. "Should we look for him first?"

Kanna sighed. "I thought about that, but I think it's best if I find the Diffusor's location. Once I know the layout of wherever it's hidden, I could set a decent trap to get the key back. Even if I found him, I don't think I can just take him head on without creating a favorable battleground first."

Jared tilted his head in agreement. "Fair point. Did Danikan at least have an idea of where it might be hidden?"

She huffed. "Sadly no. It looks like my grandfather only gave each person one piece of the puzzle. I'm guessing he thought it was best to protect everyone if they couldn't be forced to give away each other's secrets."

Jared rested his chin on his palms. "Another dead end, huh? Is there anywhere you want to start looking tomorrow?"

She sighed. "I'm not sure yet, but I'll think of somewhere I can start after I've got a good night's sleep."

Jared regarded her with a frown. "You keep saying I instead of we…"

Kanna turned her face away from him. "I'm doing this next part on my own. I can't put you two through anymore of this."

Jared leapt to his feet. "No way! You're not cutting me out of this!" he said defiantly.

She turned back toward him but avoided eye contact. "It's fine, you'll still get your payment. I can make arrangements before…"

Jared stepped forward and held her arm. "This isn't about payment, Kanna. That guy almost spiked you into the dirt, I'm not letting something…"

She pulled away and strode to the doorway, then paused.

"I've made my mind up already."

He reached forward and caught her by the waist. "Well, I haven't…"

She turned towards him and didn't protest when his hand slid behind her back. As he tugged her into his chest, she shed all her doubts and fears as their faces met, lips melting together.

- CHAPTER 20 -

CANVER

-

-

CIVIC REGION WITHIN THE
NORTHBRIDGE DOMAIN

JARED awoke in a slow blinking haze. Tilting his head to his left, he saw Kanna's velvet black hair cascading down his arm. She rustled slightly at his movement, her cheek still resting on his chest. A knock at his door burst his bemused state and brought him fully alert.

"Hey, kid, you seen Kanna? Her phone's been blowing up like crazy out here," Gillman called from the other side.

Kanna's eyes opened and she studied Jared, waiting for his response.

Jared smiled. "Did you check the garage? She might be fixing up her leg some more?"

"Yea, I'll go check," Gillman grumbled back.

After the footsteps became faint, Kanna climbed over Jared and frantically scooped her clothes off the floor.

Jared casually rolled over. "I'm guessing it's Sanzo calling?"

"Why would it be him?" she asked while pausing at the door.

"I beat you to the house, remember? I told you that glorified tricycle you peddle around couldn't touch my granny wagon."

Kanna laughed heartily. "I'll have to tell him that you stole one of his items then."

As she slipped through the door, Jared rolled onto his back. He placed his hands behind his head and sank deeper into his half-sleep.

———

Kanna casually trotted down the staircase while pulling back her hair in a simple pony tail. Early afternoon sunlight streamed in from a set of three large windows lining the living room. Rounding the corner into the kitchen, she gave a relaxing sigh after smelling a fresh pot of coffee, then flinched as something swung up towards her face.

"There you are. I've been trying to get ahold of you because your phone is blowing up," Gillman said while thrusting her Merge at her.

She took her phone from him and looked at her notifications.

Gillman sat back on a stool against the counter while taking a sip from his mug. "Who's G.S. by the way? Any chance he's got a lead for us?"

"It's Gerald Stekanstreet, but I'm not sure why he'd be calling me this much?" Kanna replied while scrolling through her phone.

Kanna sent him a vid-chat request which was immediately answered.

"Kanna! I don't have much time – has Daemon gotten to you yet?"

She shook her head. "No, but not without trying. We had a run-in with him last night."

Gerald's face grew pale. "Did he use anything on you? Even a small device?"

Kanna glanced over at Gillman, her brow furrowed in confusion. She looked back to Gerald. "I don't think he ever got a hand on us."

Gerald sighed in relief, but said nothing.

"We could use your help. Where are you right now?" she asked.

Gerald paused and adjusted his glasses. "I can't say, he's able to track my movements. Even this conversation will likely be uploaded to him at some point. Look, Kanna, everyone he's going after, he's injecting with something that links their body to the inter-web. Again, I don't have much time, this is the last stop I'm making with either phone reception or inter-web access."

Kanna bit her lower lip anxiously, knowing her next question would be a tough sell. Especially since Daemon was monitoring their transmission.

"Is there a chance you'd work with us? I know he can track you, but if we met in person and you heard me out... I think you'd trust my plan."

Gerald took in a trepidatious breath and held it. Pondering her request. After a few seconds of silence, he shook his head in disagreement. "If you've encountered him on your own and survived without a scratch... letting him track you seems like a gamble I don't want to take."

She rolled her eyes and sighed. *Why did he even bother calling if he's just going to turn me down?'*

"Well, if you won't join us, do you have any idea where the Diffusor might be? I know Johan told you about it."

Gerald pursed his lips. "That's why I reached out. Daemon was grilling me about Benwird Ottley."

Kanna's face scrunched. "Is that the reporter who was obsessed with my grandfather?"

Gerald nodded. "It is. He's been looking through old articles by him and dissecting them. He'd ask me questions about possible connections to the Diffusor. If you can find whatever Daemon wants with him, I think you'll have your answers."

Kanna gave a steady nod. "Thanks Gerald."

He smiled back. "Good luck, Kanna. I know he'd be proud of you."

The chat stopped and Kanna stood silently while comprehending everything she'd heard.

"You guys! Danikan is gone!" Jared shouted after rounding the corner and sliding into the kitchen.

"What?!" Kanna asked frantically.

Gillman crossed his arms and tilted his chin up confidently. "He did us a favor."

Jared and Kanna twisted their heads towards their elder companion.

Gillman pointed to Kanna's Merge. "You heard what he said. Daemon is tracking everyone he encounters. I'm guessing when Danikan came to this morning he probably knew that as well. Him running off is a sign that he wanted to protect us."

Jared leaned on a nearby counter. "Well, I'm not sure you'd be so enthusiastic if you knew what was missing from the driveway."

Gillman's skin around his eyelids curled. *"Damn... I liked that armored car."*

Kanna crossed her arms and looked at Jared. "Well, now that Danikan's gone, our only other lead is finding Benwird Ottley. Hopefully before Daemon does."

———————

"I knew Gerald would run off at some point," Daemon said to himself after seeing the vid-chat close.

"If all they have is Benwird to look for, I'm afraid they'll be highly disappointed at what they find."

He slowly walked up a steep set of stone stairs half covered in snow. His location was somewhere only he and one other person knew about.

"Johan, old friend. I wish your granddaughter was wise enough to hand over what I needed. However, your stubbornness seems hereditary," he continued aloud.

He reached the top step and held his posture, surveying the immense structure before him. Several large slabs of stone were interlocked together, forming a circular door that looked like an assembled jigsaw puzzle. At the center was a small port the size of a knuckle. Daemon slid the encryptor key into it and took one measured pace backward. A loud hum grew ominously from behind the stone. Soon the hum became a crackling scrape as the pieces slid apart to reveal a cobblestone hallway.

"Their devices may unlock the safe for the Diffusor, Johan... but you and I both know I'll be able to crack its code eventually without them," he said while stepping into the dimly lit entryway.

Continuing towards his destiny – which was only one latch away – Daemon opened the last article he planned to read. No longer a point of research, this periodical was a means of inspiration.

The Southbridge Gazette

southbgaz.int | Neutrino 7th, 105 P.F. | 2 Tokens

A Window into the Future's Past:
Part Three - An Interview with Devlice Karlon

Conducted by Benwird Ottley

Venturing into the wealthy hillside suburb Devlice calls home, everything here can be surmised in one word, exquisite. The buildings are a kaleidoscope of beautiful modern Lor-Rev architecture trends built of sleek glass and veined marble. I see several people – decked out in the latest wares – walking across quaint cobblestone paths, marching along with a latte towards a miniature park that's immaculately landscaped. My driver arrives – provided by Devlice of course – in a luxurious limousine painted in lacquer black.

When reaching out to Devlice, he was very eager to conduct this interview. He believed chronicling the pivotal minds in technology was the best way to build a roadmap for Lor-Rev's future. It goes without saying that Devlice views himself as the preeminent cartographer of said roadmap. In fairness, his engineering and design prowess has earned him a bid for that role. He was a pivotal designer of the sphere-ceilings employed by every major civic-region, he also accurately predicted the Merge's influence on our society, and was instrumental in helping Johan improve upon its design. Looking out the car window, I see his fingerprints everywhere in how we function daily. I realize he's become the unintentional shepherd of our culture, and he's chosen to steer us towards a more digitally connected world.

As Devlice's chauffer weaves our car further up the residential section of Torémon, I become more anxious. This is my final notch in the belt for these retrospective interviews. It's also my last chance at persuading a friend of Johan to bend his ear in my favor, and I plan to make the most of it.

As the car pulls through the front gates of his mansion, I'm surprised to see Devlice standing in the driveway. I erroneously assumed he'd wait inside his palatial home while one of his stewards escorts me to him.

"Any chance you'd be willing to complete this interview over a walk?" he says while handing me a tall ceramic mug filled with coffee.

Exiting the car and seeing the combination of his massive estate backdropped by gorgeous weather, I decide to accept his offer.

Q: When researching your career, I noticed there was very little information on how you started or even what civic region you grew up in. I'd love to hear how your upbringing influenced your decision to begin an engineering career?

A: [Smiles] It's not intentional, I'm just not much for reminiscing. I always felt my time was best spent with the press chronicling what I could contribute to the future. It's also fun carrying an air of mystery now and then.

Q: You've become such a fixture of technological design that I have to assume your fascination came at a young age?

A: It wasn't until I went to university that I became enamored with tech. When studying the known history of the Intercontinents, I noticed that before the wars, there seemed to be a more unifying purpose to our cluster of worlds.

Q: Some would say the idea of trying to unite everyone under one rule is what led to it.

A: Some may argue that, but I see it differently. I think that not having a common purpose is what drove the wedge deeper. If every corner of the Forum was shared in one collective goal, we could become so much more.

Q: Do you see that in Lor-Rev's future?

A: It's already begun here, look at how connected we all are and how that connection constantly evolves. Moving on from the Merge, while maintaining that consistent connectivity, that will inspire the rest of the Forum to adopt our way of life.

Q: How do you propose that would happen?

A: You see the projection capability of augmented reality, now imagine if you didn't have to buy expensive contact lenses or heavy visors. Instead, your mind was able to just interpret those desires as needed. Again, remove the physical devices that distract us.

Q: Do you worry that the government – or society itself – would openly reject the idea of technology being implanted? I'm assuming that's what you're alluding to.

A: That's another piece holding us back. Our three-pillar republic. The Congregate, the people, and commerce are supposed to allow for a balanced structure where everyone has a seat at the table. If one side becomes too vociferous, it shuts down another from a chance at advancement.

Q: What would you propose then?

A: [Laughs] I'm not a politician, Benwird. I understand the personal autonomy everyone is trying to maintain in Lor-Rev, though. So far, we've done a great job at keeping it. When designing or producing for the future however, I have to step back and look at everything from a higher lens. And from that angle, we – as a society – can occasionally appear like the elderly man on the porch holding onto how things were.

Q: Has that always been your philosophy for engineering?

A: I think it's become more prominent as I've gotten older, wiser, and been able to travel more.

Q: How does Johan feel about those ideological concepts?

A: [Laughs] Oh he wasn't really a fan. However, I'd argue that when we were able to come together on a project, we made better music than anyone else.

Q: Are you still discussing ideas now?

A: Yes, we definitely do. While we come from completely opposite camps, there's no denying his genius. If you're angling for an opportunity to meet him however, I'd suggest you try and have someone else refer you. He's chummier with Danikan these days.

Q: Taking a step back, when you first worked with Johan on the Merge-3, how did you become partners on that project?

A: We first met during my work on sphere ceilings. We spoke at great length on how to ensure a stable connection for slate devices. His was the most popular, so I couldn't launch the technology if [the Merge] didn't work with it. He was very guarded about privacy for his users and it took a bit to sell him on large scale connectivity not controlled by an individual like his Station.

Q: If he hadn't accepted, do you think it would have sunk the project?

A: I think it would have succeeded eventually; it was a huge leap in convenience. However, to drag that large of a user base to adopt something new takes an incredible amount of marketing, which would have been costly.

Q: After working together, when did you realize how good you two were as a team?

A: I don't know if there was a revelatory moment, but when you finish each other's programing sentences as often as we did... you know there's something special.

Q: Do you have a specific example?

A: When we incorporated projection transfer for Merge phones, the code was immense. After banging my head on a wall for days trying to compress it, he walked in one morning and pointed to a sequence, and thought of a way to do it – it was like taking the language and creating contractions for it. It was an innovation in compressing [code] that I had never imagined before. That type of discovery and execution continued with everything we accomplished. I'm proud to say I had several moments like that myself. Honestly, I know we both competed to obtain more of those, "wins," so to speak.

Q: You mentioned that you still talk to Johan. Is there any chance that one more great invention is waiting in the wings from you two?

A: That would really blow the doors off one of the conventions, wouldn't it? Well, all I can say is that we still discuss the future – and despite our different versions of them – we both see very bright ones.

We finish our tour on the walking path around his home, which leads me back to his driver. I thank him one last time before taking a seat on the plush leather interior, then begin the long winding drive down to the railway station. After a few minutes of staring out the window, I realize I fell under the spell of Devlice's charm like so many other journalists. I tunnel deeper into thought and uncover all the questions I unfortunately didn't ask. I can see why he's gotten so far in his chosen field, but I also wonder how much he's been able to conceal behind his charismatic curtain.

- CHAPTER 21 -

CHUSHIN

-

-

CIVIC REGION WITHIN THE
NORTHBRIDGE DOMAIN

BENWIRD Ottley was dead.

When researching him they found his obituary in the Southbridge Gazette. After pouring over his three-part interview series on Johan, they didn't locate any hints of the Diffusor's possible location. They were on the road once more, this time to a suburb resting on a land spire at the edge of Chushin. Hoping that Benwird's late wife might provide answers.

"Is there any chance Johan hid the interview somewhere? Maybe in one of his servers you keep tabs on?" Jared asked.

They were becoming fatigued by rehashing possible leads, but somehow a long car ride nudged the conversation to continue.

"I've dug through all of them, but I saw nothing directly relating to Benwird's articles," Kanna answered flatly.

Jared bit his lip and paused before speaking. "If he met your grandfather, but only let him do a retrospective and not publish their interview... that audio file's gotta be out there somewhere?"

Kanna shrugged in agreement. "Well hopefully his wife might have something, even if they were estranged before he died."

Jared slowed their car and parked a few feet from a two-story red house with white trim. As they trotted up the wood steps, an elderly woman answered the door. She wore a white long-sleeved shirt with a yellow sweater tied over her shoulders and black jeans. Her white hair sat in a short bob, with her pointy facial features framed by white rimmed glasses.

"Hello Ms. Evenson, I appreciate you hosting us," Kanna said while stepping inside.

"You can call me Rachel, dear. It's not often I get someone who knew Benwird around here. Most everyone he was friends with in the tech community is gone. Or they assume I'd rather not talk about him..." Rachel said before trailing off.

She gave a quick shrug – dusting away any chances of the conversation becoming dreary – then escorted them over to a seating area at the front of the home. As Jared sat on one of her rose-patterned upholstered couches, he noticed she had four ceramic tea cups surrounding a silver tray of cookies and pastries resting on a knee-high table between them.

"I can see you eyeing those, son. If you have a sweet-tooth I'd recommend the ones with a drop of jelly in the center," Rachel noted with a wry smile.

Jared huffed a chuckle at her accurate presumption and took one, munching it while Kanna continued the conversation.

"Did you have a chance to look through that storage unit before we arrived?" Kanna asked.

"Yes, I looked for anything relating to your grandfather. I only found a few extra print versions of the articles you mentioned. I also found this…" Rachel said while handing her a few folded newspaper pages.

Kanna opened them and saw one was the obituary for Benwird, and the second was an article chronicling his contributions to the Southbridge Gazette.

"I'm sure he'd want you to have those in addition to the other articles. He was incredibly fascinated with your grandfather, Kanna."

Kanna nodded in gratitude before looking them over.

Rachel folded her hands on her lap and smiled. Clearly enjoying a chance to share the work of her late husband.

She then placed a finger on her chin. "You know the funny thing about that obituary… for some reason they said Benwird had a brother. I never understood where they got that from. Of course, it could have been something he asked them to print as last little joke to his father. Once he came down with his illness, I know a few editors at the Gazette asked for his input on how he'd like to be memorialized," Rachel finished before another sip of tea.

Kanna noticed the name Harry Ottley Jr. listed as Benwird's supposed brother. She glanced over at Jared, who gave her a steady knowing look. Both silently agreeing there was definitely more than a joke behind it.

Rachel set her cup down and continued. "They butted heads on everything. Harry was a mechanic who wished Ben would've taken a more hands on career, but he was still very proud of him."

Kanna looked up from the page. "Is there a chance his father would meet with us?"

Rachel shook her head. "He passed a few years before Ben. It was a really hard loss for him."

"I'm sorry to hear that. Were they still distant when it happened?" Kanna asked.

Rachel waved a dismissing hand. "Oh no, not at all. I apologize if I gave you that impression. They were very close, but he and his father were so different. I'd say their relationship was a recipe for stubbornness. It was one of the few things they had in common. Well… that and coffee. There was one place by Harry's they would always go to," Rachel smiled and her eyes grew a faint twinkle as she reminisced, "Every time Ben would come home from there, he would complain about something they disagreed on," as she finished, she gave a quick laugh and rested back in her seat.

Jared leaned forward and set his teacup down. "Do you happen to remember where that coffee shop is? I'm a pretty big fan of coffee myself."

Rachel took another sip before she spoke. "Yes, it's in a small town called Torik, over in the Southbridge. I'm not sure if it's still run by the same family, but I remember at the time they had this sign with a goofy little lemur next to the name."

"A lemur?" Jared asked.

Rachel shook her head and smiled. "I agree, not really sure why it would go with coffee, but the family had them as pets. Their house was connected to it, so sometimes they let them run around the shop."

Jared raised an eyebrow. "Seriously?"

Rachel nodded. "Torik is known to have wild ones in the forest nearby, so it's only natural that a few would get tamed."

"I'm definitely adding that to our road trip list," Jared replied.

Kanna set the papers down on the table in front of Jared.

"Is there a restroom I could use, Rachel," she politely asked.

Their host leaned back and pointed to a hallway on her left.

"It's the second door down."

Kanna gracefully got up and strode down the hallway. The continuing conversation fell to a light murmur as she closed the bathroom door behind her. She quickly opened a browser on her Merge and began looking up coffee shops in Torik.

'Why would anyone want to live in the cold?' Nathan asked himself after reaching the top of a stone staircase.

Daemon dropped a location marker for him that was past a town just before the Southern Unallocated Zone. At first, he thought Daemon had found his father, since he fled somewhere that didn't have a signal. However, he was informed that his father was not worth chasing, and that Daemon had a much more important job for him.

He clicked on a small LED flashlight while continuing to march down a cobblestone hallway. Rounding a corner, he entered a hallway that was faintly lit by small blue lights embedded within the stone walls. Anyone else might have been lost in such a maze – as there were many wrong turns to be made – but he'd been given a map that would lead him directly towards its center.

He stopped before a large set of arched doors that were easily twenty feet tall. Approaching them hesitantly, he looked for a way to open such a massive entryway. Nathan leapt back as the doors swung open on their own to reveal a round antechamber, with long ornate columns lining the sides. Instead of uneven stone, the floor was one sheet of veined marble.

'What the hell is this place,' he thought while crossing into the next room.

Daemon hadn't told him anything about where he was headed. He'd just been given a map on his Merge and told to come immediately.

'How is this hiding out here?' he muttered while gawking at the size of the main room.

The marble from the antechamber carried over into the main hall. One side had rows of various computers and electronic instruments, while the opposite side was lined with tables, desks and seating. There were three levels of balconies on either side, with bridges running across and linking them. He continued further into the room, looking for Daemon. The sound of boots clinking from one level above signaled the arrival of his leader.

"I see you've reached my laboratory," Daemon said.

He strode down a spiral staircase and marched over to Nathan.

Nathan steadied himself and tilted his chin up. "What did you need me to do."

Daemon lifted the brim of his hat. "I need you to overcome your earlier failures."

Nathan slowly exhaled at the insult. He knew losing the Merge and Station had been costly, and would be brought up eventually.

"I know I lost those three in the East Outs, but I'm sure we can find them again. If I brought Dorian and Hunter to back me up, I know they wouldn't be able to escape."

"Hmph," Daemon scoffed, giving an unimpressed frown.

"They're not worth our time anymore. I think it's best if we just focus on unlocking the safe housing the Sphere."

Nathan squinted in confusion. "You know where it is?"

Daemon cackled and took his hat off. As he held it out, a small motorized coat rack zoomed over. He placed it on a hook gracefully along with his cloak, then walked towards a set of metal doors on the opposite side.

"There's a far-off maze with a laboratory in the center and you assume the Diffusor is located somewhere else?" Daemon continued mockingly.

The edge of Nathan's mouth slid into a grimace of frustration and humiliation. A rush of heat hit him as he followed Daemon through the doorway. Instead of the pristine white light he now saw a red glow. A large vat sat on one side of the room bubbling with a crimson liquid. The floor was a mix of metal tile inset into the rocky terrain. Nathan's heels clinked along the tile as his leader led him towards a large chest that hovered above an oversized Puck in the center of the room.

"This," Daemon said while waving a hand towards the chest, "is what holds the Diffusor."

Nathan noticed there was a line of wires snaking from the back of it to a laptop sitting on a nearby stand.

"Unfortunately, I haven't been able to create a code sequence that will open it," Dameon finished.

Nathan squinted as his eyes adjusted to the red light. He noticed two crooked lumps on the ground several feet behind the chest.

"I don't think I have nearly the programming skills you do? I'm not sure how I'd open it?" Nathan quizzically stated.

"Well, I've gotten close to what I believe is the unlocking sequence. However, when a few others tried to open it, the results were unfavorable," Daemon replied.

Nathan stepped to one side of the chest, but his eyes still hovered over what was lying on the ground beyond.

"Nathan, I need your attention," Daemon interrupted, "Without the Diffusor and Merge, I believe this chest will only open if someone Johan coded as capable does it. You're a descendant of Gerald, so I believe this palm reader I've attached will accept you when the time is right."

Nathan held his breath and nodded.

Daemon smiled and grasped Nathan's shoulder. "Good. One more thing…"

"Yes?" Nathan asked.

"Please dispose of those two in the vat," Daemon ordered before walking back to the lab.

Nathan exhaled slowly as he walked over to the mess of contorted limbs. Upon reaching them, his eyes widened and his stomach began to climb up his throat. It was Dorian and Hunter.

Daemon's earlier words rang through his consciousness.

'...when a few others tried to open it, the results were unfavorable.'

He felt tears begin to well under his lids as he gritted his teeth... then nothing. Nathan blinked and swallowed down the lump in his throat as serenity engulfed his emotions.

He stared at his hands as a tingling itch ran across the entirety of his skin.

'This must be the nanites again...'

He took another deep breath and felt a calmness beyond one capable in such a wretched moment. Then he snatched Hunter's wrist and dragged him towards the vat, doing as he was told.

- CHAPTER 22 -

TORIK

-

-

CIVIC REGION WITHIN THE
SOUTHBRIDGE DOMAIN

THAT'S definitely it," Jared said while staring upward.

Kanna and Gillman stood behind him and looked at the same sign. A smiling lemur held a cup of coffee with a single billow of steam.

"I'm guessing when your grandfather decided to split up the clues for the Diffusor, he figured no one would look here," Jared said over his shoulder with a grin.

Kanna smiled and shook her head as she stepped past him towards the glass door. A small bell chimed overhead as she entered.

241

A row of rotating high-backed swivel-stools lined a bar near an assortment of coffee makers. Kanna noticed a bright red one with a silver plated back that she'd only seen in the high-end shops of downtown Chushin. She strode past a row of small booths and took a seat on one of the stools. A few seconds later, a tall thin man emerged from behind a black curtain that sectioned off the back stock room.

"What can I make for you?" he asked.

Kanna glanced up at the wood board with stick on black letters detailing the menu.

"I'll have a cold brew please," she said.

"Any milk or cream?" he asked.

Kanna shook her head no.

The tall man looked over to Jared and Gillman as they gazed up at the menu. "And for you two?"

Jared pulled his gaze down from the menu and towards the server. "I'll get an iced compresso – just black please."

Gillman tossed a thumb towards Jared. "I'll get the same, but with some sweet cream."

The server nodded and opened a small refrigerator, where he snagged a pitcher and poured Kanna's cold brew. When he slid her the drink, she took a moment to observe him further. He had pointed facial features and slicked salt and pepper hair, with a grey beard. Behind his slim black rimmed glasses were a pair of turquoise eyes. As the man stepped over to the machine to brew the shots of compresso, a lemur crawled through a square plastic door and hopped on his shoulder. Kanna looked at Jared with wide eyes and bit her lower lip, then nodded her chin up towards the creature. Jared held a pursed smile and rolled his eyes, begrudgingly agreeing on its cuteness. He nodded in thanks as he took his drink before sitting in a booth with Gillman.

Jared pointed a finger at the server's shirt, which was patterned with miniature blue flowers. "Nice threads, where'd you snag that?"

As the server turned to face him, Jared noticed that outside the beard and eyes his features were eerily reminiscent of Benwird's.

"There's a tailor shop a block away, he's from Moncroix, so he has a few unique designs," the server answered.

"You know, I came here a long time ago with my family on a road trip and I remember there was a couple that ran this place. Are they still in Torik?" Jared asked.

The server shook his head. "No, they sold it to me a few years ago. I really enjoyed coming here myself. I didn't want it to go to someone who wouldn't keep the same vibe."

"That's great to hear, I'm Jared by the way," he said while giving a half wave.

The server nodded back. "I'm Harry," he answered before picking up a rag and cleaning the counter underneath the machines.

Kanna quickly glanced at Gillman, who nudged one eyelid towards her in a half wink. She watched the supposed 'Harry' toy around with a few of the machines before cleaning the small metal cups that held used ground coffee. Kanna rested her head in one hand while leaning on the counter and decided if being direct was the best approach.

"So how long did you know my grandfather, Benwird?" she calmly asked.

He shot her a hesitant stare. Eyelids squinting in quizzical fashion. "I'm not sure who you're talking about, do I know you from somewhere?"

She slowly sat upright. "We never met, but Johan was my grandfather. I heard you could help me find something of his?"

He lifted an eyebrow. "So, you're Kanna then?"

She nodded. "Yes, and I believe you know where the Diffusor is located."

He didn't answer. Instead, stepping over to a rack of drying ceramic coffee mugs. He picked one up and started absentmindedly drying it with a clean rag.

"If it was so important that you found it, why didn't he tell you where it was?" Benwird asked.

"I think we both know that he never consolidated his secrets," she said while rising from her stool.

She walked to the side of the counter nearest him.

"I'm sure he told you about Devlice's plans... or that he'd change into Daemon?"

Benwird looked away and started cleaning another glass.

Kanna placed both hands on the wood counter. "We already have the items to unlock it, we just need to know where it's located. I know you left that clue in your obituary as a way for us to find you."

Benwird paused and rubbed his chin before answering. "I did leave that clue behind... but my mind has changed since then. And if you have everything, then you don't need me to tell you where it is."

Kanna sighed. "We lost the Encryptor key to him, but we have two of the three. It's a bit of a stalemate at this point."

Benwird huffed. "In that case your best option is to take what you have and destroy it. Devlice already knows where the Diffusor is."

Jared stood up from his booth. "What?!"

Benwird gave him a harsh gaze. "He didn't tell you three that? And I'm really supposed to believe you're related to him?"

"We're not," Jared said while motioning to himself and Gillman, "but she is."

Jared then placed his hands on his hips and grunted while pacing around the seating area, head down. "If he already knows where this thing is... how do we stand a chance?" he looked over at

Benwird, "Wait, you're just distracting us. Johan wouldn't leave it in the same place."

Benwird gave a condescending smile. "I'm guessing he thought it would be easier to just change the locks on the most elaborate safe, rather than search for a new home."

Kanna turned and gestured for Jared to calm down.

"He can't access the Diffusor from the vault without the items we have," she said in hopes it would assuage his mounting concerns.

Benwird shrugged. "Like I said – your best bet is to smash those items. Then we can all be done with this."

Kanna glared at Benwird in frustration. "That's not going to solve anything. If he's capable of syncing his mind with a digitized one, what makes you think he can't eventually crack a safe open with enough time?"

Benwird froze in place and searched for a rebuttal, but found nothing. He turned back to his mugs and began placing them on open shelves, hoping if he ignored these three long enough, they might leave him alone.

"Benwird, please… if you know anything that could help us, we need to know. I don't understand what you're afraid of?" Kanna pleaded.

Silence sidled into the room and lingered around them for several seconds that felt like hours.

Finally, Gillman rose from his chair. "He's not afraid, Kanna. He's angry."

She turned his way and stared at him in confusion.

He'd been studying the entire conversation rather than participating, but now he believed he had an answer.

"You wanted to meet Johan more than anything, and when you finally did… it cost you," Gillman said.

Benwird barely looked over his shoulder, but stopped what he was doing.

Gillman continued, "We saw your series on Johan. At the end he let you interview him, but you couldn't print it. You just did some boring retrospective," he took a step closer to the counter, "In exchange for recording his greatest secrets you had to go into hiding. Your father was gone, you were already divorced, so you figured — why not? However, once you saw what really was at stake… you had to give up *everything* and come to this tiny little hole in hopes those fears never came true."

He then pointed ferociously at Benwird. "And by *everything*, I mean it stole the only thing you assumed could never be taken… your writing."

Benwird turned on his heel and walked around the counter, standing a foot from Gillman.

"If I've lost everything, then what reason do I have to come to your aid? Clearly helping with anything relating to Johan only brings more suffering," he said while shoving a finger into Gillman's chest.

He turned back towards the counter and waved them off.

"Again. Just smash them and be done with it. You're already too far behind and I'm done with Johan's games."

Kanna hung her head while Gillman returned to his seat and crossed his arms. He stared out the window as his brain whirred in contemplation, searching for a way to convince Benwird.

Jared stopped pacing, picked up his glass and placed it on the counter. "I'd like another one."

Benwird raised his palms in bewilderment. "What?!"

Jared pressed a finger to the counter. "Your sign says you're open for another two hours, so if we're going to have to sit here and keep thinking of reasons you should quit being an asshole… then I'm going to need a few more milligrams of caffeine in my blood."

Benwird laughed while snatching the glass. "I think service is closing early today. I've had enough of my past coming back to haunt me."

Jared tilted his face to one side but continued looking at Benwird.

"That's it! I'll trade you," Jared stated enthusiastically.

"Trade me?" Benwird asked in bewilderment.

Jared crossed his arms and stood straight. "I'll only say if you open service back up."

Benwird rolled his eyes and groaned. "Fine, I'll indulge this petty consideration. But it's your last chance before I kick you out," he said, waving a finger at him.

Jared climbed onto a stool with a broad smile on his face. Kanna leaned over and tried to whisper questions to him, but he waved her off confidently. She inhaled slowly and bit her lip to quell the annoyance of being dismissed, then walked over to the opposite side and stared out one of the big bay windows.

Benwird slammed the drink down in front of Jared, causing some to spill over the side of the glass. Jared ran his finger over the drips of iced coffee then licked it.

"You gave everything for the biggest scoop in tech history. This fight with Daemon only ends in two ways... either he finally unlocks the vault and uses the Diffusor to fix himself and enslave us all – *ooooor* you tell us where it is and we go kick his ass."

Benwird shrugged. "And..."

Jared held up a finger, cutting off Benwird.

"So, when you help us win – which we will – you can print that interview with Johan, *and*... you'll be the first person to have access to our story."

Benwird stood back and held his chin, regarding Jared's unique offer.

He shook his head. "Even if I were to finally print this, who's going to believe any of it?"

Kanna interjected. "Not to mention I can't have my name out there like that or I won't be able to protect his work anymore."

Jared leaned forward. "You're a journalist, I'm sure there's a way to tell Johan's story, *or* ours, and make sure it's packaged nicely for mass consumption?"

Benwird didn't answer, but the fact that he hadn't chased them off yet was a good sign.

Gillman got back up from his seat and joined Jared at the counter. "Look... even if you think printing this for the world is useless, think about the chance to cover real history as it happens again? Johan gave you access to his deepest secrets, now you have the chance to follow his descendant as she safeguards his work. Eventually someone is going to have to take her place, and when that time comes... we'll need someone we can trust who will be able to pass on her knowledge."

Benwird smirked. "And what makes you think I'll be around long enough to tell the supposed next generation?"

Gillman leaned forward and raised his brow. "Because you're half Malcozéan. I can tell because your skin is a mix of olive, and since you haven't dyed your hair recently – some of the red is showing underneath. I'm not sure how much of their traits you carry, but I'd imagine you'd live much longer than a Lor-Revian at least? You haven't aged from the picture I saw of you taken a decade ago."

Benwird's face went slack while internalizing Gillman's dissection of his past. He swallowed the uncomfortable revelation and went back to sorting his glasses and mugs.

"I haven't tried to hide my mother's heritage. I only changed my look when I moved here. I'm only a quarter, so I'm unsure how much that affects my lifespan," After he finished, Benwird lowered his chin and placed his hands on the back counter near the sink, "You're quite the observant one. Anything else you'd like to uncover while you're reading my palms there?"

Kanna walked back from the window and joined her two companions at the counter. "Help us, Benwird. Help us defeat Daemon and take back your legacy. Even if it's only for yourself. I

248

know you didn't write for public notoriety, or you wouldn't have kept my grandfather's secret this long."

Benwird raised his head towards the ceiling, eyes closed while ingesting everything thrown his direction by this band of travelers.

Eventually, he faced them and uncrossed his arms. "Fine, but you better win."

- CHAPTER 23 -

SOUTHERN UNALLOCATED ZONE

-

UNGOVERNED NON-CIVIC REGION

SO, he had an item in the West Outs, East Outs, and Northbridge. Too bad this thing couldn't just be hidden in the Southbridge rather than way out here," Jared mused aloud, throwing his backpack over one shoulder.

Unlike the sunny sky islands used for vacationing in the North Unallocated Zone, the Southern Unallocated Zone was uninhabited frost. The weather was harsher even than the mountain ranges of the West Outskirts. Luckily on this blizzard trek – due to Kanna's vast resources – they had snowmobiles, which considerably hacked away at their travel time. They made it three-quarters through on the first day – at least according to their map – and camped out in a cave. Despite the looming fear of Daemon possibly opening the vault if they were to arrive even one minute late, they knew reaching the doorstep of this fight bleary and exhausted would only expedite their defeat.

Jared was the first to wake and took the early rise as a chance to indulge a solitary moment.

'It all began here in the snow, and now it circles back…'

Little coincidence trinkets like this one kept his mind from lingering on fear and uncertainty. He stepped onto a rock that was peeking out from the frost, using the simple exercise of balancing on its jagged surface as another meditative distraction.

Kanna emerged from the cave next, arms crossed and chin tucked to avoid the cold flakes blowing around them. She slowly clomped towards Jared. Upon reaching him, she noticed he was staring straight ahead and hadn't noticed her.

"Hey, you ready to head out?" she asked while placing a hand on the back of his arm.

Jared blinked off his daydreaming and faced her.

"Yea," he answered calmly while stepping down.

Soon the three of them sped off, streaks of white powder surging up behind their vehicles. After several miles of hill upon rolling hill, a vast stone structure appeared in the distance. Jared revved his throttle and raced over to the flat slab of stone at the bottom of a staircase. He stepped off his ride and bent down to feel the landing. It was odd to see the entirety of their surroundings caked in white powder, but for some reason the landing and stairs only had patches of it.

"It's heated?!" Jared remarked after removing a glove and placing his palm down.

Kanna removed her helmet and shook her long ponytail free after being curled up behind her head. "I'm not sure how he could do something like that, but he did keep contacts with several important people from other Interconts."

He shot her a glance. "So, it's heated by something not from Lor-Rev?"

She shrugged begrudgingly and nodded. "Best guess I could make."

The snowfall was not heavy but still dusting, which made it hard to look very far ahead. It was only after reaching a couple of steps from the top that they noticed the entryway was completely open and unlit. Darkness stared out at them.

"At least he didn't lock us out," Jared remarked.

Gillman stepped forward and clicked on an LED lantern to light their path. Kanna unslung her rifle and Jared followed while tapping a few commands on his wrist cuff. The trio snaked through the maze of cobblestone corridors, following the directions written for them by Benwird.

————

"I need you to keep my code running while I deal with our intruders," Daemon instructed while typing feverishly.

Nathan peered over his shoulder and watched lines of code whiz by on the laptop screen.

"Is there any chance you want me to deal with them instead, boss?" Nathan asked.

Daemon stopped typing and pointed at the keyboard.

"I need you to wait for the algorithm to finish. I can't risk them destroying it. Even with their items, there's a chance Johan left behind more firewalls. Once this sequence finishes, I'll know the entire layout of the vault's code."

Daemon paused upon reaching the doorway.

"This is your chance to show your commitment to the future, Nathan. We can't accept failure."

Daemon strode into the main laboratory and held an arm out. The motorized coatrack arrived, per his command, then he snatched his hat and cloak. Nathan stood steadfast and watched until the doors shut behind his leader. He observed the computer as line after line of letters and numbers scrolled by. Anxiety crept up his chest but a light tingling overtook it and gave him peace. The nanites suppressed his emotions, but they couldn't control his thoughts. Which kept creeping back to the argument with his father.

"According to his map, we cross through this threshold and then all that's left is his lab," Gillman told the group.

Kanna lowered her rifle while staring at the immense arched doorway, clearly left open in expectation of their arrival.

"Any last ideas?" she asked the group.

"I think we have to play this one by ear," Jared replied while morphing his wrist cuff into a dagger.

He took a few practice swings and jabs with the blade that now rested on top of his hand.

"You want to draw your gun?" Kanna asked him.

"He's going to send those weird extendo-arms after me, so I'd rather have something that can deal with them," Jared answered.

They took the last corner and entered the lab in a triangle formation. Jared and Kanna each took a front side, while Gillman held an exploding orb and remained a few feet behind. They exchanged worried glances; Daemon seemed to be gone.

"There," Jared said, pointing towards the double doors on the opposite side.

"Watch the sides and I'll…"

He was quickly interrupted as the long overhead lights turned off sequentially. The bulbs hummed as they turned back on, but instead of bright white, they cast crimson. Clinking boot heels rang out, striking the steel floor of a crisscrossing bridge above.

"I see you finally decided to hand them over. I appreciate that you've succumbed to reason," Daemon said, his hollow voice echoing throughout.

"We brought a different house warming present," Jared called back while Gillman handed him an orb.

He lobbed it at Daemon and it burst in a plume of smoke. While Kanna and Gillman each ran to one side, Jared rushed straight down the middle towards the doors. A gloved hand emerged from the smoke towards him. He sidestepped the strike and swung back with his blade.

Daemon yanked his arm away and scowled. "I promise you don't want me to come down there and take what's mine. Unlike last time, you three can't run away here."

Three short indigo beams-burst fired from Kanna's rifle at him. He slid to one side so quickly it almost appeared like teleportation. Kanna steadied her sight and fired again, causing Daemon to dodge once more. They continued the dance, her shooting his way anytime he emerged from cover.

Jared reached the door and slammed the open button… but nothing happened. He jabbed it several more times with his finger, garnering the same result. He then stabbed his dagger between the doors and tried to pry it open.

"Jared!" Kanna yelled.

He barely ducked Daemon's fist, but the bottom half caught him on the crown of his head. Jared winced as he rolled along the hard tile floor. After scrambling behind a nearby desk, he felt a warm

254

wetness trickle behind his ear. Touching a finger to his wound, he found a small slice had opened up and blood was seeping out. He gritted his teeth angrily while charging out from behind the desk, then unholstered his pistol and fired on his enemy. He stalked forward while continuing to shoot, completely unafraid and no longer seeking some form of shielding. Jared was done cowering.

Kanna took note and decided to advance on Daemon as well. She continued peppering several plasma rounds his way. Unfortunately, he continued to dodge most of them. It was hard to keep frustration from spoiling her aim. She breathed deeply to stave it off, as becoming flustered would only increase her odds of missing her target.

Daemon continued to whizz between the oncoming attacks from Kanna and Jared. After sliding across another bridge, he saw Kanna sat in perfect alignment for his next attack. He extended his arms and snatched the railing underneath a bridge above, using it to swing towards Kanna. Her rifle struck him twice, but couldn't stop him. Flying feet first, he thrust his heels into her chest, sending her careening across the wide landing before slamming into a desk.

"Ghaaaaa!" she yelped in agony as her back struck against it.

As he stalked towards her, she barely swung the barrel of her weapon his direction, forcing him to duck away. While he could withstand a great deal of their assault, he couldn't take fire from that close, along with the incoming shots from Jared.

Kanna reached her knees and quickly crawled behind the desk. Looking up, she spotted the call buttons near her for elevators on the opposite wall. She hit the button for one, in case she needed a means of escape. Pulling herself up, she steadied her elbows on the tabletop of the desk and continued shooting at this unbelievably immortal monster. They were faring well for now… but she knew they couldn't continue this pace forever.

Gillman noticed Daemon was preoccupied with his friends and decided to switch roles with Jared, taking a chance to work on the door. He unzipped a pouch clipped to his belt and slapped a flat piece of plastic to the door that had a wire attached. He snaked the wire over to the open switch and began sliding it behind the plate. Before he was able to attach the final gadget, a hand caught him by the throat. He wheezed and grabbed Daemon's fingers, hoping he could pry them off, but the grip only tightened.

Gillman's eyes bulged as his feet left the ground and his body flew towards a balcony. If he hadn't clutched Daemon's fingers to stabilize himself, his neck would've snapped.

"Now, hand them over or I begin crushing bones. Starting with this one," Daemon ordered while snatching one of Gillman's wrists with his free hand.

Kanna and Jared stopped firing and quickly glanced at each other. Hoping either had an idea. When neither seemed to infer any options, their eyes darted back to Gillman, who continued to kick and swing at his aggressor in futility.

Jared inhaled and looked at his feet while unstrapping the small backpack that held the Merge and Station.

"Set him down by me and they're yours," Jared said while holding the bag by the small top strap.

Daemon's face tilted forward and a broad grin climbed up the sides of his mouth. He let go of Gillman, who fell at Daemon's feet with a thud. He gagged and rubbed his throat while rolling over to look at Jared, searching for a wink or a nod. He only received a blank dead-eyed stare.

Daemon raised an eyebrow at Jared.

Jared huffed and shook his head. "So, your arm doesn't extend far enough to reach this?"

Jared snatched the bag and walked forward while holding it in front of him, one finger hooked under the top strap. After closing half the distance between them, Daemon's arm shot forward and yanked the backpack away from Jared. Gillman started to crawl towards Kanna – who had ascended a staircase to reach Daemon's level – but was stopped in his tracks as Daemon stomped on his calf.

"You're not going anywhere until I open this," Daemon said while unzipping the backpack.

He reached in and fished around, but found nothing.

Before deciding to concede, Jared made a decision to hide the two items under a nearby desk. He now stood a few tables over from where he gave himself up, in hopes Daemon wouldn't recall where he'd been previously.

"Did you even bring them here?!" Daemon bellowed.

Jared smirked before lying. "Nope."

He aimed his pistol at the button Gillman had been toying with and fired a shock round. It hit with a cackling sizzle and the double doors leading to the vault slid open.

"Fine then!" Daemon growled.

He looked down to continue his assault on Gillman but noticed something had been stabbed into the side of his leg. A rush of electricity ran through his body, causing him to flop onto his stomach. Gillman took the opening and limped over to Kanna, who helped him to his feet.

While the two trundled over to an elevator, Jared ran through the doorway, his pistol leading the way. A lanky figure spun on heels as he entered the room.

"You again?" Jared grumbled.

Nathan backpedaled away from Jared and held his palms up. Jared regarded him with confusion, assuming he would face another onslaught.

"*Ohhhh…* I get it. You don't want me to break this thing?" Jared mused while aiming his pistol at the laptop.

"*Wait!*" Nathan shrieked, "*Please…* I just need one file."

Jared tilted his head to one side. "Why do you think *I* would help you?"

Nathan pointed at the laptop. "Please, that file is our only chance."

"Ours?" Jared asked with a chuckle.

A loud slam and several gunshots erupted in the lab behind him and his head whipped around instinctively.

Nathan lunged forward and slashed Jared's pistol with his claws. Jared yanked his hand back and noticed the barrel was severed. He barely had time to react as Nathan dove in with a barrage of furious swipes. Jared backpedaled until he noticed an opening. He tilted to one side and lodged a boot in Nathan's stomach. It barely phased him, but gave Jared a chance to regroup.

When Nathan charged in again, Jared dipped to one side and plunged his dagger into his pursuer's midsection. Nathan howled and crumpled against Jared. After catching his breath, Jared shoulder shoved Nathan off and watched as he tumbled across the floor. His skin crawled in anticipation, waiting for Nathan to eventually lurch to his feet and assault him once more.

'If he survived getting shot by Kanna...' he thought.

But Nathan just curled up and clutched his wound.

"Don't destroy it. The file... h...he can't see it," Nathan stammered.

Jared stared in confusion while leaning forward with his hands on his knees.

'What the hell is he talking about?' Jared wondered while trying to regain his lungs.

After all their travel and the gauntlet of skirmishes, his lungs were burning like seared meat. He could feel the coppery taste of fatigue in the back of his throat. Jared steadied himself and walked towards the door. His face paled after completing two steps.

Gillman limped forward and fell to his knees while holding the original Merge and Personal Station. Kanna was marching behind him, but her hands were in the air and a dark-gloved mitt had her by the hair.

"I can shove this finger through her sternum if you so much as blink," Daemon stated coolly.

Jared tried to swallow back the growing lump of fear, but it stuck in his throat.

He staggered away and raised his palms. "What do you want?"

As he gave himself up, the blade over his hand morphed back into a simple wrist cuff. Daemon shoved a foot into Gillman, who rose, then staggered over to Jared and handed him the two devices.

"I need you to open the chest. Then I'll have you remove all of Johan's disgraceful governance code," Daemon spat.

Jared approached the table with the laptop and placed his items on it. He looked at the screen, which was running lines of numbers and letters. He turned on the Merge first and started the process of wirelessly pairing it with the Station. While setting them up, he noticed the sequences on the laptop screen stopped, and it switched to a graphic interface with a set of three folder icons.

"You can worry about those when you open the vault," Daemon instructed, "Focus on what you're doing first."

After several minutes of tinkering, he finally heard a loud click from the chest. In normal lighting conditions, he would have been able to see that the swirling ornate metal that decorated the outside was a lush gold. However, amidst the red lighting he couldn't distinguish these features. Jared gently placed his hands on the lid and lifted it open.

A Puck activated inside, and an orb the size of two fists lightly rose. Jared stared intently at the Diffusor-Sphere. It appeared as if several thin, rounded blocks had been stacked together, and as he watched, the thin pieces hummed and clicked, shifting and changing places on their own. The magnitude of this moment almost made him forget the looming threat at his back.

He heard a rush of air behind him and spun around, only to see Kanna being shoved forward, her toes dragging on the ground. Daemon grasped her by the neck now, and was holding her near a vat of boiling liquid inlaid in the ground of the chamber.

"Stop!" Jared yelled, "I'll do whatever you want, ok?!"

Daemon kept his steely, emotionless gaze on Jared. "I just need room for the next step. Plug one end of that wire in the Diffusor, then the other side behind my right ear."

Jared frowned while enacting Daemon's instructions. After plugging the wire behind his ear, a squealing grind like that of a claw across asphalt sounded from Daemon's chest. A circular joint jutted from his sternum and a green light projected to the Diffusor. Daemon gasped as the procedure began, while Jared looked on in horror.

One more deep breath and Daemon lowered his eyes at Jared.

"On the computer you'll see two files, drag the one labeled initiate sequence and drop it inside the other one."

It took Jared a few gulps before he could carry out the orders. The sight of Daemon's body deconstructing itself was appalling. It was like witnessing a corpse reanimate. He coughed, shook off the dreadful eeriness rising from his stomach, and faced the computer. He noticed a third file labeled: **Deconstruct sequence**.

Goosebumps crawled across his skin upon reading it.

Why would he leave this here? Was his lackey trying to delete this file earlier, or did he plan something else? Jared wondered.

'Well, it's all I've got.'

Jared used the track pad and dragged both files inside one labeled: **Complete protocol**.

Daemon noticed Jared appeared to have finished the last instruction.

"Open the file you placed them in," Daemon said, "It only has one program inside. Once you run that, it will ask you to start the *initiate sequence* file. After that's done, you and your friends can leave."

Jared completed the request, but when he ran the program, both the *deconstruct* and *initiate* files appeared as options. He looked back at Daemon one final time, glaring with bright hatred, then doubled clicked **Deconstruct sequence**.

Daemon gasped as the projected link between himself and the Diffusor surged. He gritted his teeth and growled as the program pushed forward. Jared couldn't look away from the display. This was the first semblance of pain expressed by Daemon, which appeared as a garish mix between excitement and agony. The light snapped off and Daemon slumped to his knees.

"No, this isn't right..." he mumbled while climbing to his feet.

"I don't understand. It feels like my mind... it's slipping away?!" Daemon stammered.

He looked straight ahead and slowly brought his hands up to his face.

"NOOOO! I can't see them?!" he quaveringly bellowed.

His head tilted back and he opened his mouth to scream, but nothing came. Daemon started clawing at his face, shredding bits of synthetic skin from his cheeks as faint swaths of violet light glowed from his eyes and mouth. His body soon gave off the hissing whine of an engine reaching its breaking point. He reached out and took a step towards Jared, who leapt back and raised his arms to shield himself. Daemon tried in vain for one more stride, but his body burst into a thousand tiny pieces.

Jared sat in shock as the fragments of Daemon rained onto the jagged floor. He scooted back and reached over to the table, using it as a prop to help himself up. As he reached his feet, Kanna ran over and wrapped him in a tight hug, her arms over his shoulders.

Gillman limped over and plucked the Diffusor from its resting place, causing Jared to cast a quizzical stare his way.

"Don't give me that look. I think we've earned it," Gillman said with a smile. He then pointed behind himself. "And we can't leave it here now that *he* knows where it's hidden."

Nathan brushed the hair from his face and looked back at Gillman. "You can have the damn Diffusor; I'm done with Daemon." As his eyes turned towards the vat where he lost his friends, he wouldn't forget where following Daemon had led him. When the nanites began extinguishing his pain, he didn't stop it. He needed to keep himself together until he escaped and found his father.

Jared peered past Gillman and saw Nathan was huddled against the wall recovering. Nathan met his gaze and coughed a few times while climbing to his feet. Kanna unholstered the pistol on her thigh, but Jared gestured for her to wait.

"You can thank him for fixing this mess," Jared stated as sweat dripped from his brow. "I'm not sure when he had a change of heart, but he tipped me off on how to corrupt Daemon's software."

Kanna bit her lip and said nothing. She had plenty of questions, but would shelve them until she had some rest.

Gillman hobbled over to the door and motioned for them to follow. "Let's get the hell out of here."

- EPILOGUE -

VIRS ISLAND
NORTHERN UNALLOCATED ZONE

-

UNGOVERNED NON-CIVIC REGION

GRAB me another one of those drinks they serve in the coconut will ya?" Gillman asked while placing his arms behind his head.

"I'll get you a drink, but not one in that damn coconut. It's too expensive," Jared answered, rising from his beach chair.

Gillman lifted his sunglasses. "What do you care? Your sugar mamma over there is picking up the tab."

Jared lifted his chin and rolled his eyes. "She's not covering *everything*, Gill. We got a decent payout from her already for the job. I think we can buy our own drinks."

Gillman leaned back in his seat. "You made her buy that dumb falcon doll from Sanzo, why can't *I* get a drink?"

Jared held up a finger in protest. "First of all, she lost the bet and owed me. Secondly – being the gentleman I am – I actually had her take it from my cut instead. And finally, like I've told you a thousand times…"

Kanna interrupted Jared by handing him a blended drink.

"We know, Jared, it's not a doll," as she finished, she handed another drink to Gillman.

Jared took a long sip from his beverage. After everything they'd survived, the three of them decided to borrow Sanzo's condo in Virs. A poolside vacation was the perfect cure for all their aches and bruises.

"Alright, I'm jumping back in," Jared said while setting his drink down.

He strode off and dove in the pool. The turquoise water felt thoroughly refreshing against his skin. He plunged himself back underwater and braced his feet against the scratchy pool floor. He pushed off and rushed through the water until he had to come up for air. Emerging, Jared shook some of the water from his face, then wiped the remaining droplets from his eyes. After opening them, he saw Kanna standing at the pool's edge in front of him. He playfully swam over as she sat down and dipped her feet in.

"I got a message about something we should look into," she told him.

Jared tilted his head and motioned towards the beautifully clear sky. "We've got plenty of time to deal with that later, let's just enjoy the sun for now."

"Alright, but I think you'll be interested to know it involves an aeronautics engineer," Kanna said in a sing-song voice before taking a sip from her straw.

"Is it one who studies air travel that could take us past the Forum?" Jared asked, treading water in front of her.

Straw still between her teeth, Kanna nodded affirmingly.

"You know me so well already," Jared said with a grin.

He swam to the edge of the pool and lifted himself up, taking a seated position next to her.

"So, when do we start?"

AFTERWORD

Thank you for reading my second novel set in the Intercontinents. If you enjoyed this adventure, please leave me a review on whatever platform you purchased this from. I'd also recommend you check out my other book set in the same universe, The Assassin of Malcozé. If you would like to remain up to date on upcoming works, please visit my author site (intercontpress.com). I hope to see you soon.

- Bryan Asher